# WALK A CROOKED LINE

## OTHER TITLES BY SUSAN McBRIDE

### Detective Jo Larsen

*Walk Into Silence*

### The Debutante Dropout Mysteries

*Say Yes to the Death*
*Too Pretty to Die*
*Night of the Living Deb*
*The Lone Star Lonely Hearts Club*
*The Good Girl's Guide to Murder*
*Blue Blood*

### The River Road Mysteries

*Come Helen High Water*
*Not a Chance in Helen*
*Mad as Helen*
*To Helen Back*

### Women's Fiction

*The Truth About Love & Lightning*
*Little Black Dress*
*The Cougar Club*

### Young Adult Mystery

*Very Bad Things*

# WALK A CROOKED LINE

## SUSAN McBRIDE

THOMAS & MERCER

Published by Thomas & Mercer, Seattle

www.apub.com

Amazon, the Amazon logo, and Thomas & Mercer are trademarks of Amazon.com, Inc., or its affiliates.

ISBN-13: 9781477848647
ISBN-10: 1477848649

Cover design by Ray Lundgren

Printed in the United States of America

*To the survivors who fight their worst fears and
never give up:
Your lives are precious. Your voices have meaning.
You are not alone. You never were.*

# CHAPTER ONE

**Sunday**

It was a long way up.

She put her hands on the rungs of the rusted ladder and peered through the twilight at the old water tower. The wind whistled across its underbelly, drowning out the hum of late-summer cicadas. A loose chain clanked, metal banging metal, the sound at once tuneless and mournful. Beyond the looming silhouette, the moon's crescent yellow winked at her, then disappeared behind a cloud, as if turning its back on her, too.

Kelly sucked in a deep breath. Her canvas sneakers soaked up the damp of the overgrown grass as she hesitated.

What was she waiting for? She wasn't afraid. She'd climbed the tower before. They all had. It was what kids did around here on their very first dare and then a dozen times after until it wasn't a big deal anymore.

But this time, she needed a poke.

She closed her eyes and replayed the words in her head that she couldn't shake no matter how hard she tried to forget them.

*You're a slut. You're worthless. You're a liar. No one wants you. No one loves you. No one will miss you when you're gone.*

That saying about sticks and stones breaking bones and names never hurting? It was a bunch of crap. Words burned like fire, just as they were meant to.

"I give up," she whispered to the wind, uncurling her fingers from the ladder to wipe at tears with the back of her hand. "You win."

It would have been enough to break her heart, if her heart hadn't been broken already. Everyone she'd trusted, everyone she'd loved—they'd all left her, hadn't they?

Her dad was gone. He'd split a long time ago. He had another family in a different city, a wife and kids he loved so much that he even forgot to call on her birthday. Her mother barely seemed aware that she existed, and even when she did, all she seemed to do was spew lame advice. "You're young, Kel," she'd say, only half listening. "You'll get over it. Live and learn."

Maybe she was just fifteen, but she'd learned enough already. Like the fact that grown-ups sometimes weren't, and parents didn't always put their children first. Even people who swore they cared about you cared about themselves more. And if they wanted to—if they needed to make themselves feel better about their own crappy lives—they could take everything that was you, all that was shiny and bright, and snuff it out in an instant, like turning off a light.

She stopped brushing tears from her cheeks. Instead, she let them fall.

Like everything else, it wasn't worth the fight.

She inhaled the muggy air, filling up her lungs, and then she began to climb, not glancing down, not changing her mind. She just kept going up and up and up.

By the time she reached the catwalk, the faint purple of twilight had been swallowed by darkness. With a grunt, she stepped onto the gridded path that ringed the tower. A slim guardrail was all that stood between her and the sky. The faded black letters that spelled out PLAINFIELD across the barrel flaked beneath her touch as she trailed her fingers, moving forward. Someone had spray-painted TY + ANNA in white, and Kelly found herself wondering who Ty and Anna were. Were they still together? Somehow, she doubted it. Nothing good ever seemed to last for long.

She turned around to the night, gray clouds scudding across a navy background. A few stars began to twinkle like fireflies, tapping at the darkness. Instinctively, she reached out a hand, imagining that she could touch them.

How tall she felt, how high above it all. Windows glowed in the homes lined up in neat rows beyond the pasture. From where she stood, they appeared the size of dollhouses. Between them, headlamps swept away down the road. No one knew where she was. No one gave her a second thought. Her mother wasn't even home.

The wind plucked at her hair, tossing it into her eyes. Kelly shivered. It was colder up here than on the ground, or maybe those goose bumps were nerves. She glanced down. The grass below looked pitch-black—more a void than a cushion. She hoped it was soft, not that it would matter.

She gripped the railing and hitched herself up.

Her phone rang, and the catwalk clanked as her feet slid back down. She reached into her pocket, tugging out her cell to see who it was.

*Mom.*

For an instant, her heart seemed to stop. She thought of not answering but changed her mind and picked up. She didn't even say hello.

"Oh, God, Kel, I'm sorry." Her mother started off apologizing, something she did so often that it felt meaningless. "I completely lost track of time. Did you get yourself some dinner?"

"Yeah," she lied. Food was the last thing on her mind.

"I thought I'd be home already. I wanted to be, I swear," she rattled on. "But things took much longer than I expected."

Didn't they always?

"I just checked the baby out of the hospital, and I want to see the family settled in before I leave. He hasn't got long to go."

"I'm sorry," Kelly said, and she meant it. She was sorry for the sick baby. Sorry for herself. Sorry for everything.

"You sound funny. Are you sure you're okay?"

"I'm sure," she lied again, trying not to cry as she hung up, not wanting her mom to make more promises about trying to get home soon. Promises she wouldn't keep.

*No, I'm not okay. I'm really not okay.*

Kelly took one deep breath and then another.

But she couldn't hold it together.

A sob broke through, and she started to bawl, choking on the snot and tears. Howling like a wounded dog, she pounded her phone as hard as she could against the metal tank. When the glass had shattered and bits of plastic broke and scattered, cutting her hand and bruising her knuckles, she threw away what was left.

Then she pulled herself over the railing and leaped.

# CHAPTER TWO

*Monday*

"Is this it?"

"Yep," Jo Larsen told her partner, spotting the number on the brick mailbox and the long stretch of driveway beyond.

Hank whistled. "Nice spread. You figure it's one acre or two?" He let the car roll slowly forward, easing up to the front of the sprawling ranch house before he cut the engine.

"Yes," Jo replied equivocally. Hey, she lived in a condo. One acre or two didn't matter. It pretty much looked like a park to her.

"You can hardly see the neighbors." Hank sighed, eyeing the expanse of green beyond the windshield. "If I stand outside between my place and the house next door, I can reach out and touch both with my fingertips."

"You'd better watch it, Hank. You're drooling."

"It'd be great, you know, to have room for the girls to run around without playing in the street." He turned to Jo as he unbuckled his seat belt. "But why not have a fence? They keep kids reined in, that's for sure. I'll bet they work for dogs, too."

"I'm guessing they can't have fences in this neck of the woods," Jo said. The Winding Brook subdivision was one of the oldest in their little town of Plainfield, Texas, just a hop, skip, and jump north of Dallas. It was one of the prettiest neighborhoods, too, full of mature trees that framed the flat blue of the sky. A creek even meandered through it, at least when there wasn't a drought. "It's probably some HOA thing."

"Why?"

She shrugged. "It might ruin their scenic views."

Hank snorted. "Guess I'm lucky not to have scenic views to ruin. The joy of zero lot lines. At least I don't have a big yard to mow."

"Silver linings," Jo quipped as she let herself out of the unmarked Ford sedan. She crossed the pebbled drive, walking toward the front door just ahead of her partner.

"Tell me why we're starting the day playing Ace Ventura? We normally aren't out scouting for missing pets."

"If the dog was stolen, it's property theft," she said, glancing at him as he came alongside her. She could see the dark stains beneath his armpits, due in no small part to the mugginess of the morning. "And it's better than how we started last week. Or did you like giving a grown man a talking-to for damaging his neighbor's siding with a potato cannon?"

"Let's see. Missing pup. Potato cannon." Hank cocked his head. "Since I'm a glass-half-full kind of guy, I'll say that dog swiping is an upgrade, and it's probably less fatal than my usual breakfast in the Fort Worth PD."

"Eggs with a side of homicide?"

"Pretty much, yep."

God knows, Jo didn't want to go back to Dallas. Not that the city wasn't a good training ground, but it had done a number on her psyche. Unfortunately, leaving for greener pastures hadn't meant leaving behind the worst of human nature. Crime from inside the metro trickled its way into the outlying townships. In the past few years alone, they'd seen an uptick in hit-and-runs, identity theft, burglaries, and shoplifting, not to mention the opioid epidemic that was putting folks into caskets like cancer. Working for the Plainfield PD was a little akin to spinning a wheel of fortune on a daily basis. Detectives on a force as small as theirs tended to generalize, not specialize. They took the assignments they were given, whether they felt weighty or not, because everything meant something to somebody.

"Better a swiped dog than an OD," she reminded him and meant it. Just a week back, they'd found a car parked at a defunct gas station on the edge of town. The two adults in the front seats were unconscious, drug paraphernalia at their feet. The baby in back was crying, all of them drenched in sweat. If it had been afternoon instead of morning, all three would have baked through. So if her tone was a bit chastising, she didn't care.

"Yes, Mom," her partner drawled, like the middle-aged smart-ass he was.

"Behave," she said. She stepped on the welcome mat and pushed the bell, glancing over at Hank's hangdog face as they waited for someone to respond.

It took less than a minute for the door to swing inward. An older woman stared out at them through sleek, black glasses.

"You're Amanda Pearson?" Jo said.

"I am."

"I'm Detective Larsen," Jo introduced herself, then jerked her chin at Hank. "This is my partner, Detective Phelps. You called to report a missing dog?"

"My God, it's about time you showed up," the woman said, sucking in her cheeks. "I talked to your desk sergeant last evening, and he promised to dispatch an officer, but no one came. I had to phone again this morning to get y'all off your fannies." She looked ready to burst into tears. "Aren't the first twenty-four hours the most important when a child's been abducted?"

"A child?" Hank repeated, glancing at Jo and looking confused. "I'm sorry, ma'am, but I was under the impression you'd lost your dog. Did I miss something here?"

"Duke is my boy, Detective," Mrs. Pearson said flatly, "and he's better company than most people I know."

"I understand," Hank replied. "But I'm thinking maybe it'd be prudent to call Animal Services and some area shelters first, before involving us."

"I *have* called," she insisted. "I've phoned Dallas County Animal Services, the Humane Society, the SPCA, and every other shelter I could find within a twenty-mile radius. That seems pretty prudent to me."

With that, she turned her back on them, leaving the door wide open.

"She's right, you know," Jo said, stepping past him. "Humans suck."

"You get a cat, and suddenly you're a fur hugger?" Hank muttered as he shut the door behind him. Then they followed on the woman's heels, crossing the foyer and heading up the hallway through which she'd disappeared.

When Jo caught up to her, Mrs. Pearson was standing beside an oak pedestal table. Sliding glass doors led out back to a deck and a green yard beyond that stretched toward the horizon, cut off only by a border of evergreens beneath a canopy of power lines.

"I was told that Duke is a show dog," Jo said, thinking of what little information she'd garnered from Dispatch when she'd started her shift.

Mrs. Pearson seemed to gather herself, and her face softened as she plucked something from the breakfast table. "He was, and a very fine one, too."

"Is he worth a lot?" Hank asked.

"Only to me," the woman said, holding out a red leather strap from which metal tags dangled. "It's his collar," she told them. "I found it near the mailbox in front. Duke can't possibly have removed it himself. Clearly, he was kidnapped."

"Dognapped," Hank murmured, and Jo was thankful Mrs. Pearson didn't seem to hear him.

She was fiddling with the red collar, weaving it between fingers bare of jewelry save for a gold wedding band. "These days, thieves snatch pups from backyards to sell to laboratories or dogfighting rings. I pray that's not what's happened to Duke."

"Tell me about his glory days, ma'am. Did he win a lot of competitions?" Hank asked, giving Jo time to look around them while Mrs. Pearson filled them in on all the thousands of points and best-of-shows her dog had racked up through the years.

Stainless steel dog dishes sat atop a rubber mat, one bowl filled with water, the other empty. A large bag of dog food rested in a corner. Colorful chew toys littered the floor. Collections of photos filled the sunny breakfast nook walls. A handful showed people of varying ages, which Jo assumed were Pearson's adult children and their children. Others showed a lovely strawberry-blond dog earning ribbons at shows or merely rolling in the bluebonnets.

"He's a golden retriever," Jo said, recognizing the breed.

"Yes." Mrs. Pearson perked up. "His full name is Golden Duke of Ducat. He's a purebred from a very distinguished line, although these days he's too old for showing or breeding. When he was in his prime, he was certainly valuable. But why would anyone want to take him now?"

"Have you had any problems with neighbors?" Hank asked as he stepped over to the sliding doors and peered out at the yard. "Someone he bit?"

She let out a dry laugh. "God, no. Duke never bit anyone."

"Someone who gets ticked off when the dog barks? Or maybe Duke dug a hole in their garden or pissed on their petunias?"

"No, nothing like that. I get along fine with my neighbors. We keep to ourselves mostly, and they all have dogs of their own."

"Can we head outside and take a look around?" Hank already had a grip on the sliding door handle.

"Sure," the woman said, and Hank drew the door wide so she could lead the way.

Jo followed them out onto the cedar planks, the scent of cut grass and honeysuckle filling her nose. From the raised deck, she surveyed the landscape. To her right was a thick copse of trees and shrubbery. A single river birch stood out, its pinkish bark a stark contrast to the brown and green around it. She could hear the faint rush of water somewhere in between.

"So the creek's over there?" she asked.

"Yes," Mrs. Pearson said, pointing at the woods to the right that held Jo's attention. "It separates my property from the Engels'. They're retired and travel quite a bit." She turned due north, drawing a finger through the air where utility lines cut across the blue sky. "That's the back of my property," she told them. Below the cables, trees and brush filled a bermlike barrier. "Beyond that it's the Magees' place."

Despite all the foliage, Jo could see the extensive roofline of a two-story home with two chimneys and skylights. Hank was squinting at it, too.

"Did they tear down a ranch, or just add on?" he asked.

"Oh, the Magees razed the old place twenty years ago," Mrs. Pearson replied. "I'm surprised there are as many ranches remaining as there are. Although the Raines have stuck with their original footprint," she said and gestured to a house on their left. "I'm told they gutted the insides, though I haven't been invited in. They have a son, but the mother and father travel a lot."

"What are those?" Hank asked, pointing at three posts that dotted the landscape, like giant pushpins stuck into the earth. "Did they start to build a fence and never finish?"

He came to stand beside Jo.

"Only invisible fences are allowed around here," Mrs. Pearson said. "The family originally came from West Texas, where they had a lot of land and no rules. But once the street association sent them a warning, they stopped work."

"They left some posts, though," Hank said.

"They did," Mrs. Pearson said, and Jo heard the disapproval in her voice.

"Anything wrong, ma'am?"

"About a month back, I saw their boy tying a pup to those posts," the woman said. "The dog was a sweetheart, a pit bull mix. He'd howl and whine for hours. I felt awful for him. The next time I saw they were home, I knocked on their door to suggest they take the dog in when the weather's so hot. The boy answered, and I said my piece." She screwed up her face. "He got this horrible look on his face and told me the dog was gone, that it ran off when they were at their house in the country."

"Did they ever find it?" Jo asked, hoping there was a happy ending to the story.

"Not that I'm aware." Mrs. Pearson's eyes widened. "You don't think it was stolen, too?"

Jo glanced at Hank. "We can check for a report," she said. "Although if it disappeared somewhere outside of Plainfield . . ."

"It would have been beyond our jurisdiction, ma'am," Hank finished for her.

Mrs. Pearson nodded, gazing toward the house next door. "They have a sheepdog now. He's a bit of a growler, but at least Jason doesn't stake him to the fence post when it's a hundred degrees."

"Jason *Raine* is the boy you confronted?" Hank bounced on his heels, doing a good impression of an overly excited puppy. "The center for the Plainfield Mustangs?"

A high schooler? Jo had been imagining an irresponsible ten-year-old.

"You could be right, I guess. He's quite a big boy at that."

"Most underrated player on the team," Hank remarked. "Crispest snapper I've ever seen, and he rarely gets pancaked."

11

Jo murmured, "Stay on target."

Her partner cleared his throat. "What else were you about to say, ma'am?" he asked.

"Just that he drives a big, noisy truck with a Texas flag painted across his rear tailgate. I can hear him every time he comes and goes. The noise is enough to rattle my walls."

"He's got it modified, I'll bet," Hank said. When the woman wrinkled her brow, he explained, "You know, changed the muffler to make it louder? In these parts, noisy trucks are every teenage boy's wet dream. They don't fill 'em with gas. They fuel 'em with testosterone."

Jo waited until he'd finished with his down-home Click and Clack routine. "Could you run through what happened after you let Duke out?" she asked Mrs. Pearson. "Anything could be of help."

"Yes, of course. He went outside after dinner, like always," the older woman said. "I'd cleaned up the dishes and went to the bedroom to put on my nightgown, getting ready for bed while he did his business and sniffed around a bit in the yard. Only last night, he didn't come when I called him in. I put on my shoes and a robe, got a flashlight, and headed out. I found his collar with his tags in the street." She stopped and touched her throat, as if that alone would quell her trembling voice. "It was like he'd vanished into thin air."

"Did you see a car or hear anything?" Jo asked, because the street was kind of off the beaten track. She couldn't imagine it got much traffic from outside the neighborhood, save for the postman or FedEx.

"Nothing out of the ordinary, no."

"Does the dog have a microchip to identify him?" Jo asked.

"He does, but that counts only if someone takes him to a vet and they scan for it. Otherwise, it's useless."

Jo saw the woman's trembling hands and pulled out a nearby deck chair, in case she wanted to sit. But Mrs. Pearson waved her off.

"I'm all right," she said.

"Do you live alone, ma'am?" Jo asked.

"My kids are grown with children of their own. They're out of state. My husband is in a memory care facility. He has Alzheimer's and doesn't know who I am half the time, so I guess I've lost him, too, haven't I?"

"I'm sorry," Jo said instinctively, thinking of her own mother, who'd suffered a similar fate; she brushed off a familiar twinge of guilt.

Mrs. Pearson sucked in a deep breath and seemed to steady herself. "Ted and I built this house when Plainfield was mostly pasture. It was one of the first real subdivisions out here. I always felt safe, like nothing could touch me or my family. Now I can hardly read the news for all the tragic headlines. Makes me think my husband has it easy, being so unaware. Everything's a goddamned mess."

Hank coughed, like he'd swallowed down the wrong pipe.

"It's a big mess, for sure," Jo agreed, ignoring him.

"Duke was a godsend," Mrs. Pearson went on, "such a gentle creature. He never wanted anything from me but love." She reached for the arm of the deck chair Jo had pulled out for her earlier, sinking into it. "He must be scared to death. I can't even imagine what he's feeling," she said, choking on a fresh round of tears. "Why would anyone take him?"

"I don't know," Jo said and pulled up a chair. "We'll try to help as best we can, okay?"

"Okay." The woman nodded, wiping at her tears.

"If y'all don't mind, I'm gonna take a look around," Hank said. "I won't get shocked by the fence, ma'am, will I?"

"Not unless you're wearing an electric collar," Mrs. Pearson told him. "No need to worry. It's turned off."

"Much appreciated."

"Be with you in a minute," Jo said, earning her a loose salute before Hank ambled down the deck stairs and disappeared around the side of the house.

"I don't know what else I can do," Mrs. Pearson told her, plucking a tissue from her cardigan pocket to dab at her eyes behind her specs. "My kids want to help out, but they're so far away. They promised to get on social media and post messages and pictures, for all the good that'll do."

"It can't hurt," Jo assured her.

"Should I offer a reward?"

"You can try," Jo said. Money was as big a motivator as any, probably better than relying on kindness or character these days.

Not much else she could do but collect a photo of Duke and the dog's collar, which Mrs. Pearson put in a zippered baggie.

Then she went after Hank, figuring he hadn't gone far. With his bum knees, he never traveled very fast. And she was right. He hadn't come close to reaching the mailbox near the street where Mrs. Pearson had found Duke's collar. Instead, he'd benched himself behind the steering wheel of the old Ford. He had the door open and a leg hanging out.

As she got closer, she opened her mouth to give him hell for sitting down on the job, but then she heard him talking to Dispatch.

She caught a "Roger that" before he gestured at her to get in the car. He quickly pulled his leg in and slammed the door.

The engine coughed to life as Jo rounded the hood, inhaling the stink of exhaust as she scrambled inside.

"What's up?" she asked, grabbing for the shoulder belt.

"Someone took a dive off the old water tower."

"Who?"

"A kid," Hank grimly replied. "The human kind."

# CHAPTER THREE

Hank said little during their drive across Plainfield. His craggy face had been pensive to the point of looking pained, and Jo understood why.

Dispatch had informed them that a young woman had been found dead on the grounds of the old water tower. A dog walker cutting through the weed-infested acreage had stumbled upon her body. The fire department had dispatched EMTs, but the girl had been deceased long enough for rigor mortis to set in. They'd nixed transporting her to the local hospital, calling the PD instead.

Jo knew Hank was thinking of his own girls. They were still in grade school, not close to being old enough to visit the water tower on their own, much less try to climb it. She could see in his eyes the gut-wrenching empathy, no doubt wondering about the girl's parents and what hell they'd go through once they heard the news.

"It's like a beacon, isn't it?" he said quietly. "Kids hit puberty, and they feel compelled to climb."

Jo pushed aside the sun visor and saw what he meant.

With no tall trees to block the view, the sky seemed to widen, and the water tower came into full view.

"If I'd grown up in these parts, I would've done it. You would have, too."

"Maybe," Jo said, never having been much of a daredevil, at least not while she'd been a kid, living with Mama. She'd been in survival mode then, enduring chronic abuse from her stepfather while her mother drank herself numb.

But Hank was right that the water tower beckoned the young. Since she'd joined the Plainfield force three years ago, every season without fail, they'd ended up on the tower grounds, following reports of kids bypassing the decrepit chain-link fence, throwing beer bottles off the widow's walk, or shooting at the tower with paint guns.

"I heard they're taking it down soon," she said.

Hank snorted. "They've said that for a year, since they got the new one up across town."

"Demolition's expensive," Jo said.

"They could charge money for tickets to see that relic fall. It would pay for itself."

"I'll bet they end up bringing it down in the dead of night so they don't risk anything going wrong and someone getting hurt."

"Did you know it's a hundred and thirty feet high?" Hank remarked, his gaze fixed ahead, whether on the road or the tower, Jo couldn't be sure. The latter grew taller and taller the nearer they got. "It only pumped fifty thousand gallons in its prime. The new one's closer to two hundred fifty feet high and pumps two point five million gallons."

"That's a lot of water," Jo said, surprised by the detail, or maybe not. Hank didn't sleep much. He stayed up watching bad TV, or else he trolled the internet, reading articles about esoteric information on sites Jo had never heard of.

What she did know, because City Hall had made a point to inform the whole department, was that the new tower had a ladder on the inside and no widow's walk tempting kids to go up. It was bigger and better and safer, and it looked like an enormous round chimney.

"One hundred thirty feet," Hank repeated. "Nobody's ever survived a fall higher than eighty-five feet. Nobody. Okay, maybe, one in a billion people, like that Czech flight attendant on the plane that exploded some years back. She fell from the sky, broke a couple dozen bones, and was in a coma for, like, three weeks, but she lived to talk about it."

"Thanks, Ripley."

"I'm just sayin'. They could have prevented this."

"I hear ya," Jo said, because there was nothing else to add.

Two blue-and-whites were already parked in the graveled lot adjacent to the water tower grounds. The gate to the chain-link fence hung wide open. Jo was relieved not to see any signs of reporters. That was another plus of living outside the big city. It took a while for the Dallas media to get to the scene after they'd picked up chatter from the police scanner or from social media.

She didn't see the white van from the county medical examiner's office yet, either, but she wasn't surprised. The suspected suicide of a teen in what amounted to the distant northern suburbs didn't rate the urgency of homicide victims within the city limits. If the wait looked too long, the Plainfield PD had an arrangement with a local mortuary, which had ample refrigeration.

She couldn't help wondering what ME would be assigned to the case, and if it would fall to Adam McCaffrey, the man she'd been seeing for months. She'd fallen in love with him years earlier, when she was with the Dallas PD and he was married, making their relationship both ill-timed and impossible. Except he wasn't married anymore. He'd come to find her when he'd split with his wife, once Jo had stopped wrestling with her conscience, knowing she was better off alone than involved in an affair.

"Time to make the doughnuts," Hank said, as he released his seat belt and grabbed the keys from the ignition.

The car rocked gently as he got out and closed the door with a solid slap. Jo followed suit, rounding the hood to catch up to him as he headed toward the gate.

The sun had moved a few notches higher in the sky, and Jo felt its heat on her head and the back of her neck. Septembers in North Texas weren't very forgiving. They were less a prelude to fall than the end of an asphalt-frying summer, viciously hanging on by its toenails.

A trickle of sweat slid down the curve of her back.

She could make out at least one officer in the grass at the base of the tower, taking photographs and measurements. Jo thought of all the rules she'd learned about unattended deaths in her years on the force, and the first was to investigate as though it was a homicide. When cops assumed suicide right off the bat, they missed things. Jo didn't want to do that. She didn't want to ever let down victims or their families, because she knew how it felt to be marginalized, to not be believed or validated. Her own victimization at the hands of her stepfather never left her mind, not entirely. It was the scab that wouldn't heal and ran far deeper than the chicken pox scar on her brow.

She paused and glanced up at the tower hulking above them. She saw another officer climbing the ladder. He was about halfway up.

A sour taste filled her mouth.

Had the girl simply fallen? Was it an accident, like something from one of those teen horror flicks? A group of friends climbs the tower, drinks themselves into a stupor, and one of them falls over the guardrail while the others watch in shock.

The other option wasn't any less tragic.

Had the girl jumped? Had she come out alone and climbed up with the sole intent of ending her life?

Jo had considered it herself once or twice, back when she'd felt emotionally abandoned, stuck in a bad situation and wanting to escape. It was all too easy to go to that place in your head where making all the hurt go away sounded reasonable, even enticing, particularly when you felt alone and trapped and saw no other way out.

She hoped that hadn't been the case for this girl.

"Hey, partner, you comin'? Or are you gonna stand there all day and stare?" Hank called out, gesturing for her to hurry and catch up to him.

She didn't tell him what had been going through her head, but he seemed to read her mind anyway.

As they walked together through shin-high grass, he said, "It's a bad world for raising a girl, and I've got two of them. Between social media and reality TV, it's a constant gauntlet of piss-poor role models, body shamers, haters, and bullies. I wish to God I knew how to keep them safe."

"It was a bad world for girls even before social media and reality shows," Jo replied. "It was just easier to pretend it didn't exist when it wasn't in your face twenty-four seven."

Hank gave her a look, the kind that made her wish she could explain herself fully. But even if it had been the right time—and it wasn't—she would have been interrupted.

"Morning, Detectives," Officer Charlotte Ramsey said, nodding at them as she let them pass through the gate. She pulled it closed behind them, though it wouldn't likely deter anyone from getting in, not when it didn't even latch properly, and chain link was missing entirely in spots, leaving gaps between metal fence posts.

"What happened here?" Hank asked, his frown rumpling up his whole face. "Some teenage party gone bad? Are there witnesses?"

"No, sir. None that we're aware of, anyway."

"You know who she is?" Jo asked. "I don't see a car, so she must be local, right?"

"We know now." Ramsey's brown ponytail bobbed as she wagged her chin, eager to share. "We got a call not five minutes ago from a woman looking for her daughter. She had no clue the girl wasn't home last night."

"She what? How could she not know something like that?" Hank's voice rumbled.

"She's a home health care nurse," Ramsey explained as she led them toward the body in the grass. "She was with a family whose baby is dying. Some kind of cancer or something. She stayed with them until about three a.m. Went home and straight to bed. She woke up a bit ago and . . ."

"No daughter," Jo finished for her, as they stopped short of the victim.

Ramsey nodded. "Yep. The woman's name is Barbara Amster," she continued, while next to Jo, Hank simmered. "The girl matches the description she gave for the kid, down to the shoes on her feet."

The kid, aka the mess of tangled limbs lying in the grass.

Jo had to remind herself that what she saw was a person, a real human being still a few years shy of full grown, not a life-sized marionette that had been cut from its strings, limbs at all angles, neck unnaturally bent.

She swallowed hard. "What's her name?"

Before she answered, Ramsey checked the small notepad she'd pulled from her breast pocket. Jo appreciated that she wanted to get it right.

"Kelly Amster," she said. "She's fifteen, just started her sophomore year at Plainfield High three weeks ago. Her mom got scared when she went into her daughter's room and found a note left on the pillow. Then she tried to call the girl's cell phone but got no answer."

"What'd the note say?" Jo asked.

Ramsey cleared her throat, then read straight from the notebook: "'I love you, but it hurts too much to stay. I'm sorry. So, so sorry.'"

Jo let out a slow breath. "Well, damn."

"So we've got a legit suicide note?" Hank said, his gaze on the girl. The frustration had left his face, and instead he looked gray.

"Seems that way," Ramsey said.

"So it wasn't an accident? No one pushed her? She decided to end it all, just like that?" Hank asked, not giving the patrol officer room to answer between his questions. "I'm surprised no one live-streamed it on any of those bloodsucking social media sites," he added bitterly.

Jo tried to swallow the lump in her throat, but it wouldn't go away.

"Barbara Amster stated that she called her daughter last night to check on her. The girl answered her phone," Ramsey informed them as she tucked away her notepad. "Said she sounded off, like something wasn't right. But her guess was that Kelly was upset that she didn't make it home for dinner."

"She sounded off, huh? Like something wasn't right," Hank murmured, and he stomped down a cluster of dandelions with a boot heel.

"Did you find her phone?" Jo asked. That could answer a lot of questions. Kids these days lived and died by their cell phones. Their whole lives were wrapped up in a SIM card: texts, e-mails, search history, apps, call history, everything and everyone they loved or hated. If Kelly Amster had wanted to kill herself, she'd probably told somebody or made a video journal about it.

"We haven't found it yet, no. It wasn't on her, but we're looking. We've collected a few pieces of plastic that look like cell phone parts. We bagged them, of course, but they could be somebody else's trash. There's plenty of that around here. Got to watch out for broken glass."

"What time did Barbara Amster talk to her daughter?"

"Approximately nine thirty p.m."

"You think the girl tossed her phone from the top?" Hank tipped his head back to stare at the tower. "Or left it up there?"

"We'll know soon enough. Duncan's climbing the ladder," Ramsey said. "If there's anything there, he'll bag it and bring it down."

"Better him than me and my bad knees." Hank shifted on his feet, his gaze returning to the dead girl. "She had balls, didn't she? Getting up there's a long haul. Gave her plenty of time to change her mind. Why the hell didn't she change her mind?" He expelled a noisy breath. "Poor, poor kid."

"Kelly," Jo found herself saying. The girl's name was Kelly.

She should have been on her way to her first-period class, learning Spanish or algebra or whatever it was that fifteen-year-old sophomores studied these days. She should have been complaining about the cafeteria food, deciding whether she wanted to try out for the fall musical, dishing on the latest boy band, and forgetting the combination to her locker.

Not waiting for the van to take her to the county morgue.

Jo ignored the stitch in her chest, instead looking for something that would explain how someone so young had ended up in the shadow of the old water tower, broken beyond repair.

Her clothing looked ordinary, like every other teenager Jo saw these days: white cutoff shorts and a graphic T-shirt, this one purple with an emoji face sticking out its tongue. She had well-worn pink Vans on her feet, no socks.

Her blue eyes were wide open, brown hair splayed around a pale, freckled face. There was some blood at her mouth and nose, but otherwise nothing. The worst of the damage was beneath the skin: broken bones, a cracked spine, crushed organs. Like Hank had said, you didn't jump 130 feet figuring you'd walk away.

"Makes me want to kick someone's ass," her partner murmured.

Jo did, too. But she wasn't sure whose.

"Is there a father in the picture?" she wondered aloud.

"No," Ramsey said. "The parents divorced long ago. He remarried and doesn't live around here. Houston, I think she said. According to the mother, he hasn't seen his daughter in about five years."

"I'd die if I couldn't see my girls," Hank admitted. "It would tear me up inside."

"Your girls are lucky," Jo told him. Not every kid was. For some, childhood was more a matter of treading water, keeping your head up so you could breathe. That was how Jo saw it, anyway, and not just because of what she'd witnessed on the job too many times through the years. That was how she'd lived it.

Had it been the same for Kelly Amster?

She squatted down beside the body, pushing away grass so tall, it had gone to seed. She wondered when it had last been mowed, or if the town even cared. The old water tower was more like a grave marker, a sad memento of the past. Soon it would be gone altogether, and no one would remember who had climbed its heights on a dare, who had partied there or broken up there or died there.

Ramsey's shoulder walkie started to squawk, and she excused herself, walking away as she picked up.

Between the stalks of green, Jo could see the girl's hand: pale and slim, no rings, a thin bracelet around her wrist made of colored string. A friendship bracelet? So maybe she had a buddy she'd talked to, someone who'd be able to help explain this.

Jo leaned nearer, getting a good look at her face.

A freckled nose. Gold studs in pierced ears. Pale eyes that stared at nothing, sightless.

Ramsey stopped talking on her walkie and came back.

"Duncan said there are only bits and pieces of plastic, but no intact cell phone. Also, a couple of empty cans of spray paint and nasty old beer cans," Ramsey said. "But we'll keep looking."

"Got an address for the mom?" Hank asked, pulling out his cell phone. "Give me her number, too."

Ramsey rattled off what he needed, repeating things a couple of times as Hank did his best hunt-and-peck to input the information.

Then he squatted as low as he could on his infamous bum knees to take a few photos of the girl's face and her clothing.

"Should we close her eyes first?" Jo asked. He meant to show the pics to the mother, she knew, to confirm that it was Kelly. Would she want to see her daughter's death stare, glassy as marbles?

"Does it really matter?" he said, shrugging, before he put his phone away.

"I guess it doesn't," Jo replied. Because dead was dead, right? A mother's heart would be broken irreparably regardless.

"Let's go, Larsen," he said. "I've seen enough."

Jo rose from the grass, brushing hands on her jeans. She'd seen enough, too.

# CHAPTER FOUR

The street where Kelly Amster had lived with her mother was within walking distance of the water tower. It sat in an older section of Plainfield, and not the kind with tall shade trees and ample acreage like Amanda Pearson's. The lots were compact, and the size of the houses more akin to bungalows than sprawling ranches. Between well-tended yards with plotted flower beds and trimmed boxwoods were neglected abodes with shin-high lawns and filthy Big Wheels getting strangled by weeds.

Nearby, strip malls abounded, and train tracks ran beyond a patchwork of fencing. Jo could hear the whistle and the rhythmic clickety-clack as Hank parked the Ford and they got out.

"Being near train tracks lowers the value of your house by something like twelve percent," Hank remarked, a factoid he had probably picked up from a late-night HGTV binge. "It's about the same as being near a highway."

Jo looked at the house that had been Kelly Amster's home, and she doubted the girl had worried much about resale.

The place reminded her of where she'd grown up on Lemmon Avenue in the city. Had Kelly lain in bed at night, too, listening to the noise of passing trains, unable to sleep?

As a kid, Jo had done that often, although what she'd heard had been the sound of jet engines, taking off from Love Field and flying people to faraway places. How many times had she wished she were a passenger? Too many to count. She wondered if Kelly Amster had wished she'd been on one of the trains that scuttled by on the tracks, getting the hell away from whatever demons had been plaguing her in Plainfield.

Something must have kept her up at night. Something bad enough to make her decide to climb the tower and throw herself over the railing.

"I hate this," Hank grumbled as they walked up the path to the front door. "No, I take that back. *Hate* isn't a strong enough word."

"Yep." Jo figured that pretty much said it all.

The door opened, and a slender woman stood on the threshold, waiting.

Jo's first impression of her was the color gray: gray sweats, gray T-shirt, faded gray in her dark brown hair, deep gray circles beneath eyes the very same washed-out blue as her daughter's. There was a grayness surrounding her, too. If Jo had been more New Age, she would have called it an aura. It wasn't even that the woman appeared devastated or broken, more like she'd given up.

"Barbara Amster?" she asked, earning a quick bob of the head. "I'm Detective Larsen, and this is my partner, Detective Phelps."

"You're here about Kelly," she said, the words emerging in a slow drawl. She sounded sleepy, and her eyes seemed foggy, unable to fully focus.

It reminded Jo a little of how Mama had been in the mornings, waking up with a hangover. Did Kelly's mom drink or take sleeping pills?

26

The bleary eyes shifted from Jo to Hank. "The policewoman I talked to, she said Kelly's dead. Is it true?"

"If you're up to it, ma'am, we've got some photos of the deceased. Would you mind taking a look so you can positively identify her?" Hank said.

He waited for Mrs. Amster's nod before he drew his phone from his pocket. Then he pulled up the photos he'd taken of the girl's face and her clothing. Slowly, he scrolled through them, giving her enough time in between to digest each image.

"Is this your daughter, ma'am? Is this Kelly?"

Jo was expecting tears to come in a flood, but they didn't. She began to wonder if they'd made a mistake until Mrs. Amster let out a soft sigh.

"Yes, that's her," she said, and her shoulders slumped. She seemed accepting, not angry, like she was no stranger to tragedy. Or maybe she was just so used to dealing with sick people and death that she'd grown a callus over her emotions. "I can't believe she actually went through with it."

"I'm sorry, ma'am," Hank said, clearly perplexed. "Had she tried before? To take her life, I mean."

"Tried to take her life before?" the woman repeated, then seemed to understand the implication of her remark. "Oh, no, Detective, it's nothing like that. It's just . . . kids like to talk big to make you feel guilty. Sometimes when Kelly got mad at me, she'd say hurtful things. But it was only words until now."

So Kelly Amster *had* threatened to kill herself before? Is that what her mother was implying?

Jo started to open her mouth, to ask the woman why she hadn't paid attention to those words, but Hank stepped in.

"Forgive me, Mrs. Amster," he said, sounding far more conciliatory than Jo felt. "We're just starting to put together the pieces. If you can help us fill in any gaps, we'd appreciate it. We'd like to be sure we're not making assumptions."

"I'll try," the woman said and hugged herself. She shivered and, with a shake of her shoulders, seemed to shrug off her gray mantle and come to life. Her hand went up to her mouth, and she moaned through her fingers. "I can't believe my baby girl has left me. She's really gone?"

"I know this is hard," Jo said and resisted the urge to physically reach out, to pat her arm or her shoulder. "But can we talk to you about Kelly? We'd like to try to understand what happened."

The woman removed her hand from her mouth, lowering it to between her breasts, where she left it, a fist against her heart. "The officer I spoke with . . . she said Kelly was found below the old water tower. I think she was there when I called her last night. Was I the last person to hear her voice? Do you think it was something I said?"

"Can we come in?" Jo asked. "It might be easier . . ."

"Yes, of course." Mrs. Amster drew in a breath, as if summoning up the energy to open the door wider. "This way," she finally said and gestured inside.

As there was nothing as fancy as a foyer to pass through, they walked right into a living area with sofa and chairs set within viewing distance of a wall-hung TV. The lights were off, and in the dimness of the room, the black screen looked a bit like a window to nowhere.

Jo located the wall switch and flicked it on.

"Oh, that's so bright." Mrs. Amster groaned, shading her eyes as she plunked down on the sofa. "I wish I'd never gotten up." She pulled the cuffs of her sweatshirt over her fists, tucking them beneath her chin. "I wish I was still sleeping. Maybe I am."

"Would you rather have the lights off?" Jo couldn't find a dimmer.

"I don't know what I want," the woman said flatly and closed her eyes for a long moment. She winced as she opened them again. "I can't believe this is real. We were together yesterday morning. We both slept in. Kelly made pancakes. She knew I was having a rough time with one of my cases."

"Was that when you last saw her?" Hank asked, as he took a seat in a chair across a coffee table strewn with candy bar wrappers and fashion magazines.

Jo didn't even try to sit. She knew she couldn't stay still.

Mrs. Amster didn't appear to notice Jo moving about. Her eyes were on Hank.

"I guess it was. I left for work about eleven. I spent the day getting a baby with stage-four cancer transferred out of the hospital so he could die at home. Breaks my heart. It truly does."

"You're a nurse, right?" Hank repeated what Charlotte Ramsey had told them.

"I do mostly chronic care cases for At-Home Angels. My schedule's kind of erratic because of that. When a client's end-stage, they need me more often."

"Do you set your own hours?"

"I go where I'm needed, and I don't worry about the hours," Mrs. Amster explained. "Sometimes it's not convenient for me as a mom, but illness is never convenient for anyone, is it? Kind of like crime, I suppose. But Kelly could take care of herself. She understood."

Jo looked around the small but tidy space at the school pictures of Kelly hung on the walls, chronicling each step through life from wide-eyed kindergartener to grade-school kid with missing teeth, awkward girl with braces in junior high, and then a brilliant metamorphosis into a very lovely, fresh-faced high school teen.

Jo searched for something in the images—a sadness in the eyes, an emptiness that projected some kind of neglect—but there was nothing there. Kelly looked like a pretty content child.

"So your daughter was used to not having you around?" Hank said, the blunt edge to the question causing Jo to turn.

She expected Mrs. Amster to get defensive, but the woman didn't even bristle.

"Do I wish I didn't have to work so much?" she remarked, eyes on Hank. "Yes, Detective. I do. But when you're a single mom, you don't have much of a choice. When Kelly was smaller, I took her to jobs when I could. As she got older, she did the latchkey thing, like so many kids do. But we had dinner together every night." She glanced down, shifting position. "Well, most nights."

"But not last night?" Hank said.

"No," she answered quietly.

Jo felt a familiar ache, understanding instinctively how Kelly must have felt, growing up and having so little of her mother. Kelly's situation had been different from Jo's, though. Her mom hadn't neglected her for booze or men. She'd left her daughter in order to care for others. Had that been hard for a child to understand? And was that Barbara Amster's fault? She had to work by necessity. Single moms didn't have it easy, and no matter what politicians preached, it wasn't simple to find support.

Verna Larsen Kaufman had been a stay-at-home mom. She'd had no excuses for what she'd done—or hadn't done—to save her child and had no one to blame but herself.

Jo went back to the chairs across from the coffee table and sat down. "Had you noticed Kelly showing any signs of depression? Had she been acting different lately? Any changes in her behavior?"

Mrs. Amster half smiled. "You're not a mother, are you?"

Jo felt stung by the remark. "No, ma'am, I'm not."

"She's a teenager, Detective. Behaving strangely is what they do."

Why did that feel like a brush-off rather than a real answer?

"Was she on medication for anything? Maybe for ADD? ADHD?" Jo tried.

"No."

"Had she seen a therapist or psychiatrist in the past? What about after the divorce?"

"After the divorce, we were both better off." With a sigh, Mrs. Amster poked her missing hands from the sweatshirt sleeves to reach up, reworking her messy ponytail. "If Kelly had any serious mental issues, I would have told you already."

Jo turned to Hank, willing him to step in because she wasn't getting anywhere with the woman.

He cleared his throat. "I'm guessing since you work in the medical field that you'd know signs of depression in your own daughter," he said, pursuing Jo's line of questioning. "And, yes, I'm a parent. I have two girls. I worry about 'em every damned day."

Jo knew why he'd added that last part, and she wanted to kiss him. Barbara Amster couldn't brush him off with a dismissive remark the way she had Jo.

The woman fumbled with her reply at first. "Of course I would see . . . I mean, I'd like to think so, although I couldn't begin to know what was going on inside her head every minute." Then she shrugged off her discomfort and returned to deflecting. "Look, she was a teenage girl. There were always things that weren't right—with other girls, with boys, with me. If she didn't get invited to a party, she moped. If she *did* get invited, she'd still find something to be upset about. It drove me up a wall, but I don't find that abnormal, do you?" She looked straight at Hank.

Jo bit the inside of her cheek to keep from interjecting.

"So nothing about Kelly these past few weeks seemed out of the ordinary?" he asked, still trying to get a real answer.

"Well, I guess there *was* something," Mrs. Amster murmured, her gaze darting toward a dog-eared copy of *Elle* on the coffee table. "Even before school resumed this year, I'd caught her wearing clothes I'd never seen before. They weren't the outfits we picked out when we went shopping before the term started."

"What kind of clothes?"

"They showed more skin, you know. I told her she looked like a slut. I didn't like it, but she said it's how the cool girls dressed. I didn't have the energy to fight her." She shook her head. "She had this awful blue dress she seemed obsessed with. It was way too tight. When she lost it, she flipped out, nearly tore apart the house trying to find it. But, honestly, I was relieved. One less trampy outfit for her to put on."

Jo figured the fashion magazines were Kelly's. Maybe the candy bar wrappers, too. So Kelly Amster was a young woman who wanted to be in style, and she probably wasn't on a diet. That told her more about the vic than her own mother had so far.

"Are you saying it was unusual for Kelly to want to fit in with the popular girls?" Jo asked.

"Yes, it was. Very."

Mrs. Amster got up and crossed the room to a cabinet. She tugged open a drawer and rifled through it before she found the object of her search. When she returned, she handed Jo a photograph of a smiling Kelly sitting alongside another girl with spiral curls and braces, a gawky contrast to Kelly's emerging beauty. They were clasping hands, holding them up, proudly showing off the matching braided bracelets on their wrists.

Jo recognized them. Kelly had been wearing hers upon her death.

Mrs. Amster went on. "The Kelly I knew wasn't interested in being social. She made fun of girls who liked to draw attention to themselves. She had one good friend, Cassie Marks, and they didn't like to stand out."

"This is Cassie with Kelly?" Jo asked, pointing at the girl in braces in the photograph.

"Yes. She lives a street over. The girls have been best friends for ages. You should go talk to her . . . Oh, but she's in school right now."

Mrs. Amster's chin began to quiver. "God, poor Cass. She's going to be devastated."

Jo exchanged glances with Hank.

Why wasn't Mrs. Amster the one who was devastated?

Her partner's eyes seemed to question that, too. What was wrong with this woman? She had just lost her only child. Was she that burned out? Did death not faze her anymore?

Or, Jo wondered, were they expecting too much?

She collected her thoughts, not wanting to forget anything important. "You told Officer Ramsey that Kelly left a suicide note," Jo said. "May we see it, please?"

"It's still on her bed. I'll go get it." Mrs. Amster grabbed the sofa armrest and pulled herself up. Looking a bit wobbly, she shuffled out of the room.

Hank turned to Jo and said under his breath, "How the hell is she so calm?"

"Like they say, everybody grieves differently," Jo replied, because it was what they'd been taught. They weren't supposed to jump to conclusions. But she thought something felt off, too.

"She's phoning it in," Hank said and ran a hand over his head. "Jesus, if it were my kid, I'd be gutted. I'd be sobbing and begging to see her before they carted her off . . ."

"She's not you, Hank."

"But she hasn't asked *why*. That's the first thing that I'd want to know. Isn't she even curious? Or does she have an inkling and isn't willing to share?"

The sound of Mrs. Amster's returning footsteps silenced him.

Hank got up from the chair, and Jo did the same.

The woman clutched a piece of paper to her breasts. "Will you give it back when you're done with it?"

"Yes, ma'am," Jo said. "Of course we will."

Kelly's mom looked beseechingly at Hank, as if she required a second opinion.

"You will get it back," he told her.

Mrs. Amster handed over the note. It was written on lined white paper, torn from a composition book, with a ragged margin.

Jo held it so both she and Hank could read the purple pen strokes.

*I love you, but it hurts too much to stay. I'm sorry. So, so sorry.*

That was it. Exactly what Charlotte Ramsey had quoted from her notes. Nothing more. No explanation.

"Is this your daughter's handwriting?" Jo asked before she bagged the note and tucked it away.

"Yes, it's definitely Kelly's handwriting." Mrs. Amster blinked her tired eyes. "Are we done now? I need to get ready for work."

*She's going to work?*

Um, okay.

Jo tried to tell herself not to judge. Maybe the woman needed the distraction. Maybe taking care of a dying baby put Kelly's death into perspective for her, or she was just stoic in an "ashes to ashes, dust to dust" kind of way.

"You do what you need to do," Jo found herself saying.

And they would do what they needed to do as well.

Jo leaned toward Hank and said under her breath, "Her room? Can we take a look?"

It might pay off, she thought, to go through Kelly's space and try to dig for something more, because she didn't feel like she was getting the whole story from Barbara Amster—more like a verse than a chapter.

But Hank gave a subtle shake of his head and whispered, "Later."

Jo understood, but she couldn't walk away entirely. "Does Kelly have a tablet or laptop she uses for school?"

Barbara Amster's expression turned dull again. The gray cloud enveloped her so that her voice was a flat monotone. "She uses a laptop from the district. I don't know where it is. She doesn't have a tablet, not one I bought her, anyway."

"We may need to talk to you again, ma'am. We'll be in touch," Hank said, drowning out Jo's disappointed, "Okay, thanks."

"Well, you know where I live," the woman said, shuffling to the door and pulling it open for them.

"Again, ma'am, I'm sorry," Hank said.

"Yes, we're very sorry for your loss," Jo added, and she meant it.

"So am I," Mrs. Amster said, dry eyed, and then she closed the door.

# CHAPTER FIVE

"Did you get a weird vibe in there, or was it just me?" Jo said when they got in the car.

"It wasn't you."

She tugged the seat belt across her lap as Hank started the engine.

"I'm really trying hard not to judge," he said, but he wrinkled his nose like he was judging anyway. "Being a parent is no picnic. It's tough enough when there are two of you. I can't imagine going it alone." He hesitated, letting the car idle at the curb. "I got the impression she was kind of disconnected from Kelly, that maybe she didn't know her kid as well as she thought."

"Who knows what Kelly could have gotten into while her mother was at work?" Jo said quietly.

"Yeah, who knows?"

Jo didn't want to be judgmental, either. Her only personal experience with motherhood came from being a daughter. She'd always had an image in her head of the perfect mother: brimming with unconditional love, ever-present emotionally if not physically, overprotective, and selfless to the point of self-neglect. Yes, she understood that not all moms were enmeshed in their kids' lives. Many had high-powered careers. Even those who sacrificed a salary for full-time parenthood ended up working overtime—volunteering, managing households, and taking care of husbands, kids, aging parents, or all of the above. Others had problems with addiction or mental illness. There was nothing easy about trying to care for a life other than one's own.

Jo wasn't sure how to peg Barbara Amster. She certainly seemed dedicated to her work. She was a nurse. She took care of people for a living. So shouldn't she have noticed that her only child was headed down a dark path?

Or perhaps she *had* noticed something about Kelly's recent behavior that she wasn't willing to share. But why? It made no sense.

She sat there for a few minutes, looking up at the house.

Hank seemed lost in thought as well.

She finally spoke to break the silence. "When Kelly's phone turns up, it could answer a lot of questions."

"Maybe that friend of Kelly's, Cassie Marks, could answer a few questions the good old-fashioned way," Hank said, giving her a sideways glance. "You up for a chat?"

"Right now?"

"Better sooner than later." He put the car into gear and pulled into the street. "How 'bout a quick visit to the high school?"

Jo let out a slow breath, feeling her heartbeat accelerate.

"What's wrong? You don't want to go back to school? Don't tell me you're still having dreams about forgetting your locker combination?"

"Pretty much," she said simply, which was true enough.

She hadn't exactly *liked* school, but she hadn't hated it, either. Going meant escape for seven hours a day, five days a week. That had been a very good thing. But it was hard being a kid and having to keep a secret that was way too big. It was hard feeling different, like she was damaged goods; like what her stepfather did to her made her ugly and unlovable. She'd always been so afraid that, if the teachers found out, the kids would, too. And she'd had no one to talk to about it, certainly not her mother. Verna Kaufman had been a drunk and a liar, and she'd never taken Jo's word over that of her husband.

Once he'd died, Jo had breathed at last. With her stepdad gone, she could sleep at night. She could stop pretending. Life wasn't perfect, but it was better. Just not for Mama. She still drank like her life depended on it, and maybe it had. Jo always wondered if that was what had led to the Alzheimer's—all the alcohol pickling her mother's brain. Or else it was her punishment for pretending she hadn't screwed up her daughter's life beyond all recognition. Now poor old Verna couldn't remember anything at all.

"So you didn't like school, huh?" Hank prodded.

When she didn't explain herself, he went a step further.

"Look, nobody really likes high school, Larsen. You know that, don't you? It's the universe testing us, to see if we can get along with a mixed bag of people. You've got the geeks who speak a different language, the jocks who've got more muscle in their pinkies than they have brains in their skulls, and the spoiled young assholes who grow up to be pampered old assholes."

"So which were you?" she asked. "Because I definitely know which you *weren't*."

"I played ball," he admitted, like he was spilling a state secret.

Jo laughed. "I know. I've heard the story a hundred times about how your knees got so beat up."

"Just so you understand that I wasn't good enough at it to be a total knucklehead." He took his gaze off the road to look at her quizzically. "What about you? I'm guessing you weren't the prom queen?"

"Only in a Stephen King book."

"You get blood dumped on your head?"

"Nothing that dramatic," she said, picking invisible lint from her jeans. "I wasn't into that kind of thing, that's all."

"What?" He feigned surprise. "Social butterfly like you didn't put on a fancy dress, get pinned with an ugly corsage, and shake her booty to a lousy cover band?"

"Sounds crazy, huh?" she said.

"Seriously." Hank jerked his chin. "You were the outlier, weren't you, Larsen? The kid who wore black and cut gym class to sneak a smoke."

"Sorry to disappoint, but I wasn't that badass," she said, adding dryly, "I was just busy on prom night, stabbing myself in the eye with a fork."

"Now *that*, I believe." Hank's weathered face might have worn a half smile, but his eyes weren't laughing. They looked sober, sad even. Like he realized her childhood had been anything but normal, even though she'd never told him about the abuse, not directly. She'd had the kind of life his two girls would thankfully never know.

Jo turned to the window.

She didn't remember where she'd gone instead of prom. Had she snuck into a dive bar to hear a band? Gone to a movie alone? Did it really matter? She hadn't liked being around Mama, couldn't wait to graduate high school and leave home. She'd been an adult before she was ready. It made so many things—like going to prom—feel like a whole lot of nothing.

Thankfully, Hank dropped it. Within five minutes, they were pulling into the high school parking lot. There was a space right in front reserved for police, so they took advantage. Jo was relieved she wouldn't have to listen to him harp about walking a mile to the front door.

There were brief steps as well as a wide ramp leading up to the entrance. When they got to the locked front door, Jo noted the eye of a camera watching her as she pressed the intercom. A disembodied voice immediately said, "Can I help you?"

Jo stared into the fish-eye lens. "I'm Detective Larsen," she said and plucked her ID from her belt. She flipped it open and held it up to display her shield. "I'm with my partner, Detective Phelps from the Plainfield Police Department. We'd like to speak with one of your students if we could."

"Just a minute, Detective, and I'll buzz you in."

The door let out a telling beep, and Hank took the handle and pushed it open. They entered a wide hallway with checkerboard marble floors, doors opening to their left and right, and beyond, the hallway going in all directions.

A dark-eyed young woman with a hesitant smile stepped out of the door on the right. "I'm Margie Fox, Principal Billings's assistant. If you'll come with me, Detectives, I'll take you to her office."

"Thanks," Hank said, nodding.

They followed Margie into a carpeted anteroom hung with student-made artwork and passed several small offices with open doors before they entered a room with a heavy brown desk. A slender woman with cropped white hair and tortoiseshell glasses rose from behind it, coming around to extend her hand.

"I'm Helen Billings," she said. "You're detectives from here in Plainfield?"

"Yes," Jo said. "We're hoping to see a student of yours, Cassie Marks."

The eyes behind the glasses squinted. "Why?" the principal asked. "Is Cassie in some kind of trouble?"

"No, it's not that at all," Jo began to explain, when Hank kicked in, "We've just come from speaking with Barbara Amster. Her daughter, Kelly, was found deceased this morning on the grounds of the old water tower."

"Oh, my heavens." Helen Billings sucked in her breath. Her expression registered more surprise than they'd seen in Barbara Amster's face earlier. "Kelly is dead?" the principal said. "How? Was it an accident?"

"We're in the process of investigating, ma'am," Hank told her. "That's why we need to ask Cassie some questions, if it's all right with you."

The principal sprang into action, quickly rounding her desk and sitting down. She paused as she plucked up the phone. "If y'all don't mind, I need to call Cassie's parents and make sure it's okay. They both work, and I'm not certain if one of them might want to be here with Cassie."

Jo nodded.

"Sure, that's fine, ma'am," Hank said. "If one of 'em wants to sit in on the interview, we'll wait."

The principal hesitated with the receiver in hand. "I'll tell them I could stay with Cassie if they're agreeable."

"Yes, ma'am," Hank said. "That would work, too."

Jo nudged her partner. "Let's give Mrs. Billings some privacy."

They headed for the door as the principal looked up a number and began to dial. As Jo walked out with Hank on her heels, she nearly ran into Margie.

The young assistant had tears in her eyes. Clearly, she must have overheard the conversation. She whispered, "Is it true? Poor Kelly's gone?"

"Did you know her well?" Jo asked, ignoring Hank as he shut the door behind them. The high school had more than three hundred students, as far as Jo was aware. She figured it took some effort to become familiar with every one of them.

"I wouldn't say well, no. It's not like Kelly stood out or anything," Margie said as she gestured toward a pair of chairs off to the side where Jo and Hank could wait. "She didn't get into trouble and end up in Helen's office. Nothing like that. But she sometimes forgot her lunch and didn't have money to purchase one, and we heard from the cafeteria ladies that they were subsidizing her." Her face clouded. "When Helen brought Kelly in and asked her about it, she was so embarrassed. She didn't want anyone to know."

"Did you talk to her mother?" Jo asked.

"I think Helen tried, but she had a difficult time catching her, since she works kind of odd hours." Margie smiled hesitantly. "The principal personally took care of it. She's a good lady."

"She sounds like it," Jo said.

"Anyway, I saw Kelly on the first day of school. She seemed different somehow, more grown up, I guess." She pursed her lips. "When I asked how her summer went, she said that it had changed everything."

"Did she tell you how?" Jo asked, hoping to get some clarity.

"No, I'm sorry," Margie replied. "And I didn't ask. I just assumed it was for the good."

"Did you see her again the past few weeks?"

"I did, yes." The woman tucked short, dark hair behind her ears. "She told me she was trying out for cheerleader, maybe even student council. She seemed very focused, very determined, and I was rooting for her. She'd been such a mouse her whole freshman year, sitting on the sidelines with Cassie Marks. I sensed that wouldn't be the case anymore."

"Thanks." Jo looked at Hank. Something *had* happened. A girl didn't just change who she was overnight without an impetus.

A phone began to bleat at a desk up the hallway, and the woman's head jerked toward the sound.

"I'd better get that," she said and scurried away.

The ringing stopped.

"The summer that changed everything," Hank repeated as he settled into one of the chairs. He patted his thighs and sighed. "I'll say it did."

"Why would Kelly go on this path to be popular, then suddenly throw herself off the water tower?" Jo sat down beside him. "It hardly makes sense."

"When does it ever?"

But Jo didn't get it.

If things had been so hunky-dory for Kelly Amster, if she'd been plucky enough to want to give cheerleading a shot, why would she leave her mom a note to say "I'm sorry" and end her life?

"What happened to her between the end of summer and last night?" she wondered aloud. "Something so bad she couldn't even tell her mother?"

"Maybe she told a friend."

"Let's hope," Jo said, as the door to the principal's office opened and a grim-faced Helen Billings emerged.

Hank and Jo both stood.

"I'll take you to the conference room, and then I'll get Cassie," the woman said. "Her parents aren't worried about her talking to you about Kelly. They're more concerned about how she'll take the news that Kelly's dead."

"So the girls were that close, huh?" Hank asked.

The principal sighed. "They were like sisters."

She strode past Jo, opening the nearest door to the hallway.

Hank made an "after you" gesture, and Jo followed the principal out.

# CHAPTER SIX

Their heels clicked loudly on the tiled floors as they walked past bulletin boards, glass cases displaying photos and trophies, and hand-painted signs welcoming students back, announcing an upcoming dance, and inviting tryouts for cheerleading, debate team, and various sports.

Jo found herself holding her breath as she walked. She might have turned a slight shade of blue, because Hank caught her elbow as they neared a series of yellow locker doors.

"You okay, partner?" he said under his breath. "Or are you havin' flashbacks to pus-filled pimples and sweaty palms?"

Jo gave him the stink eye, and he chuckled.

He turned somber, though, as Helen Billings paused outside a locked door and pulled out a key. When she got it open, she gestured for them to enter.

Jo went in first, nearly running into an oval table surrounded by at least ten chairs. There was ample signage relating to taking PSATs, SATs, and ACTs, so she figured it was some kind of testing area.

"Have a seat, Detectives," the principal said. "I'll fetch Cassie and be right back."

She closed the door behind her with a crisp snap.

Within five minutes, she returned with a teenage girl in tow: skinny and angular with dishwater-blond curls and red spots on her chin. She had shiny pink balm on her lips that she nervously seemed to be chewing away bit by bit.

"Detectives, this is Cassie Marks," the principal said, making introductions. "Cassie, these are the detectives I told you were here to talk to you about Kelly."

Hank and Jo both offered muted hellos.

Cassie's wide eyes skimmed over Hank, fixing firmly on Jo. "What's going on? Is Kelly okay?"

Jo looked at the principal, who nodded. She would do the explaining.

"Come here, sweetheart," Helen Billings said, guiding Cassie to a seat and giving her shoulder a squeeze before sitting down in the chair beside her. "I'm sorry to have to tell you that Kelly has passed away. She was found near the old water tower, and the detectives are trying to figure out what happened to her exactly."

"Did she fall?" Cassie asked, glancing from the principal to Jo, her expression pure shock. "Oh, my God, she didn't jump?"

"That's what we're looking into," Jo answered, which wasn't really the answer Cassie wanted. "We're as confused as you are. We're hoping you can help us out."

The girl hugged her arms around herself, withdrawing. "I didn't think she'd really . . . I can't believe she'd do it."

"I'm sorry," Hank said solemnly. "It's hard to lose a friend."

Cassie didn't even look at him. She merely hugged herself tighter.

"How about we start over?" Jo said, sensing the girl clamming up. She could smell her fear: a mix of sweat, sticky-sweet perfume, and bubblegum lip gloss. She tried to put her at ease. "I'm Jo Larsen from the Plainfield police, and this is my partner, Hank Phelps. We're trying to figure out what was going on in Kelly's life that might have led to her death."

Helen Billings patted Cassie's hand, murmuring something to nudge her along. But the girl kept her head down.

"You were Kelly's best friend, weren't you?" Jo said, reiterating what Barbara Amster had told them. "You probably knew her better than anyone."

Cassie breathed a soft, "Yes." But that was all.

"I know it probably doesn't even seem real that Kelly's gone, but it's important that we quickly gather facts. We're hoping you can share what you know about Kelly's last few weeks leading up to last night."

"Does he have to stay?" Jo heard Cassie whisper to the principal. She was staring straight at Hank.

Her partner must've overheard as well. He shifted in his seat. The chair creaked beneath him.

"It's all right," Jo said. "He's one of the good guys."

But Cassie didn't appear to relax.

Jo pressed on. "Can you think of anyone that Kelly wasn't getting along with? Someone who might have bullied her, perhaps?"

Cassie pursed her lips.

"Is there any reason that she might have wanted to harm herself?" Jo tried again. "Think hard, will you, please?"

The girl said nothing. She just kept staring at Hank, as though he were Bigfoot instead of a slightly overweight, middle-aged man with a receding hairline.

"Was Kelly unhappy?" Jo asked, trying not to sound exasperated. "Did she tell you outright that she was upset, or maybe you sensed it?"

When Cassie didn't respond, Principal Billings stepped in. "You are not betraying a friend, do you understand? You should speak freely to the detectives. They're here on Kelly's behalf, not to get you in trouble."

Cassie nodded but continued watching Hank.

She looked terrified.

Was she afraid of men? Jo wondered. Or was it something else, like she wanted to dish about Kelly but only if it was girl talk?

Jo chewed on her cheek, trying to figure out what to do next.

Hank finally realized that he was causing a holdup. He cleared his throat and scooted back his chair. "If y'all would excuse me," he said, "I've got a few phone calls to make. I think I'll head outside to take care of them." He looked at Jo. "You got this, partner?"

"I do," she told him, grateful for his voluntary retreat.

As soon as he was gone, Cassie's demeanor changed. The hesitation dissolved. She stopped gnawing her lips, now pretty much devoid of anything glossy. A big sigh escaped her, and her eyes filled with tears as she started to speak.

"This is so messed up. Why would Kelly be at the old water tower unless, you know, she seriously meant to do it this time?" Cassie stopped talking, and her expression turned angry. A great sob escaped her throat. "It's all her fault," she said. "She should have listened to me."

*Whoa.*

Jo was taken aback, not by Cassie blaming Kelly but by the implication that Kelly had previously threatened to take her own life. It was what Barbara Amster had intimated before backtracking. Jo waited for Cassie to calm down as Helen Billings patted her hand and said, "There, there," before proffering a crumpled tissue.

Cassie blew her nose, dabbing at her eyes. When the sobs had stopped, Jo could wait no longer.

"Did Kelly talk about suicide before last night?" she asked. "Was she depressed? Was something wrong?"

Cassie took her time answering. She rubbed a hand around her wrist, as if feeling for a phantom bracelet. Jo thought of the woven braid Kelly Amster had on her wrist, even in death, and she wondered where Cassie's matching bracelet was.

"Did you . . . did you ask Barb about that?" the girl replied haltingly. "What did she say?"

*Barb?*

Not *Mrs. Amster.*

Jo raised her eyebrows. "Yes, I asked."

Cassie sighed. "Did she tell you how freaky Kelly was being?"

"Freaky?" Jo repeated. "She did mention Kelly buying clothes she'd never seen before and dressing more provocatively. She thought Kelly was trying to be popular."

Cassie sniffed and gave an exaggerated roll of her eyes. "OMG, that's classic Barb. Kelly always said she was oblivious."

Oblivious, huh?

"Why don't you explain it to me then," Jo said, since good ol' Barb was so out of the loop. "How had Kelly changed recently? What was going on with her that had you worried?"

"How *didn't* she change?" Cassie whined. "It's like I wasn't good enough for her all of a sudden, you know? It was, like, at the end of the summer break, she started acting like a stranger. She pulled away. She quit sharing stuff with me, you know, like she had so many secrets." Cassie twisted a dishwater curl around her finger. "I guess she had better things to do than hang with me."

Now she was getting somewhere.

"How did she pull away?" Jo asked, leaning forearms on the table. "Did she become withdrawn? Was she moody?"

"No, no, it was worse than that." The girl angrily wiped at the tears sliding down her blotchy cheeks. "Would you effing believe she wanted to try out for cheerleader? That's, like, totally lame, for one thing, and a total waste of time."

"Why?"

Cassie made a noise of disbelief. "Seriously? Who would have voted for Kelly Amster? Girls like us don't make cheerleader. We sit on the sidelines."

"Girls like what?" Jo wanted to understand.

Cassie grimaced. "You saw Kelly's house, didn't you? I live, like, a street away. You know all those mansions across town?"

Jo nodded.

"That's the Bubble. They're the ones that have, like, everything. We don't get the newest iPhones. Ours are crap, you know, brands nobody's heard of. We don't shop at Nordstrom, more like resale stores and GW."

"GW?" Jo said.

"Goodwill." Cassie shook her dark blond curls. "Girls like us aren't cheerleaders. We're only good enough for the spirit club or, like, the choir. Girls from the Bubble are the ones shaking pom-poms at pep rallies. But Kelly said somebody she knew could get her in."

"Who?"

The girl shrugged and looked down at her lap as she answered in a quiet voice, "Maybe whoever invited her to that party."

Compared to Barbara Amster, Cassie was the *National Enquirer*. She was full of headlines but slim on details.

Jo glanced at the principal, who gave a slight shake of her head. "What party?" she asked. "Was it held by a classmate?"

"Yeah, I guess," was all that Cassie volunteered. She seemed to be dragging her feet, and Jo didn't know why.

She tried again. "What did Kelly tell you about it?"

Cassie's head came up, and she met Jo's eyes. "She was acting shady as f—" She stopped herself, glanced at the principal, and tried again. "All I know is she got an e-mail, like, a weekend or two before school started. One of the senior Guccis was having a party, like, just for his squad. Kelly said his parents were out of the country or at their cabin in Aspen or Telluride, wherever rich people go when it's hot." Her expression turned sour. "Kelly was my fam, you know. We'd done everything together since we were kids, but she didn't ask me to go. I thought it was, you know, a joke someone was playing on her, that she was being punked." Anger narrowed her eyes. "I told her to swipe left, you know, not to do it. To go to a movie with me or something. But she went anyway. I can't even . . ." She sighed, shaking her curls again.

Jo could tell Cassie had more to say, so she didn't interrupt. She watched the girl's gaze slide over to Helen Billings.

"You do know something, don't you?" Jo said. Something she wasn't willing to admit in front of the principal, perhaps?

Cassie fidgeted. "Can we be alone?" she asked.

*Bingo.*

Helen Billings looked startled. "You'd like me to leave?"

Cassie nodded, biting on her lip.

Jo felt her pulse pick up. "Is there a chance I can speak with Cassie privately?" she said to the principal.

The woman didn't appear thrilled by the request. She pushed at her tortoiseshell specs, hardly popping out of her chair. "I told Cassie's parents I'd stay, and I want to keep that promise."

"I'm not a baby," the girl said, frowning. When she realized that didn't have the effect she wanted, she added in a more conciliatory tone, "Honestly, I'm okay. I just need to say some things without you, um . . . I don't want to throw shade on anyone."

The principal looked at Jo. "I don't know about this," she said.

"You could stand right outside, perhaps, leave the door open a bit," Jo suggested, hoping the woman would go, hoping that Cassie actually had something worthwhile to share.

The woman paused, clearly debating the request. Only when Cassie uttered a soft but insistent "Please" did she give in.

"I'll be right outside," she said, getting up and patting the girl's shoulder. "If you should need me, holler."

The principal let herself out but kept the door open, as Jo had suggested, and stood so near the jamb that Jo could see the sleeve of her navy-blue jacket.

Then Jo homed in on Cassie.

She scooted her chair nearer to the girl's, keeping an arm's length so as not to crowd her. Once she was close enough, she touched Cassie's bare wrist very gently, like they were friends sharing a confidence.

"You were talking about the party Kelly went to without you. Did something happen there?"

Cassie leaned toward her. "Yeah, it did," she whispered, glancing over at the door as if to reassure herself that no one else could hear. Once the floodgates had opened, she couldn't talk fast enough. "Kelly called and woke me up the next morning at five. She was bawling, saying there was no one else she could talk to. She'd, like, passed out at the party, and when she woke up, you know, she was in her front yard, lying on the grass." The girl paused, her cheeks turning pink. "She said she hurt *down there*, and there was blood, you know, but she didn't have her period. Her underwear was on backward. She couldn't find her keys, so she sat on the front stoop, waiting for Barb to get home from an overnight job. She kept crying and saying, 'Is it my fault? Is it my fault?'"

Jo's heart skipped. "Did she think she was raped?"

Cassie looked confused. "I don't know . . . maybe. She blacked out, she said, and she couldn't remember everything. But she'd never . . . you know . . . done it before, so she knew the blood had to be because someone at the party had . . . you know . . . smashed her while she was wasted."

Yes, Jo knew all too well.

"Why didn't she call the police?"

"I told her she should, but she wouldn't do it." Cassie fidgeted. "She said she felt responsible. She'd gone to the party, right? She drank too much. Who would have believed her?"

*I would,* Jo mused. *I would have believed her.*

"That doesn't make her any less of a victim," she said.

"Doesn't it?" Cassie replied.

Jo flinched.

Was that Cassie's opinion? Was it how Kelly had felt? Or was it just the whole "blame the victim" mentality that so many in society harbored for any woman who cried rape?

"I thought she'd totally fall apart, you know, the way she was wailing when we talked," the girl offered with a shake of her head. "But she didn't want me to come over. She said she had things to take care of. I got worried and went over anyway, but she acted like she didn't need me. She was stone-cold. I wanted to talk about it, you know. I even said she should tell her mom. But she wouldn't." Cassie paused, lifting a hand to her mouth, fingers shaking. "She said she realized she had, like, proof, and that she could get someone in big trouble if she wanted to. I wondered if there were pix or a video or something."

With every divulgence, Jo grew more furious. She found herself taking a deep breath before she pressed on. "So did she tell you who threw the party?"

"All's I know is it was a big shot, one of the Guccis."

That was the second time she'd used that term. "He's a rich kid?" Jo asked, just to be sure that they were on the same page.

"Yeah," Cassie confirmed. "She wouldn't tell me which one, even when I asked. I don't know if she was protecting him or just feeling dope to be keeping a secret." Her brow wrinkled. "Don't you have her phone? Like, can't you read her texts and figure it out?"

"We're working on it," Jo said.

Kelly's pal didn't seem to take that one well.

"So you *don't* have her phone?"

Jo didn't respond.

At first, Cassie looked worried, eyes buggy, lips parted. Then her mouth tightened, her eyes narrowing. "Maybe it's better, you know, not to dig too deep," the girl whispered. "Maybe you should just drop it."

"We can't do that," Jo told her. Especially not after what Cassie had just revealed. "For Kelly's sake, we have to look into this—"

"This what?" Cassie cut her off. "Is it better for everyone to hear that Kelly was raped at some Gucci's party? Like that would change anything? If you meant what you said, that you were doing this for Kelly, you'd stop asking questions and leave it alone." A great sob escaped her, and she started howling like the world had ended.

The noise quickly drew Helen Billings back inside the room.

"What's wrong?" she asked as Cassie pushed away from the table and stood, tears streaming down her face in earnest.

"Kelly's gone, and nothing can bring her back," she railed at Jo, her whole face pink and blotchy. "Can't you just let her rest in peace?"

Then she brushed past the principal, taking off. Jo could hear her shoes tapping on the hallway tiles at first and then nothing.

Helen Billings opened her mouth to speak, but a bell rang, drowning out any words. Then she took off, too, no doubt chasing after Cassie.

It didn't matter. The interview was over.

Jo sat still for a long moment, trying hard to steady her racing heart.

*"Can't you just let her rest in peace?"*

Wasn't that what they were trying to do? Give Kelly some peace, some resolution to the tragic end of her very short life?

Like Jo could walk away now, after learning Kelly Amster had gone to a party mere weeks ago, where—if Cassie Marks could be believed—she'd been assaulted. Was that what had driven her to suicide?

Or was there more to it?

# CHAPTER SEVEN

"You done in here?" Hank asked.

Jo's head jerked up. Her partner's bulk filled the doorway.

"Yeah, I'm done," she told him, getting to her feet. Her heart felt heavy, her emotions even more unsettled than after meeting Kelly Amster's mom. She didn't know what she'd expected to hear from Cassie Marks, but it definitely was not that Kelly had been victimized at a party just weeks before her death.

"What the heck happened? You get anything out of her?"

"More than I could have imagined." At the arch of his tangled eyebrows, she added, "Let's get to the car. Then I'll fill you in."

Students swarmed the hallways, engulfing them as they made their way out.

Jo didn't know where Helen Billings had gone, or Cassie for that matter. She figured she and Hank would pop into the principal's office on their way out. She wanted to leave her card for the principal's assistant, too, in case anything should come up.

But they'd barely turned the corner when Helen Billings reappeared. Her white hair bobbed through the sea of teenagers as they made a path for her.

"Come," she directed them over the noise of chattering voices.

She led them back to her office, past her assistant's desk, where a couple of girls in bilious pink and green Lilly Pulitzer dresses stood loudly complaining about the senior parking lot being overcrowded. The teens glanced at Jo and Hank long enough to decide they weren't important.

Once Helen Billings had closed the door to her office behind them, she flung hands in the air. "Cassie's with the nurse," she said. "She's lying down until she's calm enough to return to class. I'm tempted to call her parents and suggest one of them come take her home."

Jo stood beside Hank, keeping mum and giving the principal a chance to vent.

"I feel like the wind's been knocked out of me, yet I don't have time to rest," she said and picked up her cell phone from the desk, giving it a glance before she set it down. "I need to compose an e-mail to our families explaining that a student has passed away and call in a grief counselor for any kids who need support."

"That's a good idea," Hank murmured.

Jo just watched and listened.

"We don't expect to lose them so young," Helen Billings went on, taking deep breaths every now and then, for all the good they seemed to do her. "We'll have to issue some kind of press release, although I hardly know what to say. It's like you're not even allowed to grieve anymore before the tragedy's all over local media and social media . . ."

"You're right," Hank said, as the principal's voice drifted off. "It's a flash-mob world. Nothing's gentle anymore."

Jo wished she could say something reassuring, but she could only imagine the weight on the woman's shoulders. The school had just lost one of its own, a mere child, who likely spent more time on campus than with her own mother.

"I hope you can find out why," Helen Billings said, bespectacled eyes beseeching. "I need to know for the future, if there's anything I could have done differently . . . if I could somehow have intervened and prevented this." She slumped into her chair. "I feel like I failed her."

"I understand," Jo said. "And I am sorry."

Death had such a ripple effect.

The principal nodded.

Hank cleared his throat. "Did you have something to tell us?"

He seemed as itchy as Jo to wrap this up and get going.

"Yes, you're right, I do," she said, snapping to. "Well, it's more like something to show you." She swiveled her chair around to the cabinet behind her desk, unlocked a door, and removed a laptop with a Post-it attached. She peeled off the note and scribbled on the back before she restuck it on the computer. "This is Kelly's school-issued laptop. The district launched a program last year to make sure every kid had one for lessons and homework. Kelly brought hers by last Friday afternoon and said she thought the battery went bad, as it wouldn't power on. I was going to ask the IT people to take a look today. Now, I guess, I won't have to."

She stood, holding it out, and Jo leaned across the desk to take it from her.

"You're giving us permission to review its contents?"

Helen Billings raked white hair behind her ears. "Yes, I'm giving you permission, if you can get it to work. It's school property, or rather, property of the district. We've got filters on it so the kids can't load it with games or visit porn sites, and we maintain administrator control, so they know we can get into their accounts at any time and make sure they're not using their computers to bully or to share naked pictures."

"I'm sure the parents appreciate that," Jo said.

"They do," the principal agreed. "But there are almost too many monsters lurking online for us to protect them from everything."

"Oh, yeah, there's no shortage of monsters," Hank said, thick eyebrows cinching. "You'd think that as tech savvy as kids are today, they'd be more careful, but sometimes I think it makes them fearless. They don't believe just chatting online with a stranger's going to harm them in any way."

"If Kelly was engaged in any risky behavior, I'm not aware of it. She is . . . she *was* a good kid, the quiet kind who often slips through the cracks." The woman's voice broke.

"We won't let her slip through, ma'am," Hank assured her.

"Is the laptop password protected?" Jo asked.

"Yes, but you can bypass Kelly's password with the administrator's," the principal said, pulling herself together. "I wrote that and the username on the back of the Post-it. If you have any trouble getting in, let me know."

Jo took a moment to glance down at the fluorescent yellow square that had *K. Amster-Won't Boot* printed on the front. When she lifted it up, she noticed the mix of characters and numbers that would otherwise have made no sense.

"Thanks." She tucked the laptop under her arm so she could fish out a couple of cards from her pocket. "If you hear anything or come across anything more about Kelly that might shed some light on things, call, okay?"

"If I discover anything important, I will."

"At this point, ma'am, we don't know what's important," Hank said, earning him a solemn nod from the principal.

"Of course."

Jo thanked her for her time, and she managed to slip a card in front of the principal's assistant, too, before they got out of there and back to the car.

The sun blazed high in the sky, looking molten, and the Ford sizzled without a tree to shade it. When Jo opened the passenger door, she felt the oppressive heat, like something heavy pushing against her. She sucked it up and got inside, thankful when Hank coaxed the engine to life and the air-conditioning began to blow, even though initially, it was more hot than cold.

"I think I'm ready for Christmas," Hank said as he cranked down the windows, like that would help.

"And when Christmas comes, you'll be ready for summer," she quipped, because that was how it went.

He waited till the car cooled down and then rolled up the windows. "What happened with Cassie? She ran out on you, huh?"

"Not until she'd spilled her guts," Jo replied, belting herself in as she told him about the party that Cassie said Kelly had attended just before the start of school, and how Kelly had awakened on her lawn at five in the morning with blood in her underwear. "She had to wait for her mom to get home from a job because she couldn't find her keys."

"You're telling me the kid might have been raped?" Hank muttered. "I would've figured that'd be something her mom might have told us about. What the hell's wrong with her?"

"I'll bet Kelly didn't exactly explain."

Hank hit the steering wheel hard with a palm. "Even if she didn't give her mom details, didn't she realize that something was wrong? Seeing her kid locked out on the lawn at the crack of dawn? She's a nurse, for crap's sake. Shouldn't she be able to take care of her own kid?"

"I don't know what to tell you, partner."

"Yeah, you do. You're thinking the same thing as me. Some people aren't fit to have pets, much less children," he said and sighed, pursing his lips in a tight line as he drove the car out of the high school lot.

Jo used his momentary silence to tell him more about her chat with Cassie and how she got a sense that Cassie was pissed at Kelly, at the way Kelly was apparently trying to fit in with the cool kids. "I think Cassie felt like Kelly was leaving her behind. Kelly was wearing a friendship bracelet when she died. I saw the same bracelets on both girls in the photo that Barbara Amster showed us. But Cassie wasn't wearing hers today."

"Which means what?" Hank asked. "They had a falling out and broke up?"

"Could be."

"That's high school," he remarked. "Some kids mature faster than others. Relationships change. It happens."

"And it hurts," Jo added, because that was how Cassie had acted—a little bit spurned. "I'm getting the impression that Kelly was trying hard to move up the social ladder."

Somehow, it had backfired, Jo mused. What had the girl gotten herself into? Whatever it was, she'd been in over her head.

"Cassie said Kelly mentioned having an 'in' with one of the Guccis."

"The Guccis?" Hank turned to look at her.

"Rich kids," Jo told him, having just learned the term herself.

"You think this Gucci owed her, or she had something on him?" Hank asked. "Like, maybe the person who dumped her on the grass when she was unconscious?"

Jo was wondering the same thing.

"We need to find out about that party," she said. "Somebody knows what happened. If we could just get her phone—"

Hank interrupted her. "I heard from Ramsey."

"They found it?" Jo said hopefully. They'd be able to fill in so many blanks—who Kelly had texted, what she'd said—and get a better picture of what had been going on before her death. "That's great," she added, feeling a little giddy. "Are they back at the station? Is the SIM card intact?"

"Hey, I didn't say they found it. *You* did," her partner corrected.

Jo deflated. "So they didn't?"

"No. Ramsey said they only found some of it."

"Some?" Jo's heart sunk all the way to her belly.

"They've collected bits and pieces. Duncan's theory is she broke it before she jumped. He said there was a chunk from the back of the phone on the catwalk. Seems she had an older phone, a no-name brand that came apart more easily than the newer models."

"She trashed her phone before she leaped?"

"It sure looks that way," her partner said. "They can't even locate the SIM card. It must've come out when she beat the thing and threw it overboard. They tracked down some of the casing. The glass is busted like she pounded the thing hard against the railing or the barrel of the tower."

"Can't they use a metal detector to find the card?" Jo said, the first thing that popped into her head.

"You know how small those things are?" Hank took a hand from the wheel to pinch his fingers nearly together. "They're itty-bitty. The tower's sitting on a couple of overgrown acres that are littered with old cans, broken glass, and crap."

"I know," she said, though it pained her to admit he was right.

"On the bright side," Hank offered, "we can still get a list of calls in and out from her cell phone provider."

"But we won't get texts or e-mails or browsing history that way."

"No," Hank said. "But, hey, we have her laptop. She must have left some kind of footprint on there."

"You'd think so," Jo replied. She held the laptop on her thighs and took that moment to prop it open, pressing the power button and wishing for something to happen. But nothing did.

"So the battery's dead for real?" Hank asked.

"As a doornail." She sighed and closed the thing. When they got back to the station, she'd scrounge up an AC adapter, just for kicks. And when that didn't work, she'd call in the techs. Because what she didn't know about computers could fill the 50,000-gallon tank of an old water tower, and then some.

# CHAPTER EIGHT

When they walked through the door, their captain popped out of his office, flagging them down. He had damp spots under the armpits of his blue oxford-cloth shirt and a loosened tie at his unbuttoned collar. Jo knew the tie went on only if he had a meeting with the chief or the city council, or he had to stand before the press. Whichever it was, he looked grumpy as hell.

"In here, now," he said in his typically succinct fashion.

Jo and Hank went in and closed the door while Captain Waylon Morris perched on the edge of his desk. He crossed his arms and uttered two words: "Brief me."

Jo was pretty sure he didn't mean about the missing dog.

Hank produced the alleged suicide note they'd bagged, and Cap plunked on his specs to read the purple ink. Jo told him about talking to Barbara Amster and then to Cassie Marks, and how they were following up on the tip about the party where Kelly had gone alone before the start of school.

"Something happened to Kelly while she was there," Jo said. "If we want to believe her best friend, a fifteen-year-old girl was sexually assaulted."

"But she didn't report it?"

"No," Jo said, and he merely grunted, because that was hardly unusual.

There were a million reasons victims didn't speak up. They didn't think they'd be believed, for starters. Being threatened came in a close second.

"What else have you got?" Cap wanted to know.

She showed him Kelly's school-issued laptop that was DOA, and Hank filled him in on Ramsey and Duncan's search for the missing SIM card.

Cap, in turn, informed them that Kelly's body had been picked up by the county and transported to the ME's office in downtown Dallas to await an autopsy.

"A young girl dying like this," he said as he ran a hand over his buzz-cut hair, "it's a heartbreaker. So let's dot all our *i*'s and cross all our *t*'s before we sign off on this one. If it's suicide, we don't want to have doubts. Ditto if it was accidental."

Jo didn't even need to hear him say it. "We won't leave any questions unanswered."

"We're on it, sir," Hank assured him.

They had extra pressure to get this one right. They'd been there and done that before with a high-profile case that looked like a suicide on the surface, except it had turned out to be something else. If Jo had stopped pushing on that one, if she'd scratched only the surface instead of digging, the case would have been closed before they'd learned the truth.

"I'd like to visit Mrs. Amster again," she said, glancing at Hank. "I'm hoping she'll let us go through Kelly's room and her things. If Kelly really had proof that she was raped at a party, I want to find whatever it is. And maybe we can jog the mom's memory about finding Kelly locked out the morning after."

"It's hard with teenagers," Cap remarked. "They're not always eager to share."

Hank lifted a hand. "It's my fault we didn't hang around long enough to do a search," he admitted. "The mom was acting pretty out of it. I figured she might want some time alone to digest that her daughter was dead."

Cap nodded. "I get it." He rubbed palms on thighs. "All right, then. Go do what you need to do, and I'll handle the brass and the press." With that, he shooed them out the door.

*Good luck with that,* Jo thought.

The press had already begun knocking.

Jo had a message from a Dallas-based reporter about Kelly Amster's death on her voice mail. The woman had inquired about the possible bullying of the victim, a hot topic these days, Jo realized, but one she wasn't ready to address.

So Jo had ignored her.

But, after they left Cap's office, when she and Hank stepped into the lounge to hit up the vending machine for lunch, she caught the midday news on the TV. There on the screen was the old water tower, a blond reporter standing in the foreground, microphone in hand, remarking on the tragic apparent suicide of a schoolgirl just north of Big D. Jo recognized the reporter's name. She was the one whose call Jo hadn't returned.

*Plainfield Teen Plunges to Death,* the crawl hollered below her talking head. Then the shot shifted to prerecorded video of the reporter in front of a house that looked familiar. She was chatting up a woman in sunglasses, messy brown hair pulled into a ponytail. Jo could see a logo on her polo-collared shirt: *At-Home Angels,* it said with a little halo above the *o*.

Was that Kelly's mother?

"I still can't believe she's gone," the woman moaned. "I never thought she'd do something like this, not for real. I loved her so much. My heart is broken."

"For crap's sake," Hank muttered.

Yep, it was definitely Barbara Amster.

"So much for her taking time alone to digest it all, huh?" Jo said.

Hank groused. "She's talking suicide to the press already? Doesn't she know how to say 'no comment'? How're we supposed to investigate if she's telling everyone her daughter jumped?"

"They went to her door," Jo said, truly wanting to give the woman the benefit of the doubt. "She was probably on her way to work and got ambushed."

"Yeah, let's say that. It feels better," Hank remarked, snatching a bottle of Coke from the vending machine and handing it over. "Let's blame the reporter for jumping on a mom who's just been told a few hours before that her daughter was toast. It's like catnip to them, isn't it?"

"Yep," Jo agreed, waiting for him to hand over the crackers with peanut butter she'd given him money for. She had an apple in a drawer at her desk. "Everything's a tabloid headline."

"I wish they'd stick to covering the gubmint clowns and let us do our jobs." Hank angrily punched in the code to get himself a bag of chili-cheese Fritos. He always brought bagged lunches from home that his wife, Trish, prepared, full of cut-up carrots and tubs of hummus and other good-for-him stuff that ended up mostly in the trash.

Adam had started doing much the same thing with Jo.

Bottled tea had replaced the bottles of Coke in her fridge. Fruit and carrot sticks had suddenly appeared in the produce drawer, where she used to hide loaves of bread going moldy. But she and Hank had a pact: what happened at work stayed at work. There would be no mention of dietary indiscretions outside the break room.

Jo unscrewed the cap on her soda and took a swig, fortifying herself with caffeine. Then she nudged him. "C'mon," she said. "Let's get an adapter and see if Kelly's laptop boots up, just for kicks."

"An adapter? I think we'll need a medium," Hank said, dripping sarcasm. "You know, the kind that can talk to the ghost of a dead battery."

"That's the spirit." She gave his back a pat.

"Bad pun." He shook his head. "Really bad."

Back at her desk, Jo made quick work of her crackers and apple. She took a final slurp of her soda, then tossed the bottle in a recycling bin. She rubbed her hands together, praying for some good mojo before she started to rummage around in her drawers. She'd managed to accumulate a rat's nest of myriad cables for assorted electronics, kept on hand "just in case." Surely one of them would prove functional, if she only could disentangle them.

After an interminable few minutes of intense yanking, she extricated a couple of AC adapters. One, thankfully, was compatible with Kelly's computer. She hooked it up, plugged it in, and held her breath as she pushed the power button.

"Come on, Farmer," she said, "do your thing."

As expected, the power button never lit up.

"Who's Farmer?" Hank asked from his desk, having overheard her little pep talk.

"It's a Dell," she told him, tapping the laptop. "You know, the farmer in the . . ."

"I know." He groaned. "I know."

Then he rolled his chair over and peered across her shoulder, near enough that she could hear him crunching chili-cheese Fritos in her ear.

"You bring it back to life, Dr. Frankenstein?"

"No such luck."

She sat back with a sigh. She hated to feel defeated this early in the game. "I wonder if the hard drive crashed."

If that was the case, they were screwed.

"Didn't the department just hire a kid with a fancy computer-science degree to do geeklike things around here?" Hank said.

Yes, as a matter of fact, it had.

"Bridget," Jo said.

"Yeah, that's her." He nudged Jo's arm. "Let the she-nerd figure it out."

Bridget Morris, aka "the she-nerd," was a twenty-two-year-old pursuing an advanced degree in digital forensics at the University of Texas at Dallas with plans to join the department full-time after graduation. Cap was the one who'd pushed for the hire, asserting that they needed more technical support because of the bump in cybercrimes. The city council had given them a thumbs-up, largely because she'd start off as a lowly paid intern, saving them money. Oh, yeah, and she also happened to be the captain's niece.

"Better her than me," Jo said and shut the lid on the laptop.

"While you're dumping that piece of junk on the girl geek, I'll make some phone calls. I'll check with a few stray rescue places around town for the Pearson case, and I'll touch base with the ME's office and see if I can get a date and time for Kelly Amster's postmortem," Hank told her. "If they give the girl to your boyfriend, maybe we'll get it done in the next twenty-four."

The girl.

"Kelly," Jo said as much to herself as to him, because it was important not to forget that victims had names, even if they had no voice.

"Yeah, Kelly," her partner repeated. "That's what I meant."

Jo shook her pen at him. "You must think I have magic powers or something if I can get a PM done faster because—" *I'm sleeping with McCaffrey*, she nearly said, but mentally tweaked before she finished with, "I'm seeing Adam."

"Then what's the point?" Hank joked. At least, she thought he was joking. Chuckling all the while, he scooted his chair back to his own desk and got busy.

If Adam did catch Kelly's autopsy, the only favoritism she'd get would likely be a heads-up on the preliminary report. She doubted her relationship with one of the county's dozen medical examiners would speed things up when it seemed there was a never-ending supply of victims waiting for their turn on the table, their families all wanting answers as soon as possible.

For now, she could only do what she could do.

She frowned, picking up the laptop, and headed off to find Bridget, which wasn't hard, considering the station that housed the entire Plainfield PD was little bigger than a shoe box. She thought about all the money the town had spent on the new water tower, and like every other officer on their small but growing force, she kept waiting to get the funding promised for a new structure and more staffing. *Soon*, they were always told as their evidence room overflowed, and solitary holding cells ended up looking more like detainee puppy mills, with too many crammed into one cage.

She rounded the corner of the hallway, passed a small waiting area and the janitor's closet, and stopped at the door to the room that housed the department's server.

That was where they'd stuck Bridget.

It was the only place they'd had room to shove another desk, and it kind of made sense, considering she was the resident computer genius. Except that it wasn't exactly quiet. In fact, they'd given Bridget noise-canceling headphones from the firing range so she could work alongside the racket.

"Hey!" Jo called out as she stepped inside the room and closed the door, getting goose bumps. Not only was the server noisy, but it needed cold, too. Jo felt like she was walking into a refrigerator.

"Hey!" she tried again and raised her voice to something shy of a scream, trying to be heard over the audible whirs and hums she knew were fans within the server and the occasional hard drive rebooting.

The department had only a single server at the moment but wanted more as the need increased to store high-def video and other electronic evidence. But if it had more servers now, no way could anyone have shared the space, as the noise would have been deafening rather than merely irritating.

The headphones must have worked wonders, as Bridget didn't even turn around. She appeared to be focused on three monitors connected by cables and wired to an iPhone with its case removed. All the while, her fingers danced over a keyboard. The lines on the screen kept moving as she fed it some kind of instructions, causing code to scroll across and down. It looked like a foreign language that Jo couldn't understand.

Jo came up behind her and tapped her on the shoulder.

Bridget jumped, tearing off the headphones as she swiveled in her seat. She had wiry black hair and dark eyes and an energy that crackled off her skin like electricity, which may have been the reason she didn't wear a sweater despite the cranked-up AC.

"Hey," Jo said again loudly. "I hate to interrupt, but I need your help."

"Sorry. I was pretty focused. What's up?"

Jo held out Kelly Amster's useless laptop. "I can't make this thing boot up, and I need to get in. I'm guessing it's more than a bad battery."

"Did you try an AC adapter, just to see if it needed a charge?"

"I did, and it still wouldn't power up," Jo said, not wanting to sound like a complete idiot. "I'm looking for . . . God, I don't know what. But it's a school district–issued computer, and I've got the administrator's user name and password, so access shouldn't be a problem once we've got it working. It belonged to a student—"

"The girl who took a dive from the old water tower?"

"Yes. Kelly Amster," Jo replied, not surprised that she'd heard, considering the story had already hit the local news. And, even if it hadn't, the department was small enough that you could count the full-timers on both hands, so word traveled fast. "I'm not sure what we'll actually find on it, considering it was mainly for school use, but we're hoping for e-mails, maybe a journal, photographs, something that might shed light on what happened to Kelly."

"I'll see what I can do to get it running," Bridget said and took the laptop from her. "It could have a corrupted memory or bootloader, or maybe it's a virus." She glanced at the Post-it note stuck to the lid, checking both sides of it. "Looks like I've got everything I need. I'll let you know when I get in."

*When*, not *if*. Jo liked her already.

"May the Force be with you," she said.

Bridget smiled. "Thanks."

Well, heck, she had a Death Star pencil holder, and she was wearing a T-shirt with Yoda and the phrase, *Do or Do Not . . . There Is No Try*.

Bridget pulled her headphones back on, and Jo left her to do her magic.

She had other fish to fry.

So she couldn't get into Kelly's laptop—yet—but that wasn't the only way to find out about a high school party. She had another idea to pin down the location, and it just might work.

Jo went back to her desk and got into the department's system, doing a simple search for noise or parking violations during the last two weekends before the start of school. Since the city council had initiated a 311 call-in the year before for nonemergency incidents, residents could file complaints by phone as well as online.

Jo couldn't imagine any big-shot high school senior throwing a quiet shindig. If Cassie was right that alcohol was involved—and she'd bet that was the case, particularly if the parents were out of town—then there was probably loud music and plenty of cars parked where they shouldn't have been.

She pulled up the database, going through a litany of barking dog complaints, loud cars, loud motorcycles, ongoing construction, lawn mowers, leaf blowers, and, yes, music in the wee hours of the night. She found one incident that piqued her interest. The address was a posh neighborhood where McMansions were as plentiful as the corporate executives who owned them.

She paired the date and time with a couple of calls that came from the same hood regarding parking violations. According to the complainants, the subdivision allowed parking only on one side of the street so emergency vehicles could safely pass. But that same night, "earsplitting music" was reported emanating from a house on the block where half a dozen vehicles were parked in such a way as to make safe passage nearly impossible.

"You've been sitting there for an hour and a half without moving," said a voice in her ear, and she looked up. Hank squinted past her at the monitor. "I don't get it. You're trolling for noise infractions and parking violations. Why?"

"There's a method to my madness," she said, rubbing at her eyes, which had gone a bit blurry after staring at the screen for so long.

"You working a case I don't know about?"

"No," she told him. "It's for Kelly Amster."

His brow scrunched up. "Why? She wasn't even old enough to drive. Did she play her stereo too loud? Do kids even *have* stereos anymore?"

"I can't answer that." Jo pushed aside her keyboard. "But I do think I can answer a question that's a little more important. I know who held the party," she said, feeling like she'd won the lottery.

"*The* party," Hank repeated, looking impressed.

"I've just got one last thing to check." Jo picked up the phone and dialed.

She felt considerably less magical a few minutes later once she got Helen Billings on the line. She apologized for the interruption and asked if she might speak with another student who could possibly have information about Kelly's Amster's death.

"I'm sorry, Detective," the principal said. "But I can't help you with that."

"Oh?" Was it something she'd said?

"He's not here today. His father called and spoke with me earlier. He said his son had been up late last night with a bad stomach, so he was letting him sleep in. But if he was better when he got up, he'd be here for afternoon classes so he wouldn't end up missing football practice."

"Oh," she said, when what she really meant was *damn*.

"If you need to talk to him right away, you'd best try reaching him at home. I'll give you the number . . ."

"Yes, please."

And once she got it—and told Hank to grab his keys—they were on their way.

# CHAPTER NINE

They pulled up in front of a shiny monstrosity of a house, obscenely large by any normal person's standards but probably average-sized if you were Bill Gates.

The lot couldn't have been any more than an acre, and still the mansion seemed to dwarf it—all timber and copper and glass, like something you'd imagine finding in ski country, except no one was doing any skiing in the marginally hilly suburbs of northern Dallas County on a sticky September day.

Jo and Hank got out of the car, shutting doors one after the other with a percussive *slap-slap*.

Hands on hips, Jo stood in the middle of the cobblestone driveway, looking around her.

Yep, she could see how having a party on this street could get you into trouble. There wasn't even as much space between neighbors as in Amanda Pearson's sixty-year-old neighborhood. Despite attractive landscaping between lots, it was easy enough to view the house next door; ditto, the ones across the asphalt road.

Without difficulty, she spotted a sign stuck in the ground six feet to the left of a neighbor's driveway. It stated clear as a button: NO PARKING THIS SIDE OF STREET.

It made sense that folks nearby were upset with finding a slew of rich kids' rides taking up enough of the road to make it hard to pass.

"You really think this is the right place?" Hank asked, seemingly hesitant to take the liriope-bordered path toward the front door. "This is pretty posh company for a girl whose mom is a home health nurse."

Jo sucked in enough humid air to fill her lungs before letting it go. "Yeah," she agreed, "but it fits." She'd dug deep enough after finding the noise and parking complaints to know a little about who lived here. "Cassie said the party was thrown by someone older, a big shot on campus whose parents were out of town." She jerked her chin toward the house. "The son's a senior at the high school. He's starting quarterback for the Plainfield Mustangs. His dad's a local CEO."

"What's their name?"

"Eldon," she said, catching a shadow crossing one of the many front windows, though the way the sun reflected so fiercely off the glass, she couldn't be sure if they were being watched or if it was a momentary wave of a tree branch. "The father's Robert Junior. He's the head of a tech start-up that hit it big in security software about a dozen years back. He's got two sons. The older one is Robert the Third, aka Trey."

"Yep, yep, I know exactly who he is," Hank muttered, and his eyes brightened amid his weathered face. "Trey Eldon's got a smokin' hot arm. He's a blue-chip recruit. I heard he's been flirting with the Longhorns, although he hasn't signed a letter of intent yet."

"Let's see if he's been flirting with younger girls whose moms don't pay them enough attention," she said.

"I hope you're wrong. I've got the 'Stangs pegged to win the state championship again." Hank made an unhappy noise in his throat. "I'd hate to see a kid with so much potential self-destruct. Quarterbacks are supposed to be the smart ones."

"Even the smart ones screw up."

"You think Eldon the Third assaulted our girl and bullied her into jumping off the water tower?"

"I guess that's what we're here to find out," Jo said and started walking.

From the driveway, she took a wide paver path toward a timber-and-concrete basin with a fountain in its center. Around the splashing water they went, toward the thick-paned glass door flanked by concrete slabs—twin walls that mimicked giant bookends.

There was a strange bump on the right side of the house that looked like an old silo with a peaked copper roof. Was it meant to add a rustic touch? Through a large vertical window, Jo could see a baby grand piano lit by an interior spotlight. A round room just for the piano?

*You've got too much money,* she thought, *if you can do stuff like that.*

She'd barely reached the monogrammed welcome mat when the door came open. A man stood behind it, his eyes narrowed on her. His lean figure belied his middle age, as did the dark shade of his hair and eyebrows. Her mama would have called it "shoe polish black," and it would have looked more natural on a crow.

"Please don't tell me you're the window washers," he said with a polished Texas twang. "You're not quite what I was expecting."

"Sorry to disappoint." Jo almost smiled. She retrieved her wallet with her shield and ID and held it up for him. "We're working a case, and we think your son might be able to help us answer some questions."

The fellow squinted at her credentials, then Hank's, before they put them away. He looked even more disappointed, if that was possible. "So you're telling me that my windows aren't getting washed this morning?"

Jo couldn't decide if he was serious or trying to be funny and failing.

Hank coughed, though she thought she heard him mutter "asshole" in the midst of it. She'd been afraid that Hank would want to take the lead on this one and fanboy over Trey Eldon, the blue-chip recruit, but obviously, he wasn't going to fawn over Golden Boy's father.

*Okay, enough,* she thought.

"Mr. Eldon," she said, because even though he hadn't told them his name, he sure looked the part of a software CEO with his tailored navy-blue shirt and peg leg pants, a clunky Rolex at his wrist. "Is your son here?"

"Which one?" he asked, still not inviting them in. He crossed his arms, rocking on his heels, in no hurry to accommodate them.

"The one that's home sick," Jo said, adding, "I was told by Helen Billings that he didn't come to school today because he was under the weather. If he's up to it, we'd like to ask him a few questions."

"Why?"

Jo wondered if he was just being a dick or if he was nervous. "We need to talk to Trey about a girl from his school. She was found dead this morning—"

"You mean Kelly Amster?" Robert Eldon interrupted, and his sleek eyebrows arched.

"Yes, Kelly Amster." Jo hated that the whole town seemed to know already that Kelly was dead, even before they could definitively answer why. "So you heard?"

"Helen said Trey was going to miss an all-school assembly in the auditorium to tell the students that Kelly had passed away." He shook his head and made a tsk-tsk noise. "What a shame. I feel for her mother. I truly do."

"Is Trey here, sir?" she tried again. She could hear Hank's noisy breathing from behind her. He sounded like a bull ready to duck his head and barrel into the china shop. "Could we come in and talk to him for a few minutes? Unless he's at the doctor's office?"

"No, he's here. He woke up feeling a little sick to his stomach. I thought I'd keep him home a while, just to be cautious."

"I see. Should we go up then?" she asked, looking past him through the doorway.

"No, no, that won't be necessary. He's getting ready to head back to school soon." The man finally seemed to take them seriously. "If you'll wait a minute, I'll call him down." He started to shut the door, and Jo put out a hand to catch it.

"You'd like us to wait out here in the heat?" She glanced back at Hank, who wore a frustrated look on his face. Seemed like no one wanted to ask them in these days. "You think we could come inside?"

They didn't need tea and crumpets, just a place to wait that wasn't approaching ninety degrees in the shade.

"Yeah, sure," Robert Eldon said without enthusiasm and pulled the door wide for them. "Wipe your feet on the mat, if you don't mind. Then you can follow me."

He led them through a spacious foyer with massive beams and sunlight streaming in through uncountable windows. They went down a few steps into a living room with a floor-to-ceiling stone fireplace. Despite the toasty temperature outside, the air felt about as cold as the department's server room. Maybe that was why a fire crackled and blazed in the fireplace, though Robert Eldon grabbed a remote and switched it off in a snap, like he didn't want to waste the effect on them.

"I'll be right back," he said without inviting them to sit.

He'd barely left the room when Jo heard him yelling, "Trey! Hey, Trey, can you come on down, please?"

Within a minute, she heard a tread descending, the footsteps heavy enough to rattle glass, like a giant was taking the stairs two by two. Then Robert Eldon reappeared in the sunken living room with his arm around a younger man who, on first inspection, seemed very much like a taller, wider-shouldered, better-looking version of his dad. Jo knew from reading his stats online that Trey stood six foot two and 180 pounds. What she didn't realize from all the photographs she'd viewed of him in his red-and-white uniform, tossing a football, was that he looked downright shy: chin lowered, eyes downcast, shoulders slouched.

Adding to the effect was his pallor, although perhaps that was due to his not feeling well.

The boy chewed on his cheek, glancing somewhere past Jo and then finally meeting her gaze with worried eyes. "What's going on?" he asked. His voice sounded almost soft, far less abrasive than his dad's. "Should I know you?"

"Son, these are police detectives, here to talk to you about Kelly Amster." Robert Eldon set a hand on his shoulder, the chunky Rolex fully visible. "I was telling them I'd heard about her death just this morning from Helen Billings. Such a tragedy."

"You want to talk to me about Kelly?" Trey said, his shoulders lifting out of their slouch. "I don't understand. It's not like we were close or anything."

Jo didn't beat around the bush. "Did you have a party here the weekend before the start of school? I'd appreciate hearing the truth, as we can always talk to the neighbors to confirm it, particularly the ones who filed noise and parking complaints."

"Aw, hell." Robert Eldon's expression soured. "Go on," he said. "Tell her what she wants to know."

Jo saw him squeeze his son's shoulder and couldn't be sure if he was trying to keep Trey from talking or encouraging him to do so.

Regardless, the boy didn't respond. He shifted on his feet, like he was hoping for his dad to leap to his rescue.

And his father did exactly that. "Look, Detectives, Trey's a good kid, but he was wrong to have his friends over while I was away. They got into my liquor, and I certainly don't condone that kind of behavior. But my boy isn't responsible for what that girl did to herself."

*Hmm.*

Jo found it a pretty big leap for him to take—assuming they'd come to the house to accuse Trey of having something to do with Kelly's suicide. It made her wonder if the father knew about what had happened to Kelly at the party. Had Trey told him that Kelly had been raped?

She felt an itch to pounce on the matter, but she knew to step lightly. If she pushed too fast, she risked father and son lawyering up. "Look, Mr. Eldon, no one here is suggesting your son was involved with Kelly's death," she said, watching Trey's face and the conflict of emotions. He was trying so hard to avoid her eyes. His mouth was a tight line, nearly a wince, probably from his father's white-knuckled hold on him. "Let's start over, all right? I'm just trying to confirm that Kelly Amster was here that night."

When Trey still didn't speak, Robert Eldon cleared his throat. "As I understand it, Kelly badgered Trey for an invite. He can't be faulted for trying to include her."

"Kelly badgered him," Jo repeated. "Why on earth would she do that?"

She found it hard to believe that a quiet girl who'd avoided attention most of her school life would suddenly beg the big man on campus for an invitation to his party. It seemed contrary to what Cassie had told her.

"C'mon, Trey, be honest with me," she pressed. "It'll save us the trouble of coming back again if we find out you've lied. We'll be less likely to believe you the next time."

Trey twisted apart from his father. His hands came out of his jeans pockets and curled to fists before they relaxed. For a moment, Jo thought he was going to tell her to go to hell. Instead, he replied, "Kelly was here that night. It was her choice. No one forced her."

"Did she come alone?"

"Yeah, she was alone."

"How'd she get here?" Jo asked. "She was fifteen. Too young to drive. Did someone pick her up?"

Trey shrugged, looking down at his bare feet, so pale against the warm hardwoods. "How should I know? Maybe she Ubered."

Jo kept at him. "Why did she come at all if you weren't really friends?"

"No clue," he said flatly, raising his hazel eyes. "You'd have to ask her that."

"You know we can't."

"Right." He sighed and gazed over Jo's head toward the fireplace, just as he'd done after walking into the room. When he decided to look at her again, his eyes were focused. "I'll be brutal here, okay? Kelly and I weren't tight," he said. "She wasn't part of my squad. But, yeah, I knew her. Her mom took care of my mom when she was sick."

"Barbara Amster took care of your mother?" Jo asked, realizing only then that she hadn't seen hide nor hair of *Mrs.* Eldon, which did seem a bit unusual, considering how overprotective the father appeared. Jo hadn't done enough digging online to find out about the mom, just the football-star angle regarding Trey and, inadvertently, a bit of a scoop on his entrepreneur dad.

She found it very interesting to know there was a connection between the Amsters and the Eldons that went way back.

"She was my mom's private nurse," Trey explained.

"When she was sick," Jo repeated.

"Yes." Trey's gaze roved again, fixing somewhere past her head, and this time, she followed his eyes. "She had ALS, and it got really bad when I was in junior high."

He blew out a slow breath, staring at a large portrait of the family hung over the mantel, one that Jo hadn't given much more than a cursory glance. She'd been paying attention to the fire burning despite the warm weather, not to anything above it.

Now she took in the oversized image of the deliberately posed foursome: the delicate-looking blonde with a fragile smile sitting on a stone bench with her husband beside her, his arm around her; the pair flanked by their sons. The older and bigger of the boys was clearly Trey. The younger brother was the only one looking away, like he didn't really want to be there.

"How's your mom doing? Is she okay?" Jo asked, glancing from son to father. "Is she around?"

"Is she around," Robert Eldon repeated and made a noise of disgust.

Jo knew then she'd put her foot in it.

"No, she's not okay. She died almost four years ago," Trey said, his voice rising. "Barb . . . Mrs. Amster . . . she basically lived with us at the end, so Kelly was here all the time. The kid used to follow me around like a puppy."

Had Kelly decided to start following Trey around again, Jo wondered, maybe as a way to find the popularity she craved?

Whether she'd begged to go to his party or not didn't matter to Jo. What *did* matter was what had happened there that had ultimately led to Kelly landing on her front yard in bloody underwear.

Jo felt in her bones that Trey Eldon had the answer.

"So I guess you and Kelly have a history," she remarked. "Had y'all been in touch since your mom passed?"

"No," Trey said sharply.

"You didn't date?"

"Me and Kelly?" Trey smirked. "Is that a joke?"

"Not at all," Jo said, feeling defensive. It wasn't like Kelly was repulsive. Quite the opposite. But she let it go for now.

Though Hank remained silent, she could feel her partner's eyes burning a hole in her back. She tried to calm down the noise in her head, the little voice crying out, *Danger, Will Robinson! Alien land mines ahead!*

"I'm really sorry about your mom," she said, connecting the only way she could, understanding what it meant to go through any amount of time without the love and support of a mother. "That's harsh."

"Yeah, it was." Trey nodded.

She stared at the years-old portrait again, this time focusing on the slighter boy, the one who seemed to favor the mom's more delicate looks. "Where's your brother?" she asked. "Does he go to Plainfield High, too?"

Trey opened his mouth, started to say, "No," but Robert Eldon quickly began speaking over him.

"John's been at boarding school in Virginia since Mary passed," he said, and Jo detected a tightness in his voice. He hadn't gotten over her death, either. "They were very close. He didn't handle the loss of his mother well and had some emotional issues that I wasn't prepared to handle."

"Does he visit much?"

"No, although we take vacations together. Sometimes, he's here on long breaks." At Jo's raised eyebrows, he added, "Going away was his choice, not mine. He needed a fresh start, somewhere that didn't remind him of what he'd lost. He has a hard time being in this house without Mary, so I don't force it."

"I can understand," Jo said. Dealing with facts was easy. Dealing with emotion was rough. "Was he in town for the party?"

"He was here for a while this summer, yes. But I flew him back to school that very day," Robert Eldon replied with a glance at his fancy gold watch. "We took my private jet. If I'd been here, Trey would not have had a party and disturbed the neighbors."

"So you're at fault?"

"Sure, if you need someone to blame."

Jo swallowed down her frustration. The guy was good at deflecting. But she wasn't surprised. Folks who'd made names for themselves in business usually didn't get there because they were nice guys. They knew how to play the game, and sometimes that game involved lying through their teeth.

"So that's it?" Robert Eldon jerked his chin toward Trey, who looked even paler than when they'd arrived, if that was possible. "You can go back upstairs and finish getting ready for school. I think we're done with our little conversation."

Trey turned to go, but Jo stopped him.

"Um, no, we're not done yet," she said.

When Robert Eldon opened his mouth, Hank stepped in, clearing his throat.

"If you'd rather, Mr. Eldon, we can move this to the station," he said. "You can bring Trey down this afternoon, if it's more convenient."

"The police station?" Trey turned around. His wide eyes held panic. "Dad, I've got practice . . ."

"No, no," Mr. Eldon said. "That won't work."

"Okay, then, we'll keep talkin' now, son," Hank said to Trey, working his good ol' boy vibe, which Jo could never do without a sex change. "Just give us a handle on what happened with Kelly at your shindig. Did she drink too much? Did y'all take advantage of her? That little girl's dead," he pressed. "Why don't you man up and give us some answers?"

Trey swallowed hard, Adam's apple jumping.

Jo decided to go for broke. "Kelly called her best friend at five the next morning, crying and saying she'd been dumped on her lawn without her keys and with her underwear rearranged. Did you and your buddies drop her off when you were through with her?"

Trey did his best deer-in-headlights look and whined, "Dad . . ."

"It's a simple yes or no answer," Jo insisted.

"What the hell is this?" Robert Eldon skimmed a palm over his jet-black head. "You sound like you believe my son committed some kind of horrible offense against that girl. I can assure you that he didn't."

"You weren't at the party," Jo reminded him. "You were flying back to Virginia with your other boy."

"But I know Trey. I know my son," the man said, punctuating each word with a jab of his finger.

"It's okay," Trey started to say. "I can speak for myself—"

"No," his father snapped at him. "It's not okay for them to try to pin something on you when you had nothing to do with that girl's death. Nobody did."

Was that a roundabout way of telling Trey, "Shut up before you get yourself into real trouble"?

"Was she drinking?" Jo asked, figuring it was an easy enough question.

Trey looked at his father.

"Did she get drunk?" Jo went on, hating how passive the young man seemed, how unwilling to step forward and cop to whatever the truth really was. For a hardcore jock who let himself get pummeled by defensive linemen every week, he sure lacked nerve. All beef, no moral fiber. "Did someone slip her something in a drink? Did you see her go off with anyone? Or did she leave with someone?"

Hank stood right beside her, his arm brushing hers, as though to remind her he was there if she needed backup.

But Jo didn't want to let go.

"You invited a fifteen-year-old to your party, a shy girl who knew you from back when her mom took care of your mom. She must have trusted you. She came alone, and yet you have no idea what she did while she was here or what happened to her after?"

Trey's face flushed, the first bit of color that had come into it since Jo had met him. "I didn't hurt her," he insisted, giving a quick look at his father before he added under his breath, "It wasn't me or my friends. They were trying to look out for her when she got sick—"

"Boy," his father cut him off sternly. "You don't need to say another word."

Jo ignored him. "Give me a list of their names. Tell me who attended the party so we can interview them."

Trey turned to his father. "Dad?"

"Not another word! I said we're done here," Robert Eldon declared, his voice loud, like a blast of a car horn, meant to shut them all up.

"What are you so afraid of?" she asked, feeling Trey's unease, wondering if it was because of his father. "Kelly was a pretty girl, and all she wanted was to be popular. Did you promise her you'd help? Did things spin out of control? She told her best friend she had proof she was assaulted, so what exactly went on while your dad wasn't here?"

"Hey!" Robert Eldon snapped. "You're way out of line. My son's not that kind of boy. He's played by the rules his whole life. He's *this close* to signing with one of the best college football programs in the country. He's sure as shit not gonna throw that away for a crosstown girl like Kelly Amster." He shook a finger at Jo while he continued blustering. "So if you want to accuse him of something, you'd better have more than say-so from a dead girl's silly friend. Now, please leave my house."

"All right, we'll go," Jo said, managing to sound far calmer than she felt. She pulled a card from her pocket and held it out to Trey. "If you end up remembering anything more from that night—anything else about Kelly—call me, please."

But Robert Eldon interceded, plucking the card from Jo's fingers. "Get out," he said, as if she hadn't heard him the first time.

Jo tried to catch Trey's eye, but he turned away.

*Okay,* she told herself. She'd get what she needed some other way.

As she preceded Hank from the living room, she spied a host of photographs on a strip of wall between floor-to-ceiling windows. All of them were sports photos, every frame dominated by red and white, with one figure at the center of it all: Trey in his Plainfield Mustangs jersey. Number twelve.

*It must be good to be king,* Jo mused. *Enjoy it while it lasts.* Because it wasn't going to feel very nice when Trey got that pedestal yanked out from under him.

After they'd buckled themselves in and Hank started the engine, he paused with his hands on the steering wheel. "I don't think the Mustangs will take state this year," he said, "not unless their backup QB is a ringer. Because this kid's not gonna make it through the season."

"Not if he had something to do with what happened to Kelly Amster," she agreed. She'd felt the truth hovering there in the living room with them, dangling like the proverbial carrot. Except Robert Eldon had yanked it back before she could grab it.

*Damn, damn, damn.*

Jo was sure Trey Eldon knew something. But as long as his dad was around, she wasn't going to get a meaningful word out of him.

# CHAPTER TEN

Jo hadn't been back at her desk more than five minutes when her cell phone rang. When she saw the number, her body tensed. She considered letting the call go to voice mail, but that would only delay the inevitable.

She answered with a muted, "Hello?"

"Hey, hon," a familiar voice said in response. The two words were spoken so warmly, it should have made Jo's shoulders relax. Instead, the muscles tightened all the way into her neck, gearing up for whatever bad news was to come. Because it always did.

"Hi, Ronnie," she acknowledged her mother's best friend—more like, her only friend—and the woman who'd helped take care of Verna well before she had to be placed in full-time memory care.

To be honest, she *still* took care of Mama and visited her more often than Jo did. With Ronnie's blessing, Jo had added her name to all the paperwork for Winghaven, listing her as Mama's sister, even though she wasn't really, not legally. But she was as close to family as it got. More often than not, the nursing home called Ronnie, not Jo, when they needed a hand with Mama.

"What's up?" she asked, willing her heart to stop pounding as it did every time anything came up concerning her mother.

"Something's happened at the facility, and if you haven't heard from them already, I think you should know about it."

*Well, hell.*

"No, I haven't heard," she admitted.

"I'm not surprised."

"Look, Ronnie, I'm in the middle of a case," she tried to protest, feeble though it was. "I'm pretty tied up at the moment . . ."

"You always are," Ronnie chided. "Doesn't stop the rest of the world from turning, does it?"

No, it didn't. But Jo wished that, in Mama's case, it would.

"Is she okay?" she dared to ask.

"I don't know how to answer that exactly."

*Oh, God, here we go.*

Jo sighed as Hank glanced across his computer monitor, watching her from his desk. He gave her a quizzical look, and she shook her head to let him know it didn't have a thing to do with him.

"What'd she go and do this time?" was the only question Jo could think of asking, since Mama's problems at the home always had to do with Mama.

There'd been the Great Fork Battle, where she and a fellow patient kept poking at each other with utensils during dinner until the other had ended up with a bloody hand. And then there was the Great Shoe Theft, where Verna kept wandering into random rooms and stealing everyone's orthopedic sneakers. Oh, and pretty much weekly, she did battle with her caregivers, struggling as they tried to undress and bathe her, all the while spewing racial epithets and hitting them with her fists.

Jo braced herself for the worst, praying that Mama had not been kicked out.

"All right, here goes," Ronnie said, seeming to gather up the breath to share the sordid tale. "She pushed a woman and knocked her down, although I can't say your mama wasn't provoked. Every time I visit, this lady invades her space. She sits in her chair, takes naps in her bed, stands with her nose two inches from your mama's, and Verna had just had it with her."

"Oh, boy." Clearly, Ronnie was taking Verna's side in the matter, though Jo recognized her bias.

"Verna's only mistake was in shoving the nutty old bat right in the TV room where every danged human in the whole wing is always sittin' and drooling, so everyone could see."

Like it would have been better if Mama had knocked the lady down out of sight of spectators?

Jo rubbed her forehead, sensing a headache coming on.

Verna Kaufman couldn't do anything quietly, could she? It was all about the drama. When Jo was a kid and Mama drank like a fish, everything Verna did reminded Jo of Blanche DuBois, fanning herself and moaning about the heat, gussying herself up and leaving Jo home alone so she could play the Southern belle and get a man. Nothing was ever sane or rational. Though Mama was off the booze now, she couldn't even do Alzheimer's gracefully. Apparently, she was going to kick and scream through every stage of the disease until it killed her, which, eventually, it would.

Jo figured that would be a blessing.

"What are they going to do to her? Please don't tell me they're tossing her out." It had been hard enough finding a place for Verna that wasn't financially or geographically out of reach. Winghaven had better marks for memory care than most of the for-profit places, and Jo liked the fact that the management didn't seem to turn over every month. "She's still there, right?" Jo tried again when she didn't get an answer.

Her mother's friend sucked in a loud breath while Jo held hers.

"They've admitted her to the psych ward at the hospital," Ronnie said, sounding cross. "They claim they need her to be evaluated by a shrink. They said it's part of their procedure when a patient is violent, since they don't have a psychiatrist on staff."

Jo felt her lungs expand. She tried hard not to laugh.

*Violent?* Mama was well over sixty and weighed about a hundred fifteen pounds soaking wet. She could hardly walk more than five yards without getting short of breath. She was a pain in the ass, yes. She could engage in a mock sword fight with her fork and curse up a storm when the mood struck. But shoving someone to the ground? Jo had a hard time envisioning it. Mama had never laid a hand on her. Instead, she'd used words as her weapons of choice, usually along the lines of, *stupid little girl* and *ungrateful liar.*

"Did you hear me, Jo?" Ronnie raised her voice. "I said she's been committed."

"Yes," Jo replied. "I heard. I'm not surprised. They have to cover their asses."

That was how it worked everywhere these days, even at the department. Nobody wanted bad press. Nobody wanted to get sued.

"So what can I do? Do I have to sign some paperwork to bail her out?" Jo asked, and Hank looked over.

"Not unless you want to take her home with you."

Jo couldn't tell if that was a statement or a question. Just to be safe, she uttered, "Not really, no."

"They've got her locked up in the hospital mental ward until the psychiatrist can test her and tell the danged nursing home that she's not going to attack anyone else."

"What are they testing for?" Jo asked. "She doesn't even know her own name."

"Agreed," Ronnie said. "It's a boatload of crap."

That was as harsh a cuss word as Jo had ever heard Ronnie utter, and Ronnie's affection for her mom pinged Jo's guilt.

"Do I need to go visit the psych ward?"

"Do you want to?"

No. That was pretty much the last thing Jo wanted.

"I should, shouldn't I?" Jo said grudgingly, though Ronnie didn't answer. Because both of them knew what Jo should do, no matter if anyone said it outright.

She decided to man up, or woman up, as the case may be.

"Maybe I can go after my shift," she offered, though it took more strength than it should have to say it.

"That mealymouthed director at Winghaven promised they'd send someone over to check on her every day, not that I believe them." Ronnie harrumphed. "They also said they'd take her back as soon as she's cleared, although I just left the hospital, and the nurse said the shrink couldn't see her till tomorrow. They're not thrilled to have Verna there. They don't have room to keep her for long. They have people with real troubles they need to tend to, and they don't want to be babysittin' a woman with dementia." She clicked her tongue against her teeth. "Verna couldn't stop herself from acting like a crazy person because she *is* a crazy person."

"Amen," Jo said, because Ronnie was right about that.

Everyone on Mama's floor at the nursing home was nuts. The handful of times she'd visited, she'd seen just about everything: folks wandering around in bathrobes or in nothing at all; a woman in a wheelchair who uttered "help me" nonstop; people asleep in the dining room with their heads on the tables; patients dancing to music that only they could hear. She'd told Adam it felt like being in *One Flew Over the Cuckoo's Nest* for real, and she felt such sadness and pity for the afflicted and their families. The caregivers—the good ones—were a godsend, and Jo believed that, no matter what they were paid, it wasn't near enough.

"The aides on the floor, now they do the hard work," Ronnie said, exactly what Jo had been thinking. "But sometimes I think the people who run those places don't know what the heck they're doing."

"They probably don't," Jo said. Half the time, she didn't know what she was doing, either.

"Once they make the sales pitch and get you to sign up, they figure they've got you for good, because ain't no one going to want to have to start looking and filling out the piles of paperwork all over again."

"Yep," Jo told her, because she was dead-on.

"That's all I have to say on the subject." Ronnie didn't even pretend to be cheerful. "If you get over to the psych ward, would you take her a toothbrush? They have plenty of those Depends, so she doesn't need any kind of underpants."

"Okay."

"If you don't get out there, tell me that, too. I can go see her after dinner for a spell."

"Thanks, Ronnie."

"Now you go on back to catching bad guys, and I'll try not to bother you too much."

"Until the next time," Jo said.

Ronnie laughed. "Until the next time."

Jo didn't even have a chance to say goodbye before Ronnie hung up.

For a moment, Jo held the phone in her hand, tempted to dial Adam's number, wanting to hear his voice, to tell him that Mama was locked up like a madwoman in the psych ward at Presbyterian Hospital; to confide about getting another case with a victim who had so much life yet to live, who did not have to die.

She pulled up his name on speed dial, then changed her mind and sent him a text instead:

Mama's at the psych ward. Stopping by tonight before I head home.

Within seconds, her phone pinged.

So I should make dinner?

She smiled and returned, Sounds good.

ILY, he replied.

Ditto.

She'd barely sent off the text when the phone at her desk trilled. She picked it up.

"Jo Larsen," she said.

"Hey, Detective, I've got a woman calling about a missing dog," the front desk officer told her. "Been gone since last night."

"I know," she said, rubbing at her right temple, trying to erase the dull throbbing that had started with Ronnie's phone call. "Amanda Pearson's golden retriever. We went over and met with her first thing this morning—"

"No, it's not Amanda Pearson. It's someone else entirely. You want to talk to her? I've got her on the line."

# CHAPTER ELEVEN

Jo picked up the phone and found herself listening to a woman named Jill Burns, who could barely hold back her tears as she spoke. She'd been vacationing in California for the past ten days and had returned earlier that morning. She'd engaged a local pet sitter recommended by someone at her vet's office. The pet sitter had been paid to feed and walk Tucker, an eight-year-old German shepherd, three times a day, and Ms. Burns claimed the sitter never mentioned anything was wrong in all the times that she'd checked in.

But when Ms. Burns arrived home, she couldn't find Tucker, and after numerous calls and texts to the pet sitter, she'd finally heard back. The sitter had sounded anxious, admitting that she'd left Tucker out overnight with water and food because, according to an incredulous Jill, "She claimed he couldn't 'hold it' long enough until she arrived in the morning and let him out to do his business."

When the sitter went over that morning before Jill was due to return, Tucker wasn't there. The backyard gate was supposedly closed but not locked. When the sitter couldn't locate him, she wrongly assumed Jill had gotten back earlier and taken Tucker to the park or for a walk.

"Is she sure she didn't leave the gate open?" Jo asked.

"She swore she didn't, but it's hard to believe anything she says at this point."

"Did anyone else check on Tucker while you were away?"

"No!" Jill Burns yelped into Jo's ear. "How could she have not called me when she realized Tucker was gone? How could she be so neglectful? Now I'm a mess. I can't go to work. I can't function. I don't know what to do . . ."

"Did you call Animal Services to see if he'd been picked up?" Jo asked, not afraid of being rebuked this time, as Hank had been when he'd mentioned the same thing to Amanda Pearson.

"Yes, of course," the woman said, her voice shaky. "They aren't holding any German shepherds at the facility, and they hadn't gotten any calls about anyone finding one wandering the streets."

"Is he chipped?"

"Yes. I had my vet chip him years ago."

"Did you talk to your neighbors?"

"That's what I've been doing for the past hour, walking up and down the street, knocking on doors. No one's seen Tucker, and I can hardly breathe not knowing what's happened to him," she got out before she started bawling in earnest.

*Oh, man.*

Jo hardly knew what to do except to tell her, "I'm going to give you my e-mail address, Ms. Burns. If you'll send me a JPEG of Tucker and give me your address and the number of the pet sitter, I'll do my best to see what I can turn up."

Hank must have overheard her conversation. He mouthed from across the way, "Another lost dog?"

She nodded as she gave Jill Burns her e-mail address. She was about to wrap up the call when the woman told her one last thing.

"I found Tucker's collar," she said, "when I was going up and down the street. It wasn't far from my house, maybe three down near a stop sign. It's like someone tossed it out a car window. Would it help you to have it? To check for fingerprints or something?"

"Hold on to it, okay?" Jo told her. "Just try not to handle it too much. Drop it in a baggie or a paper sack, and I'll send an officer by to pick it up."

"Please help me find him."

"We'll do what we can."

Jo heard the pain in the woman's voice. She sounded as heartbroken as Amanda Pearson had been over her missing golden retriever. Come to think of it, both women had shown more despair at finding their pups gone than Barbara Amster had at hearing that she'd lost her teenage daughter.

Hank must have read the distress in her face as he scooted around his desk and pulled his chair up to hers. "Seriously, have we got another missing dog case?" he said, rubbing a hand over his jowls. "Is something in the air?"

"It's a German shepherd named Tucker," Jo told him. "The owner went on vacation and left him at home, in the care of a pet sitter. The sitter put the dog out overnight, and it disappeared."

"Is the yard unfenced?"

"No, there's a fence," she told him, "and the sitter swore that she didn't leave the gate open. I'd say it's coincidence, except that the owner found the collar up the street, left behind at a stop sign a few houses away."

"Kind of reminds you of Amanda Pearson's situation, doesn't it?"

"Yep."

"Both on the same night?"

Jo nodded.

"Damn." Hank paused to scratch his jaw. "Either we have a bona fide dog thief running around Plainfield, or else there's a full moon rising."

"What does the moon have to do with it?" Jo squinted at him like he'd lost his mind, which he seemed to do at regular intervals. "Have you been watching those midnight infomercials for psychics again?"

He waved her off. "No, just wondering if there's something freaky brewing, like a full-moon gathering of a cult that needs sacrificial lambs . . . or dogs . . . whatever."

"Let's hope that's not it."

Though if someone was going around Plainfield stealing dogs from their backyards, Jo couldn't imagine anything but ugly reasons. Her brain liked to jump to worst-case scenarios, and it was doing that now, envisioning some creep using the dogs for target practice or as training bait in dogfights.

She felt a blood vessel pound in her head and pressed fingers against her brow, although the ache remained.

She'd seen plenty of tragedy in her years on the force, horrible things done by humans to other humans, sometimes in a fit of rage and sometimes utterly calculated. But crimes committed against children and animals were another kind of horror entirely.

She thought of what she knew about how serial killers prepared, using animals before they trapped their first human victims. The mass shooter in Sutherland Springs had reportedly gotten dogs off Craigslist to use as target practice.

A part of her couldn't help but wonder if that was what was happening here. Was there someone in suburban Plainfield taking domesticated pups because they were easy marks? Were they dealing with a killer in training?

"Hey, Larsen, you in there?" Hank was snapping his fingers in front of her face.

"Just thinking," she told him and brushed away his hands.

"About Kelly Amster, or about the dogs?"

"The dogs," she told him. "I have an angle."

"So do I," Hank said, putting out his idea first. "There's a network of barking dog haters, and they're delivering steaks full of ketamine in the dead of night. They knock out the pups and haul 'em off to another county so they can finally have some peace and quiet."

Jo squinted. "Hmm, I think I like mine better."

"What's yours?"

"My bet's on a creep in training," she said.

"A creep in training," he repeated, and she could tell he was trying not to laugh. "That's some hunch."

"It fits, Hank." She felt miffed. "For sure, it's not animal activists stealing dogs from a medical lab. It's not someone trying to sell old dogs. Whoever took them targeted them. Older dogs would not put up a fight . . ."

"Okay." He waggled fingers. "Keep going."

"What if our dog thief was acquainted with Duke and Tucker, even tangentially, like someone from a vet's office or a part-time dog walker," she said. "They might use the same services even if they live in different neighborhoods."

"Let's look at the locations," Hank said.

"That's as good a place to start as any," she agreed.

With Hank at her elbow, she put her fingers on the keyboard and plugged in Jill Burns's address along with that of the Pearson residence, pulling up an interactive map.

"I know that street," Hank said, pointing to the road where Jill Burns lived. "I must have walked by her house a hundred times, taking the girls to the park."

"Hmm," she said as she sat back and gazed at the map, zooming in and zooming out again. She knew the area where Jill Burns lived, too, as it wasn't far from Hank's zero lot line property, where neighbors practically sat on top of one another. The Burns house was just a couple of blocks away from a community playground with an adjacent dog park, which was one reason the neighborhood was popular with pet owners and families.

But it didn't help Jo to make a connection.

"The Pearson place and the Burns house are at least five miles across town from each other," Hank said.

Jo sighed.

There had to be *something*.

They just weren't seeing it yet.

So Jo went back to her keyboard. She clicked the mouse to zoom out farther, wanting to get a bigger picture of the streets from which the dogs had disappeared and the area between them.

"The old water tower's in the middle," Hank said right off the bat.

"Yeah, 'cause it's in the middle of *everything*."

"Zoom out a little more," he urged.

Jo did but only a bit. If she zoomed too much, she'd be outside the Plainfield city limits. Heck, she'd be out of Dallas County altogether and into Collin County.

"What are you looking for exactly?" she asked her partner. He had his forehead pleated, he was concentrating so hard.

"I'm not sure. But, whatever it is, I'm not finding it," he said. "There's just the municipal buildings, the high school, a couple of churches . . ."

The phone on Hank's desk started ringing, and he sighed.

"It's okay," she told him. "How 'bout I look for barking dog complaints against the victims' pets?" she suggested, and Hank gave her a nod.

Then he rolled his chair back home and picked up his phone. "Yeah, this is Detective Phelps," he said.

Jo heard the rumble of his voice as he thanked the caller for getting back to him so quickly. But she didn't listen long enough to figure out who it was.

Instead, she fixed her gaze on her monitor and opened another window over the map on her screen. She got into the department's system, looking at old 311 complaints, just as she had when she'd narrowed down the address of the house party Kelly had attended.

But this time, she looked solely at barking dog complaints. She checked the past two days in particular, scrolling down the list of reports and the complainants, hoping to find a phone call or two relating to the dogs that had disappeared, something that could make Hank's theory pan out.

It wasn't long before she gave up.

Her partner got off the phone and stood, stretching. Then he came around to her desk with a notebook in hand and tapped it with his pen. "I just had a pretty interesting conversation with Fred Babcock over at Animal Services," he said. "I left a message for him after we talked to Amanda Pearson, and I just told him about the second missing dog report."

Jo rubbed her eyes. "And?"

"Seems they averaged twice as many calls about lost dogs in the weeks since school started versus the summer months." His eyes brightened, like he was on to something.

Jo didn't think that sounded so odd, but she played devil's advocate.

"Summer's a lazy time," she said. "Kids are home from school, and families are traveling. But once school begins, schedules get crazy. It'd be easy to forget to shut a gate when you're worried about homework and tardy slips."

He leaned a hip against her desk. "You might be right about that. But Fred thought it was odd that the disappearing dogs were all big breeds, like pit bulls, retrievers, huskies, none of those puny types. No Chihuahuas, terriers, cockapoos, or doodle dogs."

"Why's that suspicious?"

Hank glanced at his notepad. "Usually when he hears about stolen pups, they're the little ones, grabbed out of parked cars. The purse puppies are an easier resale. Top three swiped breeds are Yorkshire terrier, Maltese, and Pomeranian, in case you're wondering."

She wasn't.

"So does Animal Services think we're on to a dognapping ring in Plainfield?"

Hank blew out his cheeks. "He didn't exactly put it that way, but he did say dog flips are up."

"Flips?"

He gave her a cockeyed grin. "You'd think we were talking about house renos, right? But it's what they call it when someone takes a dog and sells it to someone else, and it's an easy way for criminals to make some money if they know what they're doing. But if the owners had their pets chipped, there's a shot some vet will find it and do the right thing. Otherwise . . ." He shrugged. "There's a good chance they won't ever be recovered."

"Great." The rate of success for finding a missing person after the first twenty-four hours got dimmer and dimmer. Tracking down a missing pet was even trickier, she realized. The dog could never talk and say where it lived or what its name was. Without collars, no one else would know, either.

"Although," Hank went on in his gravelly drawl, "Fred said they did have one dog turn up that went missing three weeks back. It was an older black Lab that vanished from his backyard a street over from Amanda Pearson's."

A street away from where Duke had been taken?

"Really?" Jo perked up. "How come we didn't hear about it before now? Was there a report?"

She couldn't always remember every call that came in, every incident, particularly if she wasn't the one who responded.

"The owner didn't file a missing property claim with us—I checked—but she kept on Fred's back for weeks, asking if her Lab had turned up. Then a few days later, Fred says, the dog did turn up in

Celina. It was found on the side of the road by someone who works at the Bethel Church."

"In Celina?" It was a town of mostly farmland, about fifteen miles north of Plainfield in another county entirely. "How'd a dog from Plainfield end up there? That's a far walk. It's twenty-five minutes by car."

"No clue, but it was on its last legs," Hank told her grimly. "Fred said the dog looked like it was hit by a vehicle. It was taken to an animal hospital, where they found the chip, but the pup didn't make it."

Jo grimaced. "Why would a backyard dog that disappeared show up in farm country?"

"Maybe he hitchhiked?" Hank joked, but it wasn't funny.

"Someone took him, that's how." She looked at the map on her computer screen and zoomed out again, so she could see the endless length of Preston Road running north to Celina. She pinpointed the Farm to Market Road, FM 455, and its surroundings. It was, as Hank had noted, full of acreage parceled out mostly for produce farms, cattle ranches, horse farms, and country property.

What did they really have, after all? Two missing dogs with their tags left behind, and the tale of another lost dog that had turned up dead in the next county.

Were the three cases connected? If so, what the hell was going on?

"So what's next, partner?" he asked.

She sat back in her chair, looking up at him. "If we can spare a couple of uniforms, they can pick up the collar at Jill Burns's house and knock on doors in the neighborhood, but it's not like we can put out an Amber Alert for missing dogs. I'm not sure what other rocks to kick over right now."

"We could call a real pet detective."

"Ha." She smiled feebly. "At the very least, we can e-mail the information on the missing dogs to the local rescue operations and tell them we'd be interested to know if they turn up and in what condition."

"Already did that for Amanda Pearson's retriever," Hank said. "I can call back and give them whatever you've got on the second dog."

"Thanks."

Jo's desk phone rang, and she jerked her head toward the noise.

"Maybe that's somebody sayin' they found a stray pup," Hank said, giving her one of his crooked half smiles that reminded her of a slightly deranged Ward Cleaver.

"Right."

As her partner wandered back to his desk, she snatched up the receiver. "Larsen," she said.

"Hey, Detective, it's Bridget from Digital Forensics," said an excited voice on the other end.

Jo smiled at Bridget's euphemism for her cluttered desk in the room with the computer server.

"What's up?" Jo asked.

"Can you come down here right away?"

"Please tell me you got into the laptop," Jo said, because surely, something had to go right today.

"I did," Bridget practically chirped, "and I think I found something interesting."

# CHAPTER TWELVE

Jo and Hank squeezed themselves into the tiny space around Bridget's desk in the server room, the level of white noise giving Hank a permanent wince. At least he didn't have reason to complain about it being hot, considering the fact that it wasn't.

Jo was too psyched to care about the goose bumps on her arms or the background cacophony of whirring and beeping and spinning.

She had her eyes glued to Kelly's laptop, which Bridget had hooked up like a deathly ill patient to a string of IVs. There were cords connecting it to another laptop and to a trio of flat screens, and even more black cords trailed in and out of various pieces of machinery that littered Bridget's desktop.

"Let me tell you where things stand so far," she announced, headphones sitting at the base of her neck. She made no move to turn around and look at them. Instead, she bent her dark head over the keyboard and started tapping so quickly, Jo felt dizzy just watching her flying fingers.

"I finally got the drive operational, although it wasn't easy," she said, voice raised so they could hear, and still her gaze didn't waver from the monitors as Jo and Hank hovered over her shoulders. "Kelly's laptop had a shutdown virus, which wouldn't let me into the registry editor."

"A what?" Jo said, and not because the words had been drowned out. She had no idea what Bridget was talking about.

"A shoot-down virus?" Hank howled in Bridget's ear. But he looked equally bewildered and dared to ask, "What the devil does that mean?"

"*Shut*down," Bridget repeated, raising her voice at least a decibel. "It kept her laptop from booting up. I had to download and install a new registry editor before I could do anything."

"Of course you did," Hank replied, giving Jo a sideways glance as if to say: *Are you sure she's speaking English?*

"What I ended up doing was going through the system and creating a restore point for everything so I wouldn't further damage any program files. I found the shutdown auto-run keys and deleted them, and then I located the execute files that had a similar name and got rid of them, too."

"Great," Jo said, waiting for Bridget to say something that she understood, although pretty much these days when it came to tech, her knowledge didn't go much beyond "on" and "off."

"Next, I cleaned up the bad files in the Task Manager and emptied the Recycle Bin, so I could feel secure about restoring the system to a point before the virus attacked. I'd like to think we didn't lose any potentially useful files, but I can't be sure," Bridget admitted, finally glancing back at Jo, like she needed to catch her breath, or maybe she was just waiting for their inevitable questions.

"So you got the thing to work?" Jo asked, hoping that was the point of all the gobbledygook Bridget had just hurled at them. "You did get it booted?"

"Yes, and I'm in." Bridget smiled, and her right hand left the keyboard in front of her long enough to push at the black specs on her nose. "I used the password you gave me from the school district to get into Kelly Amster's files."

"Now we're cookin' with gas." Hank rubbed his hands together. "Tell me she kept a diary or shared every freaking part of her life on Facebook."

"I haven't gotten that far yet," Bridget said. "I can definitely do a search on social media and see what turns up. Much of the younger crowd has deserted Facebook, but she may be there. IGen is pretty much either into Snapchat or Insta to share photos, although lots of schools use Facebook for announcements and events, and for organized groups. If she used Snapchat, we're screwed unless she made screen-shots of anything important. About as bad would be a secret group on Facebook, or if she has a Finsta in addition to a Rinsta."

"Whoa, whoa. Slow down there, sparky," Hank drawled, leaning down nearer to better hear. "What's an iGen and an Insta?"

"And Rinsta and Finsta?" Jo added, feeling like she was quoting Dr. Seuss.

"Yeah, please explain for the oldsters in the room."

Bridget swiveled so they could read her lips if they had to. She grinned nervously. "Um, well, iGen is Generation Z, whatever you want to call it. Think the next generation after the millennials, mostly people under twenty-two."

"Got it," Hank said and tipped his head.

"Insta is Instagram," she explained. "Rinsta is what kids call a real Instagram account, and Finsta is a fake account. You know, like using fake account information so they can post photos or say things they might not want attached to their true selves."

"Oh, great," Hank moaned. "More crap for me to worry about with my girls."

"They're in grade school, partner," Jo reminded him. "They're not posting naked pictures on the net yet."

"Thanks for the reassurance." Hank scowled at her before turning his attention back to Bridget. "Can you break into her accounts?"

Bridget wrinkled her nose. "You mean, like, hack them?"

"Isn't that what they always do on TV?" he said and snapped his fingers. "Takes 'em, like, two seconds to beat any password and get to the meat and potatoes."

"On TV, yeah, right. Because that's real." Bridget pursed her lips. "I can try resetting her passwords, since I've got her laptop and a valid e-mail address. We'll see if that works."

"That would be great," Jo said, then looked at Hank. "We seriously need to get back to the house. I want to go through Kelly's room . . ."

"And talk to good ol' Barb again," her partner said, finishing her thought.

"I'd like to know more about her relationship with the Eldons," Jo added. "Was Barb aware that Kelly had been in touch with Trey again? That she'd supposedly begged an invite to his party?"

"If she wasn't, she will be soon enough . . ."

Bridget cleared her throat. "Would y'all like to hear more, or you want to come back after I finally take a really late lunch break?"

Jo and Hank stopped talking.

"No," she said, as he said, "Yes."

But they meant the same thing, and Bridget seemed to get it.

"Okay then." She clickety-clacked her fingers on the keyboard, pulling up what looked like the contents of Kelly's e-mail file. "Check out her in-box."

Jo squinted at the screen as Bridget scrolled down through the dates, from most recent to oldest. She saw a handful off the bat that were clearly about homework, easy to tell by the subject headers.

"What am I supposed to be looking for?" Hank asked from over Bridget's other shoulder.

"Here," the young woman said, dragging her mouse to highlight a flurry of e-mails from one user in particular. The dates on them were all from August, after the night of Trey's party. "These aren't related to schoolwork," she said.

"How do you know?" Jo asked.

Bridget sighed, clicking on one e-mail as she explained, "Notice anything?"

Jo could see the subject header, *Advice*, which hardly rang warning bells. It had gone back and forth so many times, there were quite a number of *RE:*s preceding it. Then Bridget scrolled down the screen to the body of the e-mail.

Something was clearly wiggly-whack.

"Can you fix that mess?" Jo asked, because the text wasn't anything readable. It was just random characters, one after another, for paragraphs.

Bridget laughed, but she sounded more frustrated than amused. "No, I can't do anything about it."

"But it's nothing more than gibberish." Jo's heart crumpled in her chest. "Did the virus corrupt her e-mail files?"

"No." The young woman pushed back her keyboard, twirling in her chair to face them. "The text is encrypted. Without the key, I can't read the body of the e-mail, just the sender's e-mail address and the subject. Sometimes the program keeps the plain text once the e-mail's been read. But this one appears to stay in ciphertext when the program's closed out."

"It's encrypted?" Hank repeated.

"Yes, the e-mail program scrambles all the bits around to protect the contents," Bridget started to explain, "and only the sender and recipient have the key so they can—"

"I actually know what it means," Hank said, interrupting. "I just can't imagine why a couple of high school kids would need to use coded e-mails to send messages."

Jo gave him a look. "I could," she remarked, especially if Kelly had been raped at Trey's party, and Trey was trying to cover it up.

"You think a fifteen-year-old girl would subscribe to an encryption service? It doesn't feel right," Hank said.

"Maybe it wasn't her idea. Maybe it was Gucci Boy's."

"Gucci Boy?" Hank repeated, and then his eyebrows arched.

Jo tapped a finger lightly against the monitor in the middle, where Bridget had highlighted the sender's e-mail address. "Username 'Stang12,'" she said.

Hank whistled. "Well, would you look at that? At this rate, the boy's not gonna be playing for the Longhorns next year. He's going to be lucky if he gets signed by the University of Leavenworth."

"So you know who it is?" Bridget asked, blinking dark eyes behind her thick glasses.

"We can make an educated guess," Jo told her.

Namely, that it was the golden arm of the Plainfield Mustangs football team, who wore a number twelve on his jersey and whose daddy owned a software security company. Jo wondered if that company offered e-mail encryption.

"You thinking what I'm thinking?" Hank said.

Jo nodded. "Trey Eldon."

"Should I look into this guy's social media presence, too?" Bridget piped up.

"Please do," Jo told her. "His legal name is Robert Eldon the Third, but he goes by Trey. If we're lucky, he posted pics or video from his end-of-summer-break party. That would help us start identifying who else was there."

"That should be simple enough if he tagged them."

Jo thanked her, and Bridget promised to begin a methodical search through Kelly's electronic files, just to be sure they didn't miss a beat. Within seconds, the young woman had her headphones back on, and her fingers resumed their staccato dance across her keyboard, effectively tuning them out.

"I hope she gives us a hammer to nail that son of a bitch to the wall," Hank said too loudly as they left Bridget's quarters, emerging into the much quieter hallway.

"I can hear you," Jo said, and he tugged at his ears, like he was trying to clear them.

"Sorry," he said, lowering his voice.

"You think he's guilty?"

"Of something, yeah. He's sure acting like a guy who has a dirty little secret."

"If we can just get him to hand over the code for the encryption, we'd know what was going on between him and Kelly . . ."

Hank snorted. "They're not going to make it that easy. We can try, but my gut's screaming warrant."

"If he's as innocent as he claims, those e-mails could exonerate him."

"Well, I guess we'll have to see how helpful he is, then, won't we?"

There was so much they still didn't know about Kelly and Trey and what had gone on at that party. The sooner they figured it out, the sooner Kelly could rest in peace, and wasn't that what everyone claimed to want?

Jo thought of Cassie and of her parting shot about dropping the investigation, and a lightbulb went on in her tired brain.

"Maybe we can force his hand," she remarked, as much to herself as her partner. "Cassie Marks said Kelly had evidence she was holding over someone's head. Photos, a video, she didn't know for sure." Jo shook her head. "But I'll bet that someone was Trey. So we just have to find it."

"*It* being what, exactly?"

"The proof," she said. "It's out there." Why else would Kelly have suggested it to Cassie?

Hank smirked. "Okay, and where exactly is that proof hiding, Agent Scully? In Area Fifty-One, perhaps?"

"I don't know," she admitted.

But she had a few thoughts on where to look.

# CHAPTER THIRTEEN

Jo didn't like to walk away from her desk when there was unfinished business, but she made herself leave when her shift ended. She'd be no good to anybody if she didn't take a step back now and then. Besides, she wanted a good meal, not vending-machine crap, and some time alone with Adam. And before she could do either, she had an unwanted detour to make to the psych ward at Presbyterian Hospital, where the nursing home had sent her errant mother.

She told herself she was at a good stopping point, anyway.

Officer Ramsey had retrieved the dog collar and tags from Jill Burns to try to print them as well as the tags from Amanda Pearson. Jo had filed property theft reports for both missing dogs. She'd left a message with Barbara Amster about getting back out to the house to search Kelly's room, and she'd left a voice mail for Robert Eldon, formally requesting that Trey voluntarily give them a list of party guests. She also asked that Trey turn over the unencrypted e-mails between him and Kelly Amster.

If he didn't agree, they could pursue a warrant to force his hand. But Jo hoped the Eldons would comply and not get a high-priced lawyer involved to muddy the waters and speed bump their search for answers about what had led to Kelly Amster's death.

Before she took off, Jo poked her head into Bridget's office space but found only the department's server equipment, noisily whirring away.

So she headed out with Hank, listening to him bitch about the heat as he rolled up his sleeves. She didn't tell him where she was going, and he didn't ask. With a wave and a "See you in the morning, partner," she crossed the lot to her Mustang, keyed it open, and slipped inside.

Jo cranked up the air, waiting for it to cool down as she texted Ronnie that she was going to see Mama. Then she tossed her phone on the passenger's seat and turned on the radio. She had installed a police band in the car but left it off. Dispatch could reach her by cell, and she wanted the radio on. Switching on the classical music station, she sighed happily as Mozart's *Serenade No. 13* flowed from the speakers. She felt the tension ease from her shoulders, and she tapped a beat on the steering wheel as she slipped out of the rear lot.

She hated driving into the city at rush hour, but she had no choice. So she kept the music on and let her thoughts slide around to Kelly Amster's alleged suicide and what was behind it, to Mama and her Alzheimer's and all the paperwork Jo was slowly trying to unscramble after the sale of the house, and to Amanda Pearson and Jill Burns and what they were going through tonight, wondering about their missing "kids."

*Serenade No. 13* segued into Mahler's *Symphony No. 8*, a rather strident piece that wasn't one of her favorites, but she merely turned it down a notch. She didn't switch stations, didn't budge from her music. She didn't want to check talk radio for the latest news. She found nothing more depressing these days than crime and politics and natural disasters, and those seemed to dominate every broadcast.

Though the sun had settled low on the horizon, the sky was still fairly bright. The clouds had just begun to reflect a pink tinge when Jo exited I-635 for Walnut Hill Lane.

She didn't have far to go to reach the hospital. Once she'd parked in the garage, she took a deep breath, catching sight of her eyes in the rearview mirror. They looked so dark and serious, the pupil barely discernible from the iris beneath the dim garage lighting. They were so different from her mother's pale eyes. Jo's hair was dark, too, nearly black and full of unruly waves, whereas Verna's had always been straw yellow and straight.

Her eyes and her hair, and so many other things about her that didn't jibe with any characteristics of Mama, those were gifts from her father, she surmised; the man who'd left her to Verna all those years ago, before she'd really even known him. From what Mama had told her, and there had been much bad-mouthing, he'd walked away and found himself a new family, like Kelly Amster's father, who forgot to call on birthdays.

Jo wondered if Kelly's dad had been told of her death, and she wondered, too—although more fleetingly—if her own father knew that she was alive. Did he care?

Why did it still seem to matter so much?

Jo cursed under her breath. She got out of the car and walked into the building, brushing past the tide of others leaving. But the tower that housed the psychiatric wing seemed mostly deserted, and the elevator was empty going up.

When she hit the floor with the psych ward, she had to identify herself and whom she'd come to see before they would buzz her inside.

The lighting seemed dimmer within. She heard a TV and spied a lounge of sorts where family members sat, visiting with patients. No one took notice as she passed.

A pair of nurses—one male and one female—dressed in navy-blue scrubs looked up from beyond a countertop as she paused, unsure of where to go.

"I'm here to see Verna Kaufman," she said, and the pair exchanged glances before the male nurse came around to where she stood. "I'm her daughter, Jo Larsen."

"I'm Dimitri, the head nurse," he said, giving her a half smile.

He had his name sewn onto his shirt in simple white letters, easier to read than a name on a badge, and no dangerous pin held it on.

Though he was middle-aged, his hair faded to gray, he was in good shape with muscular arms sticking out of his short sleeves. The strange yellow lighting gave his skin the faintest tinge of green.

"How's she doing?" Jo asked. "Can I see her?"

"Your mother's actually sleeping now, which is a good thing. She hasn't eaten today, and she's been very agitated. She's understandably confused about where she is and what she's doing here."

"I'll bet she is."

"She shouldn't be here," he said, glancing over her shoulder as a gowned patient walked by, the other nurse intercepting him. "We don't have room to house Alzheimer's patients. The memory care facilities should know better than to drop them off here." He was well spoken, with a discernible Eastern European accent, which made him sound all the angrier. "They should have a psychiatrist on staff for things like this. It's ridiculous."

"Where is she?" Jo asked, looking down the hallway at a dozen doors. "Maybe I could tiptoe in and take a peek."

"I'd rather you not wake her," he said. "Can you come back tomorrow?"

Jo didn't want to be there now, much less come back.

"I don't know," she told him. "It's just that I don't live in town, and I see her so rarely . . ."

He put up a hand. "You don't have to explain. Your aunt was here. She said you're a police detective. You probably have lots of crooks to catch."

Her aunt? Jo started to say that she didn't have an aunt but caught herself.

*Ronnie,* Jo realized. He meant Ronnie.

Which made her remember something else.

"I forgot to bring her a toothbrush," she said, something she'd told Ronnie she'd do if she got here.

Dimitri grinned. "I can dig up one of those. No worries. Your mother needs sleep more than to brush her teeth, anyway."

Jo nodded, and he practically shooed her out the door. It clanked closed behind her, like it was made of some thick metal so the inmates couldn't escape.

She paused in the hallway only long enough to send a text to Ronnie:

Mama's asleep. Saw nurse who will get her a toothbrush. Heading home.

As she pressed the down button for the elevator, her phone pinged. Thx, hon, Ronnie had typed. I will go in the morning.

She went down in the elevator alone and walked to her car in the green glow of the subterranean parking.

As usual, once she left her mother, she felt an overwhelming sense of guilt—for not always doing what she should, for not insisting on seeing Mama and sitting with her, holding her hand or whatever good daughters did for mothers who deserved such attention far more than Verna did. She didn't remind herself of the things her mother should have done for *her*, long before the Alzheimer's became her sole excuse. She didn't push back against the sense that it was all her fault. She just left it there to simmer for a while, holding her hostage and making it hard to breathe until it slowly released her.

By the time she reached Plainfield, after about forty-five minutes on the crowded tollway, the guilt was gone, replaced by hunger and an ache to see Adam and Ernie.

She had begun to realize clearly that the pain of her past would never go away, but the more she loved and felt loved, the less she grieved.

# CHAPTER FOURTEEN

It was twilight when she reached her condo.

She spotted Adam's Jeep right away, and she slid her Mustang in beside it. Jo could tell that he'd turned on the living room light, though the blinds were drawn. Thin strips of yellow escaped between the wooden slats.

Before she stuck her key in the lock, she reached into the black mailbox on the porch railing and found it empty. Adam must have taken the mail inside, as he'd done often enough before when he'd beaten her home. It amazed her, how such a small action left her feeling taken care of, like finding the fridge full during a busy week—albeit with lots of health food, not the junk she was used to eating. Having Adam in her life definitely had its perks.

She got the door open in a hurry and stamped her feet on the inside mat. The noise was enough to draw Ernie, who raced toward her from across the living room, his slim, black body a mere streak, like a shadow.

"Hey, baby," she said, as the cat skidded to a stop just before he ran into her shins. Then he wended his way between her ankles as she slung her bag on the console table and dropped her keys.

He purred as she crouched down beside him.

"How're you doing?" she asked, her heart warmed by his greeting.

She thought of Jill Burns and Amanda Pearson, and her smile slipped. How lonely they must feel tonight without their close companions.

She scratched the cat beneath his chin until his eyes closed and he flopped over at her feet. "I think you missed me," she said, and her grin was back. "I'm glad to see you, too."

After a day that had left her emotionally drained, she welcomed Ernie's unbridled affection. When she'd rescued him six months ago during a case, she'd never imagined that so small a being could loom so large in her life.

She picked him up, hugging him against her chest, stroking him between his ears and trying not to think about work, about death and loss and things beyond her control.

*Let it go,* she told herself. At least for now.

She cradled the cat, rubbing his belly as she went in search of Adam.

It wasn't hard to find him in a condo that was less than a thousand square feet. All she had to do was listen. He was humming tunelessly, something that was probably old Van Halen or AC/DC. He was a glutton for eighties rock, because he said it was like him, like what he did: trying to make sense of shit that was pretty much nonsensical.

"Lucy, I'm home," she said, doing her best Ricky Ricardo impression.

He turned his head enough to give her a grin that looked boyish, despite the salt-and-pepper hair and stubble. He was standing in the kitchen, parked in front of the stovetop in clean green scrubs. His slender feet were bare. She could hear the sizzle of something cooking, and whatever it was smelled divine.

"Great timing," he said. "Dinner's almost ready."

She set Ernie down so she could come up behind him and slip her arms around his waist. She pressed her cheek against his shoulder. "What's cooking? Beef Wellington? Baked Alaska? Coq au vin?"

"Very funny," he said, leaning his head back to touch hers. "I'm no Julia Child, but I can make a mean bacon and eggs."

"You also make a mean peanut butter and jelly," she teased, giving his butt a pat through his scrubs. The back of his hair was still damp from a recent shower. She ran her fingers up into the curls that were only half-dry. "How'd your day go?"

"Never a dull moment," he said, not coughing up any details. "There's too much work. That's the problem with it. Never stops."

"I know."

"Yeah, you do, don't you?"

She thought he might say something about Kelly Amster, about who'd been assigned her postmortem, but he didn't. Maybe he was waiting for her to bring up the case first. Jo wasn't ready to talk about it yet. She wanted to pretend her life was normal, even if that lasted only through mealtime.

She went to the cabinet over the sink and pulled out two dinner plates. Then she got a saucer for Ernie. He was a big fan of Adam's scrambled eggs—heck, he would eat just about anything, from tuna fish to spaghetti—and he sat patiently nearby, waiting for his dinner to be served.

She went to the fridge and found a lone tomato. She sliced it up, adding it to their plates as Adam shoveled fluffy eggs atop them.

Ernie let out a meow, and Adam laughed. "Hold your horses, buddy. I've got yours here," he said, chopping up the eggs into small pieces before Jo put the dish on the floor.

She went back toward the stovetop and reached for a slice of bacon as Adam set them onto a folded piece of paper towel to mop off the grease.

"Be careful, it's hot," he said, stating the obvious as she juggled a piece, blowing on it before she took a bite. "Oh, yeah, and it's turkey. Healthier, you know."

"Not for the turkey," she joked. It wasn't bad-tasting stuff, though she didn't want to admit it. He was trying heroically to wean her from her diet of junk food and soda, and she wasn't protesting. Much. "At least it's not tofu. You slipped that in the pad Thai last week."

"You ate it."

"I'll eat anything I don't have to cook," she said, taking plates to the table as Adam turned off the stove and fetched the orange juice from the fridge to pour two glasses.

"If you had to see as many dead guys' arteries as I have, you'd be jumping all over tofu." He set her drink on her place mat, then gave her shoulder a squeeze before he sat down. "I just want to help you live forever."

"Thank you," she said, because no one had done that before. Maybe it was sappy, but she didn't care. How could she help but love him?

He started to eat, and she watched him, admiring the scruff on his face and sweet lines at the corners of his eyes. She thought of how they'd started their relationship: "In the middle," as she liked to tell him. *His* middle, not hers, because he was married, though she hadn't known it at first. Adam insisted it was more like he'd met her "at the end," saying his marriage hadn't been working since long before they'd ever hooked up. He'd never worn a ring that she remembered, at least not on the job, and that was where they'd connected—at her first autopsy, in fact, when she'd been a rookie cop. She had left Dallas when she'd come to her senses, starting anew in Plainfield, separating herself from Adam so he could make the choice about the future without her muddling his present.

When he'd come to her this past spring, when he'd told her his wife had left for LA and they were divorcing, Jo had felt her heart begin to beat again. She had confided in him all her worst fears—all the ugliness of her past—and he hadn't flinched. He certainly didn't pity her for it. Telling him the truth had only strengthened what they had, who they were. Jo was grateful for that.

For a girl who had never had faith in others, particularly men, it felt good to trust, good and terrifying at once.

"You hungry?" he asked, cocking his head.

"Starving."

They said little as they ate. Jo enjoyed the quiet, the time to really taste her food and relish every bite.

Once done, they switched off the lamps and settled on the couch. They leaned into each other as the light from the television flickered over them.

"How're you doing?" he asked, his hand slowly moving up and down her back. "I'm sorry about the girl who died. Kelly, right? Your captain called my boss, wanting to fast-track her post. It'll be done sometime tomorrow. I don't know if it'll be me, though."

"It's okay," she said, "if it's not you, I mean. I just need it to be done."

"You think she jumped?"

"I do." Jo nodded, feeling all sorts of things bubbling up inside her. That was all it took, and she unloaded on him, describing how she'd felt seeing Kelly Amster lying broken in the field and knowing that, even if no one else had been up in the tower with her, making her leap to her death, something had pushed her to that edge. Something so real and damaging and painful that she hadn't told anyone.

Not her best friend. Not her mother.

But someone knew.

Someone always knew.

They were in bed when she heard the phone vibrate.

She'd dozed off with Adam's arm across her belly. Ernie's ten pounds pinned down her legs, so she couldn't easily move until Adam rolled over, startling the cat off the bed as he reached for his phone in the dark. But the vibrations continued.

Jo sat up. "Is it yours?"

"No," he murmured, setting the buzzing object into her lap before he dropped his head back onto the pillow.

Her screen lit up in the pitch-black, and she saw the *Blocked Caller* notification before she answered.

"Hello?" she said, rubbing her eyes.

She heard Adam's rhythmic snoring resume.

"Detective Larsen?" a male voice whispered, and she imagined a child, sounding very small and scared.

"That's right."

"It's Trey Eldon." Not such a little boy, after all. "I need to see you. The sooner, the better."

She squinted at the tiny clock on her phone. It was half past eleven.

"Now?" she asked in a whisper, puzzled by his urgency to meet and wondering if it was in response to the message she'd left his father about the encrypted e-mails and the list of party guests. Was Trey feeling the pressure? Or did he just need to unload without his daddy in the room? "Can it wait until morning? You could come to the station, or I could go—"

"No." She heard his sharp intake of breath before he replied with an angry, "Do you want to talk or not?"

"Yes," she said. "Very much."

"All right, then. Listen up."

She waited through his instructions and agreed to meet him, despite the hour. She knew that if she didn't go, she'd miss her shot. He sounded desperate to get something off his chest, and Jo needed to capitalize on his guilt. If she waited until the bright light of morning, he'd probably decide to clam up.

"If you're not there in fifteen, I'm gone," he told her before he hung up.

*Well, hell.*

Despite her misgivings and her madly pounding heart, Jo got out of bed, careful not to wake Adam. She dressed quietly in the dark, adding her holster and sidearm beneath a loose jacket. She stood by the bed, tempted to lean over and wake her man, to whisper where she was going. But she didn't. She would be back soon enough.

She tiptoed out of the bedroom, halfway up the hall before Ernie appeared out of nowhere, tripping her. She cursed under her breath, catching herself and scolding him softly. "Go back to bed," she hissed, patting his soft head before she slipped out the door.

# CHAPTER FIFTEEN

Jo met Trey at a park a few miles away from the old water tower.

Was there some hidden meaning behind the location? Did he need the tower to be evident, looming nearby in the dark, a visible reminder of how his actions—or maybe his inaction—had consequences?

Or, more likely, she was reading too much into things, and he'd picked the spot because it was far away enough from home that his daddy couldn't eavesdrop.

Once she'd turned into the entry lane, she spotted the black Silverado with *Stang12* on the vanity plates tucked into the graveled lot. She pulled in beside it. As far as she could tell, no one else was around, though it was hard to see. The widely spaced streetlamps didn't cast much light on the grounds, not at nearly midnight, when the park was officially closed.

Jo sat in the car for a moment, her phone in hand. She'd dialed Hank's number and was waiting for him to pick up.

"Where are you?" she asked the second he answered. She'd called him once before already, telling him about the meet, and he'd agreed to back her up, albeit hiding in the shadows so as not to spook Trey. "Are you near?"

"I'm still home," he grumbled. "I was about out the door when Cora started throwing up."

That was his four-year-old, Jo knew.

"Trish said she'd handle it, but then Grace started puking."

His six-year-old.

"Can you put the Third off?" he suggested.

Jo sighed. "No."

"I don't like this one bit . . ."

"Hey, I'm a big girl," she said. "I can do this by myself. Just keep me on speaker, okay, in case I need you."

Hank grumbled something about Trey needing a kick in the ass, which she took as an affirmative.

"I'm putting you in my pocket," she said.

"You must have a damn big pocket," he joked.

"It's bottomless, like a clown car," she told him, garnering a quick laugh. "I'm heading into the park, so expect a bit of radio silence until I can fish you out again."

"Roger that. And, Larsen—"

"Yeah?"

"Watch your back."

"Thanks, Dad."

There was a gentle pop as Jo pushed the door open. She slid out and let her eyes adjust to the night before she took a step away from her car. Then she began to walk toward the shadowy figure sitting atop a picnic table just across the grass.

He was hunched over, his feet on the bench below, arms resting on his bent knees, though he straightened up when he realized she was there.

"Hey," he called softly.

"Hey," she said, surveying the area as she approached. She felt sure that he'd come alone, but that didn't stop her from being apprehensive. It had been bred into her bones through the years.

"Have a seat." Despite his muscular frame, he moved agilely, slipping off the table and scooting onto the opposite bench.

Jo sat down, removing the phone from her pocket. She set it on the bench beside her, out of Trey's eyeshot.

The branches of nearby trees rustled as a vague breeze blew, scudding clouds across the night, obscuring stars. The hum of cicadas surrounded them like noisy chatter in the background. Usually, she found the sound reassuring, but not now.

She was on high alert.

Casually, she unzipped her jacket and slipped her hand underneath to unsnap the holster on her sidearm.

She waited for him to speak first. This was his show. He'd set it up. He must have a load to get off his chest if he wanted to see her badly enough to sneak out of the house beneath his father's nose.

"So here's the thing," he said after a drawn-out sigh. "Kelly knew stuff about me, about my family . . . stuff my dad wouldn't want anyone to know. You can't understand how hard it's been. No one can."

Jo sat stock-still, afraid that if she twitched, he'd turn tail and run.

"Kelly knew my dad cheated on my mom when she was sick. She knew my brother jacked Mom's pain meds. She knew I drank too much. Watching my mom—" He paused and swallowed. "Watching her die . . . We were all, you know, doing things to numb ourselves. We lived in a fog."

"I'm sorry," Jo said, because she was and because he hesitated, seeming to expect something more from her. "My mom's sick now," she went on. "It's painful to see."

She wasn't sure if that was what he wanted, but she guessed it was close enough, because he continued.

"I'd pushed it away to somewhere in the back of my head. We had to move on, you know, keep going. I hadn't even thought about it lately, not until Kelly got in touch toward the end of summer break. She wanted me to help her, give her things, and if I did, she said she wouldn't talk." He hung his head, wiping at his eyes. "I didn't realize how much she saw back then, how much she remembered. It scared me, you know, imagining her blowing up our world."

Jo was still skeptical. "Why? What did she want from you?"

He laughed, rubbing his hands together before he clasped them atop the table. "What didn't she want?"

Jo wasn't sure what he meant.

"Did she ask for money?" It was the first thing that came to mind. But then she remembered what Barbara Amster had said about Kelly wearing outfits she hadn't bought her. "Did you take her shopping?"

"I paid for a few things, yeah," he said, "but she wanted more."

She shook her head. "More, how?"

He smiled weakly. "She wanted to be popular, you know, part of my squad. She said she was tired of being invisible. She acted like I could snap my fingers, and she'd be a cheerleader or have any friends she wanted." He shrugged. "It's not like I could refuse."

"You felt blackmailed by her?" Jo asked, surprised that Kelly Amster had had it in her. Not that she approved of the girl's tactics, but it must have taken guts.

"I guess I did. Kelly and her mom had dirt on my family. I wasn't going to risk it." He steepled his fingers together. "I'd gone through it once, you know, and I didn't need any reminders of how much it sucked . . . how lost I was when my mom was dying. If I gave Kelly what she asked for, you know, I could breathe easy. I thought it'd be simple, except it got complicated really fast."

Now it was all starting to make sense. "She asked for an invitation to your party?"

"Two, actually. She wanted to bring that girl with her, the one with bad hair and braces who's always tagging along."

"Cassie Marks."

"Yeah. I told her no way could that woofer come," Trey admitted. "That was a deal breaker."

So the pretty girl got a pass, but not her unattractive friend. How unenlightened of him. Jo doubted that Cassie had known the facts behind her lack of invitation. She seemed to blame it all on Kelly wanting to go it alone.

Too bad Cassie hadn't tagged along. Maybe things would have been different.

Jo leaned in, bumping her rib cage against the table. "What happened that night, Trey? What did Kelly get herself into?"

He stared into the dark, toward the black silhouette of the water tower. "I didn't think she'd actually show, you know, but she did. She even rang the frickin' doorbell." He laughed. "Nobody does that. My bros just walk in like they own the place, even when my dad's home." The smile died. "I said hey and got her a beer. I had a few myself. After that, you know, I barely saw her. She wasn't really on my radar."

"I'm surprised to hear that," Jo said. "She was lovely."

"Yeah, I guess she was. But I don't tend to go for girls like that."

*Girls like what?*

Did he mean too young or too poor?

After having seen the ostentatious glass house and meeting Robert Eldon, Jo had a feeling it was the latter. But that hardly mattered now. It had nothing to do with the truth she was after.

"Was Kelly drinking?" she asked.

"Everyone was."

"So you were drinking. She was drinking. Maybe you weren't thinking so much about her not being your type," Jo suggested. "Did you push things too far and give her yet another nasty secret to hold over your head?"

"Hell, no. Lady, you're not even close," Trey said, and his voice rose defensively. "We drank too much, yeah, but I wasn't pushing anything, not with her. She was outside, hanging with a couple of my bros by the pool. Like, an hour in, they said she was puking on the patio. All I did was stash her upstairs in a guest room to keep her from trashing the place."

"Did you figure someone with a conscience might call 911, thinking she had alcohol poisoning?"

"Um, no." He gave her a look.

"Kids can die from it, you know."

"But *she* didn't die from it, did she?"

Jo didn't quit. "So you left her unconscious in a house full of wolves?"

The sneer turned into a nervous grin. "There were chicks there, too, a few of the cheerleaders Kelly fangirled over."

"Great. I'd like their names, along with your buddies' . . ."

The smile died. "You're not listening to me! *She* started this. She brought this on herself." He shook his head and started to move, slinging a leg so he straddled the bench, like he was going to leave.

*No, no, no.*

Jo couldn't afford to lose him, not yet.

"I'm listening," she told him. "Really," she added, unable to keep the urgency from her voice. He seemed to be her best shot at piecing together Kelly's last few weeks on the planet. Jo didn't want this to go sour. "Please, tell me what happened next. After you left her in the guest room."

What did he see or do? What exactly did he know?

Trey sighed. "Can't we just let it go? Can't we let her rest in peace?"

*Wow.*

That was precisely what Kelly's best friend had suggested as well, and it made Jo mad as hell. Why did everyone around Kelly seem intent on keeping the curtains drawn over the final act of her life? What had everyone so afraid?

"C'mon, Trey," she cajoled, "you have enough balls to stand out on a field every week and get pummeled by bigger guys than you, but you're afraid to tell me who was at your party? Because nothing you've said so far has convinced me that something ugly didn't happen there." She had a hard time keeping the frustration from her voice. "When Kelly blacked out, did someone go in the room with her? Did one of your *bros* rape her and then dump her in her front yard so you wouldn't be held responsible?"

Trey's jaw clenched. "For the hundredth time, I did *not* hurt Kelly that night. My bros did not hurt her. I swear it on my mother's life."

"Your mother's dead, Trey."

"You know what I meant!"

"You didn't answer my question."

He crossed his arms. "I don't have any more to say."

*Yes,* she thought. Yes, he did. He had a lot to say, except he wouldn't.

"Did you take pictures or make a video of the assault? Did you threaten her with them to get her off your back?"

He balked. "What the hell are you talking about?"

Had she struck a nerve?

"Did you send encrypted e-mails to Kelly warning her that if she went to the police, the taped assault would go viral? Was that why she killed herself? And don't deny you sent her coded messages, because we've got her laptop and the e-mails from you. Stang12, right? Just like your vanity plates."

Jo was breathing hard by the time she finished, so worked up she could have exploded. Trey seemed pent up, too, from the curl of his fists on the table to the visible shake of his shoulders.

And then his dam burst.

"I didn't make a rape tape, because I didn't rape her!" He stood, banging fists on the table, shaking it. "Where'd you hear something like that? From that loser she hangs with? Because it's a lie."

*No, because you're a spoiled rich kid who thinks he can get away with anything,* she wanted to say but didn't.

Jo kept calm. "You said she was blackmailing you. Be an easy way for you to turn the tables."

Even through the dark, she could feel his fury radiating through the night air, giving off a stink like raw sweat and humiliation. But it hardly unnerved her. It felt like vindication.

Very calmly, she told him, "If you didn't make a video, if you weren't threatening her, then you can easily prove it."

His voice was pained. "How?"

"Surrender your cell phone, then give us the key for the encryption, and let us read any and all communications between you and Kelly since she contacted you about your party. We'll find out pretty quickly if you've been holding out on us."

"You're joking."

"No," Jo said. Far from it.

Even with Trey's face shadowed, she could see he was torn. *Come on, do it,* she willed him. *Give me your damned phone. It really is that simple.*

"Go to hell," he said instead.

Then he stepped over the bench and headed off, his agitation obvious in every shake of his head, every toss of his arms.

*Well, crap.*

That was it? Their midnight gabfest was over, just like that?

*Over,* she told herself, *but not done.* She wasn't giving up.

She rose, stepping over the bench to the grass. She turned to pick up her phone, expecting to hear the slam of Trey's car door, the noise of his engine revving. But instead, she heard the quick succession of muffled footsteps and his noisy breaths as he ran back.

Before she could face him, he grabbed her from behind, knocking the phone from her hand. He pinned her arms to the small of her back, holding on so tightly, Jo gasped.

"Are you ready to listen?"

"Let me go, Trey," Jo said through gritted teeth.

But he didn't.

"You might want to consider one fact you're missing," he told her, his breath in her hair, the heat of his body penetrating her clothes. He pushed her forward, over the picnic bench, so Jo's face glanced off the wood as she turned her head.

"Hey!" she yelped.

"Listening now?"

"You want to go to jail for assaulting a police officer?" she hissed, the grain of the wood rough against her cheek. She tried to kick at him, but his thighs pinned her. Then he leaned into her harder, and full-blown panic began to set in.

"I just want to make you hear me," he said under his breath. "If I really wanted to *assault* you, I could. You know that, right? Just like I could have done whatever I wanted to Kelly that night. But I *didn't*."

"Let me go now," she intoned, wondering if Hank could hear her from wherever the phone had dropped, if he was even listening at all instead of tending to a sick kid. "Damn it, Trey, this is not the way . . ."

But he just shushed her.

His weight pushed into her, crushing her lungs against the bench, turning her breaths shallow. She swallowed hard, hating the helplessness, feeling like she'd felt every time her stepfather had come to her room all those years ago, had forced his way into her bed and held a hand over his mouth to silence her until she'd given up and given in.

"I want you to get this, Detective," Trey told her, his pelvis pressed against her backside. "Are you listening?"

Jo gritted her teeth, nodding as best she could, hoping to hell that was his belt buckle poking her and not an erection. Son of a bitch. If she could have reached for her sidearm, she would have taken a shot at whatever it was.

"The girl is dead," he said into her ear. "Kelly's dead. She offed herself, and that's all there is to it. Nobody pushed her. Nobody made her jump. So get off my back, keep away from my bros, and leave my family the hell alone. You got that?"

He waited until she said, "I got it."

With that, he let her go and took off in a sprint.

Jo pushed up from the table and turned, trying to catch her breath and feeling sick. She put a hand on her weapon, and she started to move, thinking she could chase him down on her wobbly legs.

But she couldn't.

Before she'd managed to go ten feet, the pickup's engine ignited, the headlights flashing on, swamping her in their glare.

Jo listened to the tires skitter on gravel, and then the overly bright beams swung away. She stood in the dark for a moment, waiting until the flashes of light disappeared from her eyes, hearing the thud of her own heartbeat before it was drowned out by the cicadas. She placed her hands on her knees and bent over, spitting the bad taste from her mouth.

*Damn it,* she cursed herself. He'd done what he'd come to do, hadn't he? He'd made her feel like a victim. Made her feel powerless. Was that his intent all along? Did he think she was Kelly Amster? Did he imagine she'd react like a fifteen-year-old girl and stay quiet out of fear?

If he did, he'd thought wrong.

Pretty dumb move for a quarterback.

Jo rubbed a sleeve over her mouth, wiping away any traces of bile. Slowly, she walked back to the picnic bench, stooping over to hunt for her phone. "Hank," she said aloud, thinking if he could hear her, maybe she could hear him. "Hank, are you there?"

A muffled voice said her name.

"Jo?" Tiny, tinnish, like someone very far away. "Jesus, Jo, what the hell's going on?"

"I can't find you," she told him. "So keep talking."

"Um, okay, did you know that flu viruses kill up to half a million people on the planet every year, which is nothing compared to the

Spanish Flu pandemic that toasted around five hundred million people in 1918? And, er, the Spanish Flu was called the Purple Death because it starved the lungs of oxygen, and it turned people blue or purple . . ."

Jo rummaged until her hand touched glass and plastic, nestled in the grass below the bench. She snatched up the phone and put it to her ear. "Got it," she said. "You can stop now."

"Are you okay?"

"Yeah." That was only partly true. "That asshole threatened me," she said, her voice as unsteady as the rest of her, hating that she'd let Trey get the upper hand.

"You hurt?"

"No, just shaken up," she said, rubbing her cheek, wondering if she had a splinter in her face from the picnic table.

"You want him picked up?"

"Not yet," she said, despite everything. Calm settled in her chest, erasing the ebbing panic. "We'll get him soon enough. He knows what happened to Kelly. I'm sure of it. We just have to find a way to the truth. If it's not through him, we'll go around him."

*Whatever it takes,* she thought. *Whatever it takes.*

# CHAPTER SIXTEEN

*Tuesday*

In the morning, Jo awoke slowly to the noise of running water.

*Is it raining?* she wondered, until the rush of water stopped with a soft groan of pipes, and she realized Adam was in the shower.

Too bad, 'cause they could have used the rainfall.

Yawning, she plumped her pillow and turned on her side. She squinted as light squeezed through the crack of the not-quite-closed door. Then it burst wide open, spilling into the bedroom. Adam's footsteps on the carpet quickly followed, and she watched him enter the room, towel wrapped around his hips.

"Morning, sunshine," she said, sleep still in her voice. "You gonna wear that to work? It would make quite a statement."

"Ha." He smiled. "You sleeping in today?"

"I wish."

He leaned over to kiss her, droplets from his wet hair landing on her face. He wiped them away with a soft brush of his thumb, apologizing. He paused for a moment, glancing at her cheek. Jo wondered if she had a bruise.

"What's wrong?" she asked.

"You have a scratch."

"Oh." Jo touched her face but didn't explain.

He sat down beside her, and she reached for him, setting her palm on his bare chest.

"Come back to bed," she said.

"If only I could." He sighed. "But I've got a full caseload . . ."

"Kelly Amster?" she asked, her heart skipping a beat.

"I don't know," he admitted. "I've got a case review meeting in an hour, so it'll probably be assigned, since she was brought in yesterday afternoon. You have doubts about how she died?"

"No, not about how." Jo withdrew her hand from his chest, sitting up higher. "Just why. Is it possible to find evidence of rape in a post-mortem, if the assault occurred weeks ago? She was supposedly a virgin before it happened."

Adam let out a puff of breath. "It would be pretty difficult, yes. If she'd had any tearing, she would have had some time to heal before her death."

"You would know if she'd had sex, though, right?"

"Only if she has an STD," he said. "Can't tell a virgin just by an intact hymen when some females are born without and some stretch more than others—"

"Thanks, Dr. Ruth," she cut him off, having heard enough.

"Hey, you asked."

He gently touched her cheek. Then he got up. He tossed the towel over the back of a chair and went to the dresser, opening the bottom drawer—the one she'd ended up sacrificing for him—and he pulled out clean boxers, socks, and a white tee. He'd left his scrubs hanging over the arm of a chair, and she figured he'd wear them again, changing at work if need be.

Jo sighed as he slipped on the boxers, wishing they could both stay in bed all day. She was tired and hadn't gotten much sleep after her disturbing encounter with Trey.

"Did you go out last night?" he asked, turning around as he tugged on his shirt.

"What?" The question jolted through Jo like a shot of caffeine.

He'd been asleep when she'd left and when she'd returned. She had taken great pains not to jostle him. But, somehow, he knew regardless. Maybe Ernie had squealed on her?

"Did you go out?" he tried again. "Your car's in a different spot this morning."

It was. He was right about that.

"I was going to tell you," she said, and it was true. She just hadn't planned to tell him at that very moment. "That call that came late . . ."

"Yeah?"

"It was a high school kid who might know something about Kelly Amster," she said.

"You didn't go out alone?" He got that look on his face, like he was about to give her hell for taking a stupid risk.

She blurted out, "No, no. I called Hank. He was supposed to meet me there, but both his kids got sick."

Adam's jaw tightened. "So you did go alone."

"I had Hank on my cell the whole time, just in case."

"I could have gone with you." Adam looked miffed.

"You needed your sleep," she said, which was the God's honest truth. "Hank knew where I was, so if anything had happened . . ."

She stopped, catching herself. She'd been ready to lie to him, or at least lie by omission. But they'd sworn off secrets, hadn't they? They'd promised their relationship would be built on trust, not fear—fear of pissing off the other person, fear of being rebuked, fear of the past.

Jo let out a slow breath, patting her palms on the sheet. "It was a high school kid, a football jock," she told him. "I thought he'd gone, but he came back. He pinned me to the picnic table, which is how I got this." She touched her cheek where Adam had seen the scratch. "He didn't hurt me, not physically. He just reminded me that I'm the weaker sex," she said dryly, having a hard time meeting Adam's eyes. "I wanted to shoot his balls off."

"Jo," he said, clearly having trouble finding the words. He came back to the bed to sit beside her. "You're hardly weak, but . . ."

"But I'm no match for a hundred-eighty-pound muscle head."

"You should have known better," he started, but stopped himself. "Look, it's just that there are some things a woman shouldn't do alone."

"Like meet a witness in a public park?"

"It was after dark—"

"So I can only go out alone in broad daylight?"

Adam sucked in his cheeks. "It's the world we live in. There are just men who don't respect boundaries—"

"Boundaries?" she interrupted him again. "I'm a police officer. I have a shield. I carry a sidearm. Why should I be afraid of a high school boy?"

"You said it yourself. Because he's bigger than you."

"So I should be afraid of anyone who's bigger than I am?" she said sharply. "I can't trust that there are men out there who haven't been trained to think rape is okay? Who don't think all girls are whores and we ask for it?"

"C'mon, Jo." Adam put a hand on her thigh, a lump beneath the covers. "You know I'm not saying that."

But she wasn't done with him yet.

"I get it. I was like Kelly Amster going to a party alone, at the mansion of a rich white kid—the same kid who asked me to meet him." Her anger bubbled to the surface, and she snapped at him, despite knowing it wasn't his fault. "Why shouldn't we have felt safe? Why should she— why should I—have felt afraid?"

"Hey, I'm not your enemy." Adam took her hand, holding on when she tried to pull away. "I agree with you. No woman should have to live in fear. You should all be able to walk down a dark alley in a miniskirt at midnight and not expect to be attacked. But I'm only one man, okay? I don't control the pack. I can control only what I do." He frowned at her. "And I know for damned sure that I don't control you."

"Do you want to?"

"No." He shook his head. "Hell, no."

Jo glanced down at her fingers as she intertwined them with his. "I just don't like you taking risks."

"I get it. I do."

"Next time, wake me up, okay? I'll go with you. Shit, I'd hide in the bushes if that would keep you safe."

She understood. She did. It was a scary world out there. Scary for women, for kids, for folks who looked different from everyone else, for anyone wearing a badge. Abuse, rape, mass shootings, sex rings, terrorism in all its ugly forms. You walked out the door, and you were taking a risk.

"I love you," she said, because it was true, and it was better than an apology when she didn't feel she owed him one, not for saying what she meant. She kicked off the covers, scooting to the edge of the bed and wrapping her arms around him. "But sometimes I need to do things my way, even if I make mistakes."

His arms covered her, holding them closer together as he whispered, "I love you, too, unconditionally."

She closed her eyes, breathing in the smell of him: the soft scent of soap and the musk of his skin. She realized why he'd tacked that word on. Because he knew she needed reminding. He understood she walked on tenterhooks half the time, sure that something she said or did would make him leave.

He kissed the top of her head. "I've got to run. Work, remember?"

"I remember," she said, parroting his earlier words with a smile.

He let her go, and then he finished dressing.

Jo got out of bed and stripped off her T-shirt and underpants, heading for the shower.

By the time she'd finished running hot water over her face and scrubbing yesterday off her skin, Adam had taken off, trying to beat the rush of traffic south into the city.

She took care of Ernie, grabbed a banana, and was out the door herself not twenty minutes later. She had work to do, too.

# CHAPTER SEVENTEEN

Jo drove to the station early so she could talk to the captain about what had happened with Trey Eldon the night before. As it happened, Captain Morris was on his way out the door when she got there.

"Hey, Cap, got a minute?" she said, attempting to get his attention as he practically brushed past her with his head down, trying to knot his tie as he walked.

He stopped, looking up as he pulled the tail end of his tie through and cinched the knot up to his throat. "Ah, Larsen, I've got a day full of meetings at City Hall," he said, pushing up the cuff of his jacket to check his watch. "Can it wait?"

"I'll make it quick," she said. "Trey Eldon called me last night. He hosted the party Kelly Amster attended alone. We're pretty sure she was assaulted there, after she'd had too much to drink."

"By Trey Eldon?" Cap squinted. "He's quarterback for the Mustangs."

"Yeah." Jo wet her lips. "He wanted to meet at the park. He sounded like he had something to get off his chest about Kelly and what happened."

Cap frowned. "You go alone?"

"Hank was supposed to meet me there, but both his girls got some kind of virus so he couldn't get away. I had him on speaker, but Trey kind of caught me unaware, Cap, and I dropped the phone—"

"Oh, crap. I'm already five minutes late." Captain Morris checked his watch again. "Can we finish this later?"

Jo nodded. "Sure." Like she had a choice.

He gave her a quick salute before he took off, boots tapping down the hallway.

Jo stared at the back of him until he'd disappeared around the corner. Then she went to the vending machine, tossed a coin to decide whether to get water or her usual Coke, and ended up saying "to hell with it," going for the caffeine.

Soda in hand, she settled at her desk, intending to do a little research on social media before Hank arrived.

Since she was most familiar with Facebook, she went there first, entering via the department's community relations pages. She did a quick search for Kelly Amster and found half a dozen comments where her name had been mentioned or tagged. There was one public page using the name, and it was Kelly's.

She pulled it up, scrolling down through recent posts, finding only a few photographs from the past three weeks. The most recent post was dated the day after the start of school. It was a selfie, taken in front of the poster for cheerleading tryouts. *Y not?* she had captioned it. A user identified as Angel had commented: *Because they don't want u.* Kelly had replied, *Says who?* Then they'd gone a few rounds back and forth, with Angel telling Kelly that she needed to stop trying to be someone she wasn't. *U r changing*, Angel told her, *and not 4 the good. Go back to who U were, ho, or lose urself.*

Kelly hadn't responded, and Jo was pretty surprised she hadn't deleted the exchange altogether. But maybe she had banned Angel from her page, as the only remarks Jo found from her were older, like the comments on Kelly's selfie dated the night of Trey's party: a mirror shot of her wearing a skintight blue halter dress. That caption read: *Party dress!*

*Going 2 ho it up 2 nite?* Angel had remarked. *If u keep on this road, u will lose yourself.*

*Jealous?* Kelly had replied.

*No, sad 4 u that u think being a slut is the way 2 go,* Angel had answered.

*Who are you?* Kelly had asked.

*Friend of a friend. U need 2 listen and turn back, or u might as well jump 'cause u will be all alone, if u aren't already.*

Jo clicked on Angel's moniker, finding a page with a banner that had an expanded graphic of the cute cherub statue with wings that Angel used as her profile photo. There wasn't much information visible, just a gmail address. The About section had been left blank, and Jo could find only a handful of posts from the past month, all of them inspirational quotes likely cribbed from Google Images, along the lines of *Don't change so people will like you . . . be yourself so the right people will love you* and *Real friends don't fall through the cracks.*

*Hmm.*

Jo would have to ask Barbara Amster and Cassie about Angel. Kelly didn't seem familiar with her—*Who are you?*—and yet she'd engaged with her instead of deleting her comments. Did Kelly feel she had something to prove? Or did Angel's remarks feed into Kelly's lack of self-esteem? Angel hadn't been on Facebook for long enough to have made many friends, although her comments on Kelly's page had elicited a handful of likes.

*Harsh.*

Had this Angel gotten onto Facebook just to harass Kelly?

Jo made herself a note to follow up. She couldn't imagine having grown up in this age where cowards could insult you online and verbally rip you apart to make themselves feel good.

How Jo wished she could have talked to Kelly and told her to stand strong, to not let herself get beaten down, to push back and push through. The girl had been too young to understand that being fifteen lasted mere moments in the grand scheme of things.

All Jo could do at this point was try to make things right for Kelly, to make her life count and maybe save somebody else a world of hurt in the process.

"Hey, Larsen. You talk to the captain yet about Eldon the Third getting rough with you last night?"

She turned at the sound of Hank's voice. He must have just arrived, as he had his keys in hand.

"Sort of," she said.

"Sort of? You need me to go talk to him, back you up?" He started to pull open a drawer to drop his keys in. "I'll do that before I even buy my first bag of Fritos."

"No!" Jo scrambled to her feet.

"No on the Fritos? Or you don't need me to back you up?" Hank looked confused.

"No, as in don't put those away," she said, gesturing at his key ring.

"We going somewhere?"

"Yeah, to see Barbara Amster."

"Does she know we're coming?"

"She will when we get there."

# CHAPTER EIGHTEEN

By 9:00 a.m., they were standing on the Amsters' doorstep.

This time, Kelly's mom opened the door and let them in without preamble. She didn't look foggy, merely exhausted.

"I'm making coffee, if you'd like any. I won't get through the day without it," she said, her face drawn, dark gray circles beneath her pale eyes.

Jo declined the offer, as did Hank.

If Jo looked hard enough, she could see the resemblance to Kelly. Barbara had probably been as pretty once; but the years—and maybe her work—had not treated her with kid gloves. Her skin was porous and shiny, and she had deep grooves between nose and mouth, aging her beyond her years.

Jo wondered if she'd seemed attractive to Robert Eldon four or five years ago, when she'd started caring for Mary. Or had attractiveness not even mattered when Mr. Eldon had turned to other women while his wife had been dying? Jo wouldn't be surprised if he'd sought solace from Barbara Amster. Trey had suggested both Amsters knew about his father's affairs. Maybe one of those affairs was with his mother's nurse.

"I'm glad you came," Barbara said, fatigue in her voice. "I realize I wasn't much help yesterday, but I was in shock. I want to know what happened, too." Her eyes teared. "So if y'all would follow me, I'll take you to Kelly's room."

"Thank you," Jo told her, eager to get going.

There weren't but five rooms in the entire house. The kitchen was to the left of the living room, and a short hallway took off to the right. Barbara Amster led them toward the latter, bypassing a bathroom with baby-blue tiles and tub, clearly from another age. Next up, Jo saw a darkened room with a tousled bed and dirty clothes on the floor, but Kelly's mom didn't stop there.

Across the hallway, there was a closed door with a handmade sign in its center. The border consisted of pink and purple hearts. The printed letters looked identical to the handwriting in the suicide note and proclaimed: *My Room, My Rules, Keep Out!*

Barbara paused for a moment, like she was reluctant to breach Kelly's privacy. "I tried to give her space. I wanted her to trust me."

"You're not breaking that trust," Jo assured her. "You're helping her now, when she can't help herself."

"I guess you're right." The woman sighed. "It's not like she's got anything to hide anymore."

Jo thought otherwise.

Barbara put her hand on the knob and turned. Pushing the door open, she flipped on the light and backed up so they could enter.

Jo stepped past her into Kelly's domain. Hank came in afterward, looking oversized and masculine amid the feminine touches: a slim bed with a bohemian quilt in shades of purple and gray, the gauzy pink canopy draped above it. A small chest of drawers sat beneath the only window. To the side of a curtained closet door was a desk made of plastic crates with a painted plank across the top.

The walls were filled with quotes, printed with bright markers in Kelly's identifiable handwriting, centered on large white paper:

*Be who you are, not who the world wants you to be.*
*You are a strong girl, never ever forget that.*
*She believed she could, and so she did.*

Jo felt a twinge in her chest, as she imagined Kelly gazing at the words every morning, pumping herself up to start the day. Even those poster-sized pep talks had not been enough. They were just words. That was all. Unless she'd believed them.

"I know it's not much," Barbara Amster said, as if inferring criticism from the detectives' silence and feeling the need to defend the small size of the room or the brown stain on the ceiling. "But Kelly rarely complained, not even after seeing some of the really big houses I worked at. 'Mama, why do they need all that space?' she used to ask me. 'Don't they get lost?'" A smile fleetingly touched upon her lips, and then it was gone.

"I feel the same way about big houses," Jo said, taking the opportunity to bring up something on her mind. "Like the Eldons' place, for instance. We were there yesterday. It's kind of ridiculously huge. But then, you'd know that, wouldn't you?"

Barbara gave her a puzzled look.

"You worked for Robert Eldon a few years back," Jo said, because she knew it for a fact. "His wife had ALS. He has two sons. One of them went to school with Kelly."

"Yes, of course. My God, that seems like a lifetime ago. Poor Mary was going downhill so fast and with two growing boys who needed her so badly." Barbara paused. "But what does that have to do with Kelly's death?"

"Kelly was at a party at Trey Eldon's house shortly before school started," Jo began, giving Barbara ample opportunity to jump in with anything she knew. "She showed up alone, and some hours later, before dawn, she was deposited on your front lawn, barely conscious. Did you know anything about that?"

"I didn't realize . . . no," she said, blinking rapidly.

"As a parent, that'd be something I'd remember," Hank said quietly.

"You sure Kelly didn't mention the party to you or anything that went on there?" Jo pressed.

For a moment, the tired eyes panicked. "I just knew that she was going out. I didn't realize it was to Trey's house. So Kelly went to Trey Eldon's party? That's something," she murmured. "He's such a big football star at the high school. I didn't figure he even paid attention to her. He mostly ignored her back when, but they were younger. I'm sure he's changed a lot, like Kelly. She grew up so much this past summer. She got too pretty for her own good."

*Oh, she grew up, all right,* Jo mused, *some of it not by her own choosing.*

She waited for more, for some acknowledgment that Barbara Amster understood that her underage daughter had been drinking with older kids, had purportedly gotten herself so drunk that she was incapacitated.

But Kelly's mom didn't add a lick to the conversation. So Jo tried to drive the point home, remarking again, "Trey said your daughter got pretty drunk that night. Did Kelly tell you she passed out?"

"No," Barbara replied. "Would you have told your mom?"

That would have been tough, Jo was tempted to retort, when Mama was the one who drank herself into a stupor.

"Kelly told Cassie she woke up on the grass, with her panties on backward." Jo figured that bit of information would be hard for Barbara Amster to overlook.

But, again, she was dismissive. "If Kelly had been drinking, maybe she put them on wrong after she used the potty."

Jo looked at Hank, who wore his best stony face.

Did Barbara Amster not want to upset the apple cart, knowing the Eldons were involved? Was that worth more to her than the truth?

"Your daughter told Cassie she couldn't find her purse when she woke up on your lawn." Jo dug her heels in. "She didn't have her key to let herself in. She thought she might have been raped—"

"She what?" Barbara Amster said, stammering, "Y-yes, I-I remember finding Kelly on the front step early one morning, maybe the weekend before school had started. She looked like she'd been crying, but I thought that she was just mad at me because I hadn't been home to open the door. She definitely let me have it."

"Did you ask where she'd been?"

"I don't think I did. I'm sure I thought she'd gone out with Cassie and spent the night. She did that often on weekends when I was working."

"She never said a word to you about being assaulted at Trey's house, even though she mentioned it to Cassie?"

"You figure I could have forgotten something like that?" Barbara Amster said, pale eyes narrow. "What kind of mother do you think I am?"

Jo didn't respond, sure that the woman wouldn't like what she had to say.

But Barbara apparently took Jo's silence to heart.

"You're blaming me, aren't you? I'm the mom, so it must be my fault, even if Kelly was old enough to be responsible for herself." Her cheeks flushed. "I wish I could recall every detail of one particular night weeks ago. I guarantee you, I was tired as hell when I got home. I always am. But Kelly was so upset that I wasn't there, and we argued. No, she did not say, 'Hey, Mom, I got drunk at Trey Eldon's party, and somebody dropped me off 'cause I couldn't find my keys.' What I remember most vividly is that she was wearing that tacky blue dress that made her look like a two-dollar whore. If she put it on to catch the eyes of the older boys, I guess it worked, then, didn't it?"

Hank coughed, like he'd swallowed down the wrong pipe.

Jo stared at her, speechless.

Did the woman even know what she was saying? Was she blaming her fifteen-year-old daughter for going to a party alone? Did she think Kelly's outfit had encouraged an assault? And all she worried about was whether she looked like a bad mother.

Seriously?

If Jo could have forgotten who she was and why she was there, she would have let loose on the woman; instead, she held it in, breathing hard, her frustration like a weight on her chest.

"Please, don't look at me like that." Barbara Amster dragged a sleeve across her cheeks, though Jo hadn't seen any tears. "I don't know what you want me to say. I tried my best with her. She shut herself off from me, from Cassie. All I wanted was for her to be who she was again."

"You don't have to say anything, ma'am," Hank said, finding his voice first. He jerked his chin at Kelly's mom. "We'll take it from here if you want to go make your coffee. We'll let you know if we need you, okay?"

Jo had more to ask Barbara, but she had to take a step back. Hank was giving her that space, and she didn't stop him.

"Coffee, yes. I'll do that." Barbara Amster nodded, biting her lip. She stood there a moment, looking past them at her daughter's room. "I loved her," she said softly. "I truly did, no matter what you think. None of this would have happened if she'd stuck with Cassie instead of trying to make her life feel bigger."

Jo gritted her teeth.

Barbara Amster nodded to herself, pushed away from the door-frame, and left them there in her dead daughter's room.

When she was gone, Jo shut the door. "Lord, help me," she said, her pulse still racing. "Cassie was right. The woman's oblivious."

"Better to wear blinders than take responsibility for your own kid, especially the bad stuff." Hank grunted. "You had that look on your face like you wanted to shake her."

"I did. I still do." Jo surveyed the small bedroom. "But I don't have time for a suspension. I've got work to do. Want to divvy things up?"

"Sure."

"I'll take the bed and the dresser drawers."

"Which leaves me with the desk," he said, adding with a wince, "and the closet. Though I'm a little afraid of that, partner."

Jo could see what he meant. There was no door on the thing, just a curtain pushed askew. It wasn't big, but there were clothes crammed onto hangers on two rods, one above and one below. Shoes and other detritus bulged out from beneath, like Kelly had kicked things in just to hide them and keep her room looking neat.

"She could have stashed a library's worth of diaries in there, and we'd never find them. Not without a machete," he quipped.

"C'mon, positive thoughts."

"Booyah," Hank said sarcastically.

"Look for notebooks, letters, papers, thumb drives, anywhere that she might have recorded her feelings or made notes about people or places."

"Yes, ma'am." He offered her a pair of latex gloves plucked from his pants pocket, and Jo tugged them on, rolling them down her fingers.

Then she turned to the bed, pulling back the comforter and sliding her hand between the box spring and mattress. She checked inside pillowcases and peered behind the headboard, looking for anything taped to the wood. She got on hands and knees to inspect the area beneath the bed as well and ended up pulling out random sneakers and inside-out socks.

"You got anything?" Hank asked.

"Nothing," she said, moving over to the dresser. "What about you?"

She glanced across the room, seeing him remove the wooden plank from the milk crates and check both sides before he put it back in place. He started on the cubbies.

"Girl sure kept a lot of magazines. If I needed to figure out an outfit for homecoming, I'd be in the clover," Hank remarked, dumping a pile of *Vogues* and *Elles* on the floor. He riffled through the first one, shaking it upside down, though Jo didn't see anything fall out beyond subscription cards.

"Keep at it," she said, doing the same.

She pulled open the top dresser drawer, deciding that Kelly was fairly organized for a teenager. There were socks, underwear, and bras split by dividers. No contact paper or shelf paper lined the bottom. She stuck her fingers into every sock capsule, inspected each bra cup and the half dozen pairs of underwear.

Nothing.

Then she moved down to the next drawer, filled with T-shirts and shorts, clumsily folded. Jo went through each piece of clothing, checking pockets, and continued through the bottom two drawers until she was done. She even reached beneath the dresser, finding dust and a couple of tangled cords from the nearest wall outlet tucked out of sight.

She finished, having uncovered nothing stranger than a horde of assorted chocolate bars stuffed into an empty tampon box and shoved into a drawer with faded jeans.

So Kelly had a sugar fix. That seemed harmless enough, way better than turning up prescription bottles of Vicodin or codeine pilfered from her mom's medicine cabinet.

When she turned around, Hank was putting books and magazines back into the milk crates that made up the base of Kelly's desk. "You done there?"

"Yep," he told her. "You got anything?"

"No drugs, no booze, nothing squirreled away except a stash of sugar."

"If this girl had a dark side of her life, I'm not seeing it," her partner said, filling a crate with what looked like old textbooks.

Jo went over to help him stuff the last cubbyhole. She got on her knees and picked up a heavy dictionary and a thesaurus. "I didn't think anyone had these anymore. Don't they look up everything on the internet?"

Hank took the books from her and put them away. "Hey, I got a set of hardcover encyclopedias for the girls so they can leaf through 'em. I want them to turn pages when they learn about stuff. Everybody does too much scrolling and clicking these days."

Jo smiled. "Good for you."

He handed her a notebook next, a cute pink one with white polka dots. "It's not a diary," he said, "but it says something about our girl Kelly."

She took it from him, cracking open the cardboard cover to find page after page of drawings on the lined paper. There were dresses and shoes and handbags, all sketched with colored pencils. And they weren't half-bad.

"Maybe she wanted to be a fashion designer," Jo said, flipping through the pages until she ran into a slew of empty ones in the back. "She could have been the next Michael Kors."

Hank scrunched up his brow. "She's going to make fashion for beer brewers?"

"No, wrong Coors," she started to correct him, but what was the point? Hank's idea of high fashion was wearing socks that matched.

She returned the notebook so he could stick it back in the milk crate. Then he picked up a pink box. "I thought you ladies kept these stashed away in the bathroom," he cracked.

Jo reached for his arm, stopping him from putting it back. "What's that?"

"You have to ask?" he said, eyeing it and then giving her a funny look. "Did someone miss getting a lecture about the birds and the bees?"

Hardly. It was impossible to miss the bright pink color or the silhouette of a dancing female on the front. "It's a box of tampons, smartass. I can see that. Did you open it up?"

"I'm married to a woman." Hank squinted. "I know what tampons look like."

Jo snatched it from him. "I want to see what's inside. I found another tampon box with a stash of candy bars. Maybe she's got a phone she keeps out of sight from her mother."

"'Cause who'd check inside a box like that, right?"

"Not you, apparently," Jo said dryly. The top had been taped closed, so she peeled the adhesive strip away and opened the flaps.

*Oh, God, could it be?*

She poked at the contents with a gloved finger. Yes, it was. It was exactly what she'd thought. She sat back on her haunches, the breath knocked out of her.

"What've you got? Is it a phone?" Hank asked. "Please, let it be a phone."

"Not even close," she said, holding the box open for him to see.

Stuck inside was a baggie with a date written on the white label in black laundry marker, a date Jo recognized as the night of Trey's party.

Hank let out a whistle.

Carefully, she used gloved fingers to extricate the contents of the bag: a pair of pale blue panties.

*"She said she realized she had, like, proof, and that she could get someone in big trouble if she wanted to."*

"Scully, you were right. It was out there," Hank said.

"Kelly's proof," Jo remarked, excitement bubbling in her chest. "It's not pictures or a video. It's DNA."

# CHAPTER NINETEEN

"Can you run it down to the ME's office?"

"Now?"

"Yes, now," Jo said, putting the panties back in the baggie and getting up off the floor. She hoped to God that any potential evidence on the fabric—any blood or semen or bodily fluids that might yield the name of Kelly's assailant—hadn't degraded. "Adam said they were assigning Kelly's autopsy today. The lab should get this ASAP."

"You want me to go without you?" Hank looked at her, bug-eyed.

"I'm not done here," she told him. She really meant that she wasn't done with Barbara Amster.

"How'll you get back to the station?" He took the baggie from her, and she began to shoo him into the hallway.

"Call Dispatch and have them send a squad car to pick me up in twenty minutes, okay?"

"If you're sure."

"I'm sure."

Heck, it was only a couple of miles to the station. She could walk if she could ignore the heat.

She steered him through the living room and to the front door. Pulling it wide, she walked out with him, though he paused on the cracked sidewalk, looking back at the Amsters' house.

"You okay with going back in there alone?"

"Of course I am." What was she? Five?

"Don't pull a Floyd Mayweather and knock her out or something."

Jo dryly replied, "I'll do my best."

He had concern in his eyes and written across his middle-aged face with all its comfortable creases, but he nodded, just the same.

"Go get her, tiger," he said, and then he gave her his back, heading toward the car at a pace that suggested his bum knees weren't bothering him too much that day, or maybe it was just the adrenaline rush of finding something meaningful.

Jo went back inside, back to Kelly's pink room.

Jerking aside the curtain draped over the closet, she began to dig.

She moved shirts and skirts, pants draped over hangers, targeting a dozen dresses in every color but blue.

*Where was it?* she wondered, the blue dress that Kelly had worn to the party, the one Barbara Amster finally had remembered her daughter wearing when she'd found her crying on the stoop. Was it the same dress she'd mentioned when they'd first interviewed her yesterday morning, the one she'd disparaged, too?

*"She had this awful blue dress she seemed obsessed with. It was way too tight. When she lost it, she flipped out, nearly tore apart the house trying to find it. But, honestly, I was relieved. One less trampy outfit for her to put on."*

Where had it gone?

Only one way to know.

She went to find Barbara Amster in the kitchen.

"Where is the blue dress Kelly wore to the party?" she asked point-blank, as the woman put down her coffee cup, though she made no move to rise from the tiny, two-seat table. "The one you hated because it was too tight. What happened to it?"

"It's gone. That's all I know." Kelly's mom pushed at hair that had escaped her ponytail and fell in her face like a frizzy halo.

"Gone where?" To the dry cleaner? To Cassie's house on loan? To Goodwill?

"A few days before . . . before Kelly died," she started slowly, "I came home to find the back door unlocked. Nothing looked out of place except in Kelly's room. It was a mess. I was so tired that I couldn't think beyond cleaning up. When Kelly got home from school, I yelled at her for being a slob. I asked what the hell had gotten into her, but she swore, 'It wasn't me, Ma.' She was so panicked about it that I believed her. Her stuff was all there, she told me, everything but the blue dress, which makes absolutely no sense. I thought she'd misplaced it, maybe left it at Cassie's house, but she went nuts. Was it that important?"

"It could be," Jo said, particularly if there was evidence on it, tying Kelly to someone who'd been at Trey's party.

What if Trey had known about it? Maybe that was part of the discussion in their encrypted e-mails. Kelly had left her purse at the party, which was why she hadn't had her keys when she'd awakened on her front lawn. Had Trey made a copy before he returned the purse, with Kelly none the wiser?

"Tell me about your daughter's relationship with Trey Eldon," she said.

"What relationship?" Barbara Amster let out a dry laugh. "It's not like they were dating. I already told you that I was Mary Eldon's nurse at the end, but that was years ago. Trey's a football star. To him, Kelly was a kid. She wasn't even in his orbit."

"Perhaps they were seeing each other in secret," Jo said, though Trey had already denied it, insisting that Kelly wasn't his type. Clearly, Kelly's mom believed that, too.

"I'm not sure Kelly even liked him much," she remarked. "Trey wasn't the brother that Kelly played with when I took her over to the house. He didn't treat her as well as the other one."

"The other one?"

"The younger boy, John." The puffy face softened. "Trey was kind of cold, like his dad. He didn't talk much. He mostly gave Kel a hard time when she followed him around. But John was different. He had a heart. His mama's death near to broke him, and he got into drugs. He did crazy things after she passed."

"Like what?"

"He crashed one of his father's fancy cars into a fence. He swallowed a bunch of his mom's leftover pills and almost died. He was disruptive at school, mouthing off to the teachers and the principal. I heard a rumor that they would have expelled him, except his dad donated so much money to the school association."

"How old was he then?" Jo asked.

Barbara Amster paused to think. "He must've been twelve, right in the throes of puberty and without his mother to guide him. Kelly was a year younger. I think the last straw was when John showed up here one night. Kelly caught him looking in her bedroom window. He was"—she hesitated—"pleasuring himself."

Kelly had caught an adolescent John Eldon masturbating outside her window?

"Did you report the incident?" Jo asked, already anticipating what Barb's answer would be before she shook her head.

"No. I called Robert."

Of course she did.

"And that's when John was sent away?"

Barbara Amster wet her lips. "John . . . he needed focus. He was such a lost soul. I realize that now."

Hadn't Robert Eldon said that going away had been his son's idea? But, if what Barbara Amster said was true, it sounded to Jo like the

Eldons had been caught between the proverbial rock and a hard place. What better way to get rid of a problem son than to ship him off to boarding school out of state?

"When did Kelly last see John?"

Barbara squinted. "Four years ago, at Mary's funeral."

"Did she keep in touch with him?"

"She had no reason."

No, Jo thought, maybe she didn't. But Kelly *did* get in touch with Trey, and she had plenty of ammunition to use against him and his family, enough to score some new clothes and the promise of popularity. It was no wonder Trey had agreed to her requests, and it wasn't exactly surprising that he wasn't grieving over her sudden death.

With Kelly alive, he had so much to lose. Having her out of the way had to be a relief for both him and his dad.

"Is that all, Detective?"

Jo started to nod but remembered something. "Do you know a girl named Angel?"

"Should I?"

Barbara Amster was damned good at answering with nonanswers.

"She was on Kelly's Facebook page," Jo explained, "though all she did was criticize. She told Kelly to go back to being who she was and that, if she didn't, she'd be all alone."

"It's too bad Kelly didn't listen, don't you think?" Barbara said, and her face closed off. Her eyes met Jo's, and there was real pain in them. "Will you tell me when I can bury my daughter? Will I get her back soon?"

"Yes," Jo promised. "You'll have her back soon."

"Thank you."

Barbara Amster made no move to get up, so Jo let herself out. She half expected a blue-and-white to be waiting for her at the curb, but it wasn't a car she spotted as she came down the front stoop.

A slim figure stood on the sidewalk, one hand on the rail of the chain-link fence that ran along part of the Amsters' front yard. The sunlight on the dishwater-blond curls made them look almost red, so she didn't recognize the girl at first, not until she turned her head, and Jo saw her face. The eyes seemed puffier than yesterday, the skin even blotchier, as though she'd spent the better part of the morning crying.

"Hey, Cassie," Jo said as she approached.

"Detective Larsen, right?" The girl gnawed on a glossy lip. "What are you doing here?"

Jo wanted to ask her the same thing.

"Shouldn't you be in school?" she said, and the young woman smiled nervously, giving a rare glimpse of her plastic braces.

"Mom and Dad thought I should stay home today, because of Kelly dying and all. I didn't sleep much last night." She yawned on cue. "But they both went to work, and it felt weird being home by myself. I thought I'd come talk to Barb. Is she doing all right?"

"She seems to be taking Kelly's death pretty well," Jo remarked, which seemed an understatement.

"Oh, she's good at hiding things," Cassie told her. "Barb's not one to show her emotions. Kelly was the opposite, always a nervous wreck."

"They weren't close?"

"You'd think they would be, right? Since they kind of had only each other. But Kelly felt like they never really connected, not with her mom working all the time. They hardly saw each other."

Jo nodded, glancing out to the street. Still no sign of the cruiser. Had Hank forgotten to call Dispatch?

"Did you get into Kelly's phone?" Cassie asked, drawing Jo's attention back to her. "You said you were looking for it yesterday."

"No, not yet."

Cassie nodded, her eyes brightening. "What about the guy who threw the party? Did you find him?"

"We did," was all Jo would say.

159

The corners of Cassie's mouth twitched. "I think I figured out who it is."

"Really?" Cassie had told her the day before that she didn't know.

"It's Trey Eldon, isn't it?" The girl tightened her fingers around the fence rail. Her painted nails looked short, the shiny green on them chipped. At Jo's raised eyebrow, she scrambled to add, "Since Kelly jumped, people at school have been talking."

"Oh, yeah? What are they saying?"

Cassie seemed all too eager to share. "Trey's boys have telling people that Kelly was puking up her guts by Trey's pool at the party. Were they the ones who tossed her on her front lawn the next morning?" Cassie squinted across the fence into the tiny yard, and her knuckles whitened where she clutched the railing. "Those Guccis make me sick. They act like they're better than everyone else, but they're a whole lot worse."

Jo had already figured that out, but she wanted to hear more. "How's that?"

Pale eyes narrowed. "They have their own gang," she said. "They call themselves the Posse, and they think they're thugs underneath all that white bread. Stupid rich kids who figure they'll get away with anything."

"Did Kelly tell you about a blue dress?" Jo asked, taking a shot in the dark.

Cassie swiped her hand beneath her nose, which had begun to run. "She and I weren't talking as much after the party. She ghosted me, you know. She quit taking my calls, so I burned her stupid bracelet. I thought she was dumping me for them so she could be popular. And look where it got her."

"Do you know Angel on Facebook?" Jo asked, and Cassie's eyebrows went up.

"Did Barb tell you about that?"

Jo cocked her head. "Did Kelly talk to her mom about the mean comments?"

If that was the case, why hadn't Barbara said something when Jo had asked?

"She didn't have to," Cassie replied, then she looked away, toward the street.

What did that mean? Jo sighed and glanced past Cassie's mop of curls to see a cruiser rolling up the street.

Cassie stiffened. "More cops?"

"No, one less cop," Jo told her. "I'm leaving."

"Hmm," the girl said, her shoulders relaxing. She uncurled her hands from the fence and dropped skinny arms to her sides. "I'll go check on Barb. I'll bet she could use a hug. I'll hang out with her till she goes to work."

"You do that."

"It's hard, you know, realizing you won't ever see someone again, someone you used to love." Cassie stared at the house. "I wish things had been different."

"I do, too."

The girl came around the fence, passing Jo on the sidewalk, allowing Jo to read the words on her graphic tee: *Born to shine*, they said.

She hated to be so cynical, but she couldn't help wondering if Cassie could shine brighter now, since the best friend who'd outshone her was dead.

Maybe she'd just been working this job for too long, but she found herself wondering as well if Trey Eldon wasn't the only classmate letting out a sigh of relief now that Kelly was gone.

# CHAPTER TWENTY

Cassie's question about Kelly's phone was one that nagged at Jo as well. So on the way back to the station, she had Dispatch track down Officer Ramsey to get an update.

She had her on the phone within a few minutes. "Hey, Charlotte, any sign of Kelly Amster's SIM card?"

"You mean the needle in the haystack?" the officer replied. "We're back out here looking. We even borrowed a canine from the county that's supposed to sniff out electronics. We're hoping he might turn it up, even though it's a long shot. Cap said to give it another day, then shut it down. We're already starting to get kids out here, trampling the scene, tying balloons to the chain link and leaving homemade sympathy cards and teddy bears and candles. It's getting tough to keep it secure."

"Just do what you can," Jo said, having already figured the captain wouldn't let them tie up resources on the SIM search forever.

"We're good for now, unless it rains or someone from Public Works decides to mow this old patch of cow pasture when we're not around."

"They'd have to hack through that jungle with a scythe first," Jo joked, doubting the city would preen the acreage before they took the old tower down. As for rain, water would likely be about as bad for the chip as the blades of a riding mower. "You find anything else?"

"Nothing that changes the suicide scenario," Officer Ramsey said. "You have any doubts she killed herself?"

"No," Jo replied, finding it hard to say. But it was the truth.

"Then I won't beat myself up if we can't locate the card."

"No, don't beat yourself up."

The cruiser that had picked her up in front of the Amsters' house deposited her at the station before taking off. Jo hadn't even gotten through the back door when her cell phone rang.

"Jo Larsen," she said by rote, hoping it wasn't another reporter asking about Kelly Amster's alleged suicide and where they were in their investigation. She had her patented "no comment" ready to go, just in case.

But instead of a barrage of questions, she heard only what sounded like a quiet weeping.

"Hello?" she tried again. "Can I help you?"

"Yes," a woman replied between sniffles. "It's Amanda Pearson. You were out at my home yesterday after my Duke went missing . . ."

"Yes, of course, Mrs. Pearson."

The weeping started again, so Jo could pick up only the tail end of a garbled sentence, something along the lines of "some news about Duke."

"I'm sorry. I should have been in touch sooner," Jo said, flinching. "It's been kind of crazy around here, but I'm sure you want an update."

She told Mrs. Pearson that she'd had one of their officers pull prints off the dog tags, recovering only a few barely useable partials. She wasn't sure it was even worth it to have the owners come by to print for comparison. Finding possible matches on AFIS was a long shot anyway, unless the thief was already in the system.

She paused as Mrs. Pearson blew her nose. "I want to assure you that we're still trying our best to find Duke," she said when the noise had stopped.

"You don't need to find him."

"What?" Jo asked. "Why?"

"He's already been found."

Hank couldn't get back from downtown Dallas fast enough to join her, so Jo took her own car and picked up Amanda Pearson at her home, driving her across county lines to a vet's office in Celina.

Not much was said along the way, just enough so that Jo knew where to go. Mrs. Pearson didn't seem to have much information besides the fact that Duke was in extremely critical shape. He'd been picked up along FM 455. Jo recalled Hank's story about another dog in critical condition being found on the same farm road about three weeks earlier.

Maybe it was a coincidence. But she had a gut feeling it wasn't.

Within twenty-five minutes, they'd arrived at the clinic of Cynthia Hooks, DVM, in Celina, just off North Preston Road.

They found a waiting room filled with barking dogs on leads and howling cats in cages. Jo didn't bother to find a seat. She walked right up to the receptionist and showed her shield and ID. She explained that she'd driven Amanda Pearson, the owner of Duke, the golden retriever who'd been brought in by a Good Samaritan.

"Do you have proof that he's yours?" the young woman asked, and Mrs. Pearson nodded, fumbling inside her enormous black bag and producing more than enough paperwork to be convincing.

The receptionist paged the vet, frowned, and murmured an affirmative before she got up and ushered them into the doctor's office.

Jo hardly had time to assess the framed diplomas on the wall or the family photos on the credenza before a bespectacled woman with short gray hair and white lab coat came in, offering her hand to Mrs. Pearson.

"Oh, my goodness, I'm sorry to meet you under these circumstances," she said, patting the woman's hands and holding on to them. "Your beautiful golden was made as comfortable as possible, but he left us about fifteen minutes ago. Please know that he was not alone."

Mrs. Pearson let out a whimper from low in her throat. "I want to see Duke now," she said, voice quivering. She'd been fighting back tears for the last half hour, and they suddenly began to fall.

The vet looked at Jo, as if it was up to her.

She nodded, despite the full-blown ache in her chest. It was the reason they'd come, after all, to reunite the dog with his human mother.

The doc grabbed a few tissues from a box near the sink and handed them to Mrs. Pearson, who pushed her glasses into her hair to dab at her eyes.

"If you'll both follow me."

Dr. Hooks led the way out of her office, up a brief hallway, the cacophony of yapping dogs and mewing cats filling the air and drowning out the elevator music being piped through ceiling speakers.

Jo held on to Mrs. Pearson's arm, and the woman leaned into her, like she'd given up pretending to be strong. Jo thought she was holding it together remarkably well, all things considered, but there was fear in her eyes as they approached a door marked SURGICAL SUITE.

"Excuse me a moment." Dr. Hooks went in before them, and Jo heard her telling someone, "She's here." Then she reappeared to hold the door open wide, and she helped Mrs. Pearson into the room.

The lights had been dimmed, the room chilled by air-conditioning. Jo breathed in the antiseptic smell mingled with the scent of damp dog, though she doubted either was to blame for the churn of her stomach.

Mrs. Pearson hung back at first, and Jo touched her arm gently. She had nothing to say, no words to comfort her. She just wanted the woman to know she was there.

"Sarah?" Dr. Hooks asked, motioning at the vet tech who sat beside the table upon which the dog lay, a blanket atop him.

The ponytailed woman in scrubs quickly hopped off her stool and reached for Mrs. Pearson's hand, guiding her toward her boy. Jo stayed in the room just long enough to see the woman stroking him, murmuring to him in the sweetest of voices.

Tears sprang to Jo's eyes, a pain in her chest as real and raw as the one she'd felt upon seeing Kelly Amster's body on the grass.

"Detective?"

She felt a touch on her elbow.

Dr. Hooks whispered, "Let's leave them alone for a bit."

Jo swiped at her cheeks and followed the woman outside the room, waiting in the hallway as the door was closed partway.

"What the hell happened to him?" she asked, keeping her voice low. "Was he hit by a car?"

"He was hit by something," the vet said quietly. "If it *was* a car, it hit him more than once. His skull is fractured in several places. Ribs are broken. The pelvis is fractured. I don't know if he managed to crawl to the highway or if he was dumped there."

"Was he used as bait in a dogfight?"

"I didn't find bite marks. He wasn't attacked by another dog or even a pack of dogs," Dr. Hooks assured her. "He was battered, plain and simple."

"Battered? Like beaten?"

The vet blew out a breath. "That's my guess."

"What could do that much damage?"

"I don't know. A tire iron, a shovel." Dr. Hooks frowned. "I started out my career at a rescue organization, and I saw some pretty horrific cases of abuse that ranked right up there with this."

"You really believe someone did this?" Jo asked.

"Oh, believing's the easy part." Dr. Hooks sniffed. "Sadly, these days, anything's possible. You must know that as well as anyone."

Oh, yeah, she knew.

Jo forced herself to breathe.

She thought of what Hank had told her, about another missing pup that had turned up near death in Celina, and she asked the vet, "Have you come across any similar cases recently? Any other dogs found in this condition?"

"Not at my clinic, no. I would've reported it." Dr. Hooks cocked her head. "But I read a sidebar about keeping pets safe in the local paper three weeks back. It mentioned a dog found on the side of the Farm to Market road, said he looked like he'd been hit by a Mack truck. When I saw Duke, I did have to wonder if the two dogs were connected in some way . . ."

She stopped, jerking her head toward the door of the surgical suite. *"Oh, my baby, my sweet, sweet baby . . ."*

Jo turned, too, her heart breaking all over again at the agonized sobs of a woman whose whole world had just been blown to dust.

# CHAPTER
# TWENTY-ONE

Jo ended up leaving Mrs. Pearson at Dr. Hooks's clinic in Celina. She didn't want to, but the older woman insisted on staying with her beloved Duke and riding with him in the van that would transport him back to his personal vet in Plainfield. Dr. Hooks even volunteered to accompany them, making sure Mrs. Pearson was returned home thereafter.

"I'm so sorry we couldn't find him sooner," Jo told Mrs. Pearson, feeling like she'd failed her and Duke, that she'd been too slow to save a life.

"Just tell me you'll get the sons of bitches who did this," the woman said, gripping Jo's hands so tightly. "Promise you'll do that."

She started to say, "I'll try," only to stop herself, reminded of the movie quote on Bridget's T-shirt. *Do or do not . . . There is no try.*

*Damn Yoda.*

"I will," she said, not making excuses. "I'll get them."

"Good. You find them, and you kick their asses to kingdom come." Mrs. Pearson nodded, patting her hands before letting them go.

*Kick their asses to kingdom come.*

Jo put that at the top of her to-do list.

Before she left Celina, she asked Dr. Hooks to e-mail copies of any records she'd generated in her examination of Duke. Then Jo walked out the door, hesitating at her car.

She stood for a minute in the parking lot, heat rising from the asphalt, baking her feet through her shoes, and she looked up at the blue sky, sniffing away tears that didn't want to stop falling.

*It's just a dog,* she tried to tell herself. *A dog, not a child.*

But that didn't work.

A life was a life, and they mattered, every single one of them.

With the exception of the assholes who took lives, like they were nothing. *Those* didn't matter, not to her. Not at all.

*Keep going. This isn't over,* she told herself, sucking in a deep breath and filling her lungs with muggy air. It didn't exactly feel good, but it helped enough that she could calmly settle herself into the driver's seat. She started the car, turning on the police band, listening to a bit of chatter about a shoplifting suspect nabbed at the Warehouse Club for slipping prime rib beneath a fake baby in a stroller.

Jo pulled out of the lot, her head hurting. Her heart hurt, too.

Two deaths in two days—a teenage girl with a lost soul and a lost dog as beloved as any child. Maybe that shouldn't have been grief enough, not for a cop who'd worked the city beat for ten years. But she'd gotten used to a slower pace in Plainfield, to a body count measured in months, not in days or even weeks.

Hank liked to say she was a dog with a bone. Sometimes he even called her a hard-ass. And, sure, she played it on occasion, convincing everyone but herself that she could handle any horror without flinching. But, at her core, she wasn't hard at all. She wasn't Superman but Lois Lane, falling through the sky, vulnerable and all too mortal. She shared the grief of the survivors. She felt the pain of the victims, because it was her pain. It would never let go.

She liked to tell herself it made her a better cop, a better advocate. But, the truth of the matter was, she'd spent her childhood putting walls around herself, hiding how she felt, keeping in the most horrid and hurtful of secrets. She'd trained herself to be stoic, except her armor had cracks; and the more she lived and breathed, the more they showed.

If there was anything that therapy—and being with Adam as well—had taught her, it was that, if she didn't allow herself to feel, she was as good as dead. Sometimes it made her job harder when her heart got too involved. It became a crusade—a cause, not a case. But was that really so bad?

Only if it clouded her judgment, she told herself. Only if it made her miss the details. And *that*, she didn't want to do.

If she was going to keep her promise to Amanda Pearson, what she needed was a clear head, not a catch in her throat.

So she pulled herself together, donning her suit of armor, dinged as it was, and ten minutes into her drive back to Plainfield, when she glanced in her rearview mirror, her eyes were bone-dry.

She was back within the Plainfield city limits when her cell phone rang.

"Where are you, partner?" It was Hank.

"I'm nearly at the station," she told him, the phone stuck in a cupholder so she could keep both hands on the wheel. "I left you a message about going to Celina with Amanda Pearson. Duke was found along FM 455, just like that other dog your pal at Animal Services told you about."

"Jesus, Larsen. Is he okay?"

"No. He's not okay, Hank."

"Well, damn." Her partner sighed. "This is starting to sound like something, you know? Not just some puppy resale ring."

"I know."

"So what've we got? Did anyone do an autopsy on Duke?"

"I've got the Celina vet sending us exam records," she told him as she sailed through an intersection on a green light and put on her right blinker, ready to turn into the parking lot. "Maybe Adam can look them over."

"How's Mrs. Pearson?"

"She's beside herself."

"Any sign of that other pup, the one you got a call about last night? The German shepherd?"

"No."

Hank was so quiet, she thought she'd lost him.

"Where are you?" she asked, imagining him in the old Ford, stuck in traffic somewhere on the Dallas tollway. "Did you drop off Kelly's underwear at the crime lab?"

"I did, and I'm still here."

"Okay," she said, wondering why he wasn't on his way back. "What's up?"

"I saw your boyfriend. He said he didn't get assigned Kelly's case, but he's offered to assist so maybe we'd get answers faster."

"So you're hanging out with Adam?" she said.

"I thought I'd stick around for the autopsy."

"Really?" Jo knew how he hated attending postmortems.

"I might have some questions," he said. "It's easier to ask them during the post than to decipher the reports. You okay for a few hours without me?"

"Of course I am," she told him, prickling a bit, although she realized he wasn't questioning her ability, merely doing his best impression of an overly protective brother. "Call me if you learn anything that can't wait."

"You got it."

She hung up, then cut off the ignition. Grabbing keys and phone, she went inside. She checked to see if the captain was in yet—he wasn't—and then almost ran headfirst into Bridget.

"There you are!" the young woman said, appearing out of nowhere. "I've been trying to hunt you down. Got a minute?"

"Sure."

Bridget beamed, her eyes shining behind the sturdy black glasses. She had her dark hair shoved under a knit cap with a peace sign patch, even though forecasters were predicting another near-triple-digit day. Her graphic T-shirt de jour featured Princess Leia and the words *Girls Run the Galaxy*. She was definitely rocking the hipster-tech-geek look, and it made Jo like her all the more.

"Come into my lair, though it's sadly lacking in dragons," Bridget said, rolling her chair through the door into the server room.

Jo didn't feel as bothered by the noise of the server this time around. It was a nice distraction, helping to drown out Amanda Pearson's devastated cries, still on repeat in her head.

Bridget had pilfered a small stool from somewhere, and she indicated Jo should sit. It was a tight squeeze when she pulled it up beside Bridget's chair at the table that held the trinity of monitors.

"What'd you find?" Jo asked.

"Little appetizers," she told her. "Not the main course yet, I'm afraid."

"I like appetizers."

"Good."

Kelly's laptop was still hooked up like an ICU patient, and Jo noticed a Facebook page featured prominently. But it wasn't Kelly's. The banner background was the Texas flag, painted on the tailgate of a pickup trick. To the left was the group identifier: *the Posse*, it said.

*"They call themselves the Posse, and they think they're thugs underneath all that white bread. Stupid rich kids who figure they'll get away with anything."*

Jo thought of what Cassie had told her, about Trey Eldon and his squad. Was this their gang?

"What's the Posse?" she asked Bridget, trying to square how it fit in with Kelly Amster and their investigation.

"You asked me to look into Trey Eldon on social media, right? So I did a search for his name, and this came up through a few intriguing tags that were cached on Facebook."

"Is it a group he's in?" She leaned forward, trying to get a better look at the administrator information and the tiny roster of members before Bridget changed the image on the screens.

"First things first, okay? Let's focus on Kelly Amster, since I've been working on her social media presence all morning. I reset her passwords, which was the easiest part. Finding anything that explains her death is going to be trickier." Bridget clicked her mouse so that one of the screens showed an Instagram account. "Here's what I found on her Insta. Looks like a bunch of pics with her bestie up until about a month ago."

She scrolled through large photos with Kelly's freckled face pressed alongside Cassie Marks's pimpled cheeks and spiral curls. The captions were simple, lots of things like, *Froyo with my bestie*, and pics of painted toes and fingers alongside descriptions: *Green mani-pedis!* Each notation was followed by hashtags like *#BFFs* and *#chillaxing*.

"She liked clothes, I guess, because she has lots of pics of shoes and blinged-out mannequins in store windows. There's the occasional cute puppy or squirrel upside down on a bird feeder," Bridget said as she continued to scroll. "But something changed around the first weekend of August. It's like the happy pics dried up after this one."

She stopped moving the page up and down when she got to a selfie taken in a mirror. It showed Kelly in a slim blue dress that hugged her body all the way down to her knees. Beneath, Jo glimpsed sneakers on her feet.

In the caption, two hashtags: *#partydress* and *#bignight*.

There was the infamous blue dress again, the one Kelly had worn to Trey's party and that had mysteriously disappeared.

"Hold it there," Jo said, noting comments to @kellyam:

*More like #slutdress*, one said.

*#askingforit*, said another.

Both were posted by Anonymous.

"Can you trace those?"

"Just to the Instagram accounts," Bridget told her. "But they weren't tied into any other social media accounts, and if they used fake names and fake phone numbers . . ."

"It'll make it that much harder to find them," Jo filled in.

"Yeah," Bridget said.

"Is there more?"

"No, after that, there's nothing."

Jo nodded, considering how Kelly must have felt the day after. She and her best friend weren't speaking. Trey Eldon was sending her encrypted e-mails, probably telling her to keep her mouth shut. Her mom was busy taking care of other people's children. It made sense that Kelly had felt disconnected.

*C'mon, Kelly,* Jo willed, trying to conjure up a *Ghost* moment. *You've got to show us more than that. Tell us what happened to you, what made you take a flying leap.*

"She has a Snapchat account," Bridget said, "but it looks like she abandoned it, too. I did find her on Facebook . . ."

"So did I," Jo said. "I got on her page this morning. She had some rough comments left by a girl named—"

"Angel, yeah, I saw," Bridget told her. "I looked into that account as well. I think it's a shell. I could try to get the IP addresses for you."

But then they'd have to prove to a judge that the bullying online was threatening enough to get a warrant. Jo wasn't sure they had that much, not yet.

"So what'd you find on Trey Eldon?" she asked, pressing forward.

"Plenty," Bridget said, "for Trey and his dad. I Googled them both, actually. There's a lot about Mr. Eldon, though it mostly involves his cybersecurity company. I skimmed through the business articles on him and through the endless football stats and game scores for Trey. Not surprisingly, Trey's public presence is almost exclusively sports related."

"He wouldn't want to screw up his chances for a football scholarship."

"I found a lot of pics and rah-rah captions from football games and pep rallies," Bridget went on, looking unimpressed. "Though why anyone would willingly play a game that beats you up like a car wreck, I will never understand."

"I wouldn't say that too loudly," Jo joked, "or they might kick you out of Texas."

"Right." The young woman half smiled. "I couldn't even find many pics of Trey with the opposite sex. He's probably playing it safe there, too. But he does have a bunch of selfies with him and his buddies watching sports, drinking beer, hunting. Nothing crazy."

So they'd hit another dead end?

Jo sighed, disheartened. "Is that it?"

"He was tagged in a few posts that referenced a closed Facebook group called the Posse," Bridget said and tapped her mouse so that now all three of her monitors were filled with the Texas flag tailgate banner that had been on the screens when Jo entered the room.

"So it's Trey's group? He's the administrator?" Jo asked, noting the tiny profile pic and name. She could also view the names and profile pictures of three other members, who all appeared to be male. The group was labeled a "Club" and had only a one-word description: *Brotherhood.*

*Brotherhood?*

Was the Posse a secret fraternity?

"Can we get into the page to take a look?"

"Not unless we belong." Bridget pushed at the bridge of her glasses. "Only members can see content, unless someone posted a photo or video without double-checking the privacy settings. If they left any open, I can probably find them. I'll work on that today, in case there are any pics posted from Trey's party that slipped through the security cracks."

Jo nodded, frustrated. No matter how patient she tried to be, it always felt like things never moved fast enough.

"Whatever you can do," she said, staring past Bridget's shoulder at the closed-group page for the Posse. She squinted at the names listed beneath Trey's:

*Scott Gray.*

*Dan Trent.*

*Jason Raine.*

Jo got that prickle at the base of her neck. She'd heard that name the day before.

"You see something, Detective?"

"Jason Raine," she said.

"Ring a bell?"

"Yeah, a loud one."

*"He drives a big, noisy truck with a Texas flag painted across his rear tailgate. I can hear him every time he comes and goes."*

Could be that very painted tailgate in the Posse's Facebook banner.

"His family lives next door to Amanda Pearson, a woman whose dog was snatched the other evening," Jo said. Snatched and found dead up in Celina. "Apparently, the Raines had a dog vanish, too."

"Weird."

"Yeah."

"I intend to look into the Posse members' personal Facebook pages," Bridget told her. "But I haven't had enough time. I figured you'd rather have me poke around in Kelly's laptop, anyway."

"Yes, definitely. How's the code cracking going, by the way?" Jo asked. "Have you reset the password to read the encrypted e-mails?"

Bridget frowned. "I wish I could. But there's a PIN involved as well, and I can't reset that. You might want to ask Robert Eldon if he can help out. It's his company's encryption software."

Of course it was. Jo had suspected as much. No wonder Trey hadn't seemed too nervous about coughing up the code for the e-mails—or anything else, for that matter. Daddy held the key, and Daddy probably took care of all the Third's messes.

"It's okay," Jo told her. "Keep digging into Kelly's files."

"Will do," Bridget said. "I'll e-mail you all the passwords I reset for her social media, in case you want to look around some more."

"Great, thanks," Jo murmured, but her mind was somewhere else.

*"We drank too much, yeah, but I wasn't pushing anything, not with her. She was outside, hanging with a couple of my bros by the pool."*

Was Kelly hanging with Jason, Dan, and Scott, or some combination thereof? Did one of them go up to the guest room after an unconscious Kelly had been deposited there?

*"I did not hurt Kelly that night . . . I swear it on my mother's life."*

Too bad for Trey that Jo wasn't gullible enough to take his word for it.

"You okay, Detective Larsen?" Bridget asked.

Jo realized she'd been staring at the screen but seeing nothing. She shifted her eyes away to look at the other woman. "Keep at it, will you? Try to see if you can get into the Posse's closed page. I want to know what they're hiding."

Bridget chortled. "They're hiding, but they're not *really* hiding."

"How's that?" Jo waited for her to say more.

"Well, it's kind of surprising they didn't make their group secret if they were so bent on nobody finding it." She shrugged and reached for her noise-canceling headphones, hooked around the back of her chair. She hesitated before she put them on. "It's like they wanted people to know it existed. They just needed to be able to keep them out."

That sounded illogical. Or did it?

Why *would* Trey Eldon and his buddies set up a page on Facebook that wasn't open to everyone, that exposed nothing but its outermost layer, just enough for people to recognize that it existed?

Did it make them feel more powerful somehow, like they were holding a prize beyond everyone else's reach?

Was it enough that classmates *knew* about the Posse?

Did it make them feel, what? Jealousy? Fear? Admiration?

What exactly *was* this posse, and what were they trying to get away with?

# CHAPTER
# TWENTY-TWO

Jo went straight back to her desk after she left Bridget's office. She got on the computer, digging into the department's database and pulling up driver's license information on each of Trey's buddies. She studied the DMV photos of their clipped hair and blandly handsome faces, and she wondered who they were at the core. Maybe they were great kids, respectful of their parents and teachers, kind to old folks and children, and concerned about the environment.

Or, maybe they were silver spoon–fed brats completely devoid of conscience.

But did they have it in them to rape and threaten a fifteen-year-old girl, driving her to suicide? Was one of the boys a dognapper, too? Did that explain the disappearance of Jason's pooch, as well as Amanda Pearson's?

Unfortunately, those answers weren't stored in the DMV's files. But she learned a few facts, at least. Trey Eldon, Scott Gray, Dan Trent, and Jason Raine were all eighteen. Also like Trey, they either owned pickup trucks or SUVs. None of them had registered as organ donors, not that the latter told her anything except they probably weren't thinking about dying anytime soon.

Next, she delved into county property tax records. She was not surprised to find each lived in a home at or above 3,000 square feet, though Trey's was the largest, eking its way just past 10,000 square feet. Once she knew more about where they lived, she brought up the map she'd used to pinpoint the dog-theft locations. She overlaid the addresses of Trey's buddies, curious to see if any others lived in the neighborhoods where pups had disappeared, like Jason Raine and his next-door neighbor, Amanda Pearson.

She let out a little "Hmm" at finding that both Dan's and Scott's houses bordered the park not two blocks from the residence of Jill Burns.

Just another coincidence?

Jo was beginning to have serious doubts.

About an hour and half into her probing into the searchable lives of Trey's crew, Hank phoned her from downtown Dallas. He murmured something about Kelly's autopsy not being over yet, but that he'd slipped out when they'd stared cutting the scalp so the flesh could be rolled back and muscles beneath examined.

Jo knew that meant the surgical bone saw would be coming out soon enough, and all kinds of chips and bone dust would go flying. It was not a pretty sight and involved stepping away from the table a safe distance so as not to get bits of corpse in your eyes.

"You know how I don't like that part," he grumbled.

Did anyone?

"Learn anything?" she asked.

"McCaffrey said they're looking for bruising or blood beneath the scalp and any signs of skull fractures so they can rule out if she had a seizure or head injury before she fell from the tower."

Jo doubted that they'd find anything. "If she'd seized up there or if someone hit her on the head, she'd probably have ended up on the catwalk, not on the ground beneath, not unless she was tossed."

"McCaffrey said they'll check her neck muscles to look for signs of strangulation, like if someone tried to choke her in a fight before she went over."

*McCaffrey said. McCaffrey said.* Jo had to smile. Adam would get a kick out of hearing he was so imminently quotable.

"Any surprises?" she asked.

"Not really. She didn't look so bad on the outside, but her insides looked like they'd gone a round or two in a blender. Bits of her ribs cut up her lungs. Her heart was carved up like a pumpkin, sliced clear through by splinters of bone, ditto her liver and her spleen. The pelvic girdle was shattered."

Jo took a breath, leaning over her desk to rest her head in her hand.

"So far, it's all consistent with death by severe blunt-force trauma. The ground's so dry from lack of rain that it's nearly as hard as concrete."

It wasn't as though she didn't believe Kelly had killed herself. It was the "why" part and what had come before that troubled her.

"ME's doing the usual specimen collection so they can work up a tox report," he said. "Then we'll know if she had any alcohol or drugs in her system."

Jo didn't think she would. If Kelly had been a drug user, they would have found some evidence of it already.

"Her mom asked about getting the body for burial," she said.

"It won't be long," Hank replied. "We've got the manner of death down pat."

Jo nodded. "The blunt-force trauma from the fall."

"Yeah. But it'll be a few days before the ME can sign off on a cause."

*Which would be suicide,* Jo was thinking. There was nothing to suggest that anyone had been up on the water tower catwalk with Kelly, and they had the goodbye note she'd left for her mom. It was all pretty cut-and-dried.

"Did you see Emma Slater when you dropped off the panties at the lab?" she asked next.

"Yeah, and she said to tell you 'hey' and that she'll do her best for a quick turnaround, but they're kind of backed up, so . . ."

"Don't hold my breath," Jo finished. It was the same-old, same-old, though Emma was the best evidence tech Jo had ever met. She'd known her from her years with the Dallas PD and trusted her instincts and her expertise.

"What about you?" Hank asked. "Any progress?"

"I might have something," she told him. "But it can wait until you're here."

"Give me another hour or two. I'm about to head back into the chop shop. Just hoping they put away the bone saw and the full-on face shields. Makes me feel like I'm in a horror movie."

"Go get 'em, partner," she teased, and he grunted before hanging up.

She sat back in her desk chair and rubbed her eyes.

Her mind sifted through an overload of images and information: Kelly Amster's body lying broken beneath the tower, the suicide note, the strange behavior (*was she raped?*); the missing dress (*stolen?*) and the panties she'd hidden away (*her proof of assault?*); the abducted dogs and the dead dogs (*beaten to death?*).

The soft spots at her temples started to thrum.

Was everything tied together somehow? Was she just missing the connection?

She had no evidence of anything, just a lot of feelings and conjecture.

She sighed. Were they tilting at windmills? Was Cassie inflating what Kelly had told her after the party so she could get more attention? Was the real truth more akin to what Trey had suggested—that nothing had happened at the party except Kelly getting drunk, then being dropped off at home the next morning, albeit unceremoniously?

So why couldn't Jo convince herself that it was all a big nothingburger?

*She believed she could, and so she did.*

Kelly's handwritten quote wormed its way into her brain.

She couldn't give up, not yet. If Kelly had felt let down in her life by the people around her, Jo wasn't going to let her down in death.

*Pity party over,* she told herself. *Get back to work.*

She found the passwords Bridget had sent to her e-mail and used them, logging on to Kelly's accounts and into her Facebook. The wall had spontaneously begun to fill with comments relating to her death. At least a dozen had popped up so far, though, as Jo watched, others quickly appeared. *Rest in Peace,* a few said, and another, *Jesus is the answer, not suicide!*

Jo didn't see anything from Angel.

Cassie Marks had posted on the wall, sharing a photo of herself and Kelly with broken-heart emoticons beneath. *I love and forgive U,* she had typed. *I know U R in a better place.*

Jo scrutinized the words, confused. She forgave her?

*What did Kelly need forgiveness for?* she wondered. Killing herself? Going to Trey's party solo? Trying to come out of her mousy shell?

She stared at the screen for a moment longer, finally clicking on Home and going to Kelly's news feed. Not surprisingly, she found a lot of posts about Kelly's death, links to news reports, even photographs of Kelly with classmates. Was Kelly's suicide the latest entertainment, like one of those Kardashians pushing butt padding or lip gloss? Or was Kelly truly missed? Where had all the interest in her been before her death, when she had to twist Trey Eldon's arm to get attention?

A few trolls appeared to have tagged Kelly in their posts as well. *Loser!* one said, and another, *Who was this duster? One less ho on the planet.*

Jo wished technology had advanced enough that she could shoot a Taser through the screen and jolt the angry trolls into silence.

*Next,* she told herself, leaving Kelly's page to search for Jason Raine's and finding it easily, thanks to the familiar Texas flag tailgate he used as his profile pic and the Plainfield, Texas, locale.

Since Jo had logged in as Kelly and Kelly wasn't on his Friends list, she couldn't see much. But, apparently, they had at least one friend in common—Trey Eldon—which doubtless was the reason Jo could read the few tidbits that weren't hidden from prying eyes.

Jason noted in his bio that he was "Gunslinger's Right Hand," which Jo assumed referred to his position as an offensive lineman for the Mustangs. It also explained the broad shoulders and neck as thick as his skull. She viewed a few older posts with pics: Jason lifting up Trey after a win; chugging a Shiner Bock by a fire pit; and dressed head to toe in camo, a dead buck at his feet, holding up its antlers like he'd won a prize.

She couldn't view much beyond the most recent posts. It wouldn't let her access anything older, though she wanted to go back a month or so and see if he'd mentioned losing the pit bull mix that Amanda Pearson had mentioned.

Jo didn't find anything illicit in what she'd viewed except underage drinking, and that wasn't even a crime if he was hanging out on his own property and his parents didn't mind.

From everything Jason Raine put out for public consumption, he appeared to be the poster child for high school jocks. He was athletic. He was popular. He'd probably even thank his mom when he signed a letter of intent with a Big 12 university.

But Jo never trusted what she saw on the surface.

He had to have been at Trey's party. Even without Trey providing a guest list, she was sure that Jason, Scott, and Dan had attended. They were Trey's posse, after all, right?

She kept going, gathering as much intel as she could from looking at their social media via Kelly's accounts, thinking they all seemed too good to be true. Did she want to pin some blame on Trey so badly that she was misjudging his friends?

The only way she knew how to fill in the blanks was old-fashioned footwork. So by the time Hank returned, Jo was ready to hustle him right back out to the car.

"Where are we going this time?" he asked.

"To the Winding Brook subdivision," she told him.

"Amanda Pearson's house?" he said as he got the motor running on the old Ford, and Jo belted herself in. "You want to pay our condolences to Duke?"

"No. We're going next door."

She had a lot of questions to ask Jason Raine, and she wanted to be sure to get to him before he had any more time to talk to Trey and change his story.

# CHAPTER
# TWENTY-THREE

On the way to Jason Raine's house, Hank filled her in on the rest of Kelly's postmortem.

"They didn't find any signs of epidural hematoma, so it wasn't a head injury that killed her. But there was some kind of intracranial bleed. McCaffrey said that shows her head was the last thing to hit the ground. No evidence, either, that someone grabbed her hard to throw her over. McCaffrey said they would have seen some type of indentation in the strap muscles. Her neck wasn't even broken," her partner finished, one hand coming off the wheel to touch his throat. "When the blood work comes back, they'll rule on cause. But, off the record, your boyfriend said it looks to be what it is."

"Suicide," Jo said, because it was what she'd expected to hear, and at this point, it had about the least to do with why they were still investigating.

Jo told him what she'd learned while he'd been gone—about Kelly's missing blue party dress, the swipes from trolls on social media, and the existence of the Posse, the mysterious brotherhood formed by Trey Eldon and three of his buddies: Dan Trent, Scott Gray, and Jason Raine.

"They're all players on Trey's squad, aren't they?" Jo asked.

Hank nodded.

"It's a good bet they were all at Trey's party. Cassie Marks said she's heard talk that Trey's crew has been bragging about seeing Kelly there, falling-down drunk and throwing up by the pool."

"So they're a bunch of disrespectful pigs who may have raped a teenage girl?"

Jo felt Trey's grip, holding her arms behind her back, pushing her down on the picnic table, and the hairs stood up on the back of her neck. "Anything's possible," she said.

Maybe Robert Eldon believed his son walked the straight and narrow.

Jo had her doubts.

She found herself staring out the window as they pulled into the long, snaking feeder road that took them into the Winding Brook subdivision. It would have been hard not to think of Amanda Pearson, since they were fast approaching her house.

She tried to see things differently this time around. Instead of admiring the sprawling ranch houses and the oversized trees shading the large lots, she noted that the path they were taking was the only way in or out of the neighborhood. There was another street that split off from Winding Brook called Creek Side, but it ultimately dead-ended. The next street over did not connect.

So there was no true grid, no roads running perpendicular, like in so many neighborhoods. If anyone came into Winding Brook to commit a crime, there wasn't an option of parking on the next street over or slipping out a back way.

It stood to reason that whoever took Duke was familiar with the area. The perpetrator knew that Amanda Pearson had a dog that was let out to roam in the evening. It wasn't like she lived on a main thoroughfare, where someone could park and observe without being noticed. Whoever took Duke hadn't attracted undo attention. No one had reported a suspicious vehicle in the area the night he was taken.

"I think Mrs. Pearson has visitors," Hank remarked, and Jo cut short her mental meanderings.

As they slowly passed by the Pearson house, she felt a catch in her throat. Indeed, there was a car in the driveway—a rental, from the looks of the Enterprise sticker on the bumper.

"I hope it's one of her kids," she said. "She needs the support."

Hank grunted his agreement.

He eased the Ford ahead, pulling past the Pearsons' mailbox, near to where Duke's tags had been found. They rolled alongside grass and a few rosebushes and fencelike hedges that marked the edge of Mrs. Pearson's property.

Then they were at the next lot, the brakes letting out a prolonged squeal as Hank stopped the car on the street, taking care to keep tires on the asphalt instead of trenching the lawn, although the grass looked pretty brown at this point. The summer wasn't over yet, and an acre was a lot to water.

Jo got out of the car, her gaze focused on the house, which wasn't all that different from Amanda Pearson's: part brick and part siding, shaded by thirty-foot oaks and maples. She heard the woof-woof-woof of a dog barking. Activity on the left side of the structure caught her eye, and she jerked her chin in that direction as Hank came around the hood of the car.

"You want to knock, see if the parents are home?"

"He's eighteen," Jo said. "He doesn't need a chaperone."

They started walking up the long driveway. The barking got louder, as did music that streamed from around the back of the house, something that sounded like countrified pop, or maybe popified country.

As soon as they turned the corner, Jo got the full impact of Jason Aldean riffing about cornbread and biscuits while a large gray-and-white dog barked his head off at them, growling as they got closer.

Mrs. Pearson had mentioned a newly acquired sheepdog, and Jo figured that was it, although its fur was mostly shaved, giving it the appearance of an oversized poodle. With a loud bark, it lunged toward them from the grass but was yanked back by a bungee cord tethered to a zip line so it could run back and forth for about twenty feet across the backyard.

She was just glad it wasn't running loose on the property, hemmed in by an electric fence. That would hardly have stopped it from shredding the pair of them.

A big ol' pickup with extended cab sat on an area of asphalt the size of a small parking lot. The tailgate had a Texas flag painted on it, exactly like in the Facebook banner. The side of the house loomed two stories above them, a solid wall of red brick. She saw a brick wall of a human as well. He was using a hose to fill up a bucket that was close to overflowing with soap suds. Nearby sat a Big Gulp cup that looked to hold about forty ounces.

Jo figured washing his truck made him mighty thirsty.

The garage door was open behind him, and she glimpsed plenty of stuff: ladders, shovels, rakes, shelves filled with camping gear, stacks of plastic pots, even a couple of dog crates. But she didn't see any other cars. For all she knew, the parents were on vacation, giving Jason free rein.

Hank whistled. "Nice truck," he said. "Country lift, thirty-five-inch mud tires."

"Down, boy," Jo said under her breath.

Jason looked up, frowning, before they'd even called out a hello.

The pipes let out a squeak as he shut off the water. He tossed a sponge into a bucket and ambled toward them in knee-length swim trunks and an old football jersey with the sleeves cut off.

"Hey, what's up? You sellin' something?" he asked in a rumbly West Texas drawl. "'Cause if you are, we're not buying."

He had a lump beneath his bottom lip where he'd stuffed a wad of dipping tobacco. Sure enough, he reached down to scoop up the Big Gulp cup and spat into it.

Jo winced. *Ugh.*

Guess he wasn't that thirsty after all.

"You're Jason Raine?" she said, as he wiped the back of an oversized paw across his mouth. She removed her wallet, flipping it open to show her ID and shield. "Detective Larsen." She gestured at Hank. "My partner, Detective Phelps."

"You're the po-po?" he said, brow wrinkled. He crossed thick-muscled arms over his broad chest. "Did I run a red-light cam?"

Jo nearly laughed. Like Trey hadn't told him the police were asking questions about the party, about Kelly.

"We're not here about your driving record," she said and glanced at Hank, anticipating that he'd want to take over. "So you can relax about the red lights."

"Uh-huh." Jason eyed her skeptically.

Guys like Jason didn't often want to listen to a woman, even one with a badge. But Hank gave her a nod, encouraging her to go for it. She was ready for this. She had more information in her pocket now than when she'd talked to Trey Eldon yesterday.

She eased into things, asking a simple question first. "Are your folks around?"

"Naw." Jason shook his head. "My dad has business overseas. He took my mom along for a second-honeymoon kind of thing."

"You're home alone?"

He smiled, showing spots of brown between his teeth. "You think I need a babysitter?"

*Maybe not,* Jo thought. But he could have used a good flossing.

"Did you know a girl named Kelly Amster?" she asked, watching his face as the smile faded from his lips.

He squinted. "She's the one who jumped off the water tower?"

"Yes," Jo said, "and she was at the party you attended at Trey Eldon's house." He started to open his mouth, probably to play dumb. So Jo added before he could rebut, "I heard you and your crew have been talking about Kelly being drunk and throwing up by the pool."

"Who told you that?"

"A friend of Kelly's."

He didn't deny it, merely ducked his head, scratching at his crew cut.

"What happened to Kelly at Trey's party?" Jo asked.

He turned his head and spat, hitting the ground near Jo's left boot. "Sorry," he said. "My bad."

Jo didn't flinch. She waited for him to answer.

"Um, yeah, so what happened was that T carried her upstairs." Jason shifted his gaze to Hank. "T's dad had spent, like, six grand on this big-ass teak daybed with a frickin' canopy. That chick would've ruined it with one heave."

"You don't say," Hank murmured.

"So did you go up?" Jo pressed. "Did you check on her?"

He hung his head, going all "aw, shucks," as he apologized. "Gosh, ma'am, I guess I kind of forgot about her once she was out of sight, you know. Never saw her again. End of story."

Jo wasn't sure she believed him. "Did any of your friends go up?"

He wrinkled his brow. "Now, why would they do something like that?"

"I don't know." Jo shrugged. "Because she was a pretty girl who was unconscious? Because y'all figured it'd be easier to get in her pants if she couldn't fight back—"

"Hey, back up the bus there, Sarge," Jason interrupted, and his bulky arms unfolded to wave dismissively. "You think one of us raped her post-puke? Is that where you're goin' with this?" He looked over at Hank, eyes pleading. "No way. I don't Cosby girls, okay? And neither do my bros."

Hank gave the kid a nod, like he bought that argument.

Jo sighed, impatient.

"Whoever it was, we'll find out soon enough," she said. "That blue dress Kelly wore at the party, that wasn't all she had on her rapist. So whoever broke into her house to steal it didn't finish the job. Kelly had the smarts to hold on to other evidence. The crime lab's working it up now."

Jo met his eyes, dared him to look away.

He didn't.

"Blue dress? Breaking in? Sorry, ma'am, but I've gotta plead ignorance," he said. He shifted his gaze back to Hank, who'd taken to walking around the truck, running a hand over the tailgate, peering into the bed. "Swear on the Bible, I didn't touch her. That's not my thing."

"What is your thing, Jason?" Jo asked.

Hank glanced around, found a stick, and went back to the truck bed, picking up something that looked like a dirty old blanket.

"My thing?" Jason repeated, doing a good impression of befuddled. "You mean, like hobbies?"

No, that wasn't what she'd meant at all.

He was watching Hank like a hawk and didn't appear too keen on having the po-po checking out his ride. The dog had stopped barking but paced back and forth, panting and slobbering.

"Hey, Larsen," Hank said, holding the blanket on the stick like a flag. It was covered in dark stains. "That look like blood to you?"

Jo nodded. "Yeah, it does."

"Hey, man, you can put that back, all right? It's my property."

"What'd you do?" Hank asked in his rumbly voice. "Cut yourself shaving?"

"I hunt. Got a license and everything," Jason explained. "You mind giving that back?" He strode over to Hank and reached for the blanket. Hank let it go. The boy quickly rolled it into an untidy bundle and went to the garage, pitching it atop one of the dog crates.

"What do you hunt, son?" Hank asked when Jason came back. Jo's partner stood beside the truck, leaning against the bed with his arms crossed.

"Mostly white-tailed deer. Sometimes duck," Jason said, squaring off with him. Feet planted apart on the pavement, arms similarly crossed.

"You go on public land or private?"

"We've got a spread up north, about a hundred acres."

"Sweet," Hank said. "Whereabouts?"

"West of Weston," Jason told him without missing a beat. "Eastern edge of Celina."

"Is that where you lost your previous dog?" Jo asked him, and his face seemed to crumple, like she'd hit a sore spot. "What happened?"

Jason clutched the back of his neck with a hand as big as a bear paw. "I crated Shale and took him up to our country place, I guess about a month back. I let him out to run around while I put away the truck. But when I whistled for him, he didn't show." His hand came off his neck as he sighed. "It was dusk, but I went out looking for him. Called the sheriff, too, to see if he'd help. But Shale never turned up."

"Did you hear that Mrs. Pearson's dog went missing on Sunday night?" Hank said, and Jason nodded.

"Yeah, she was over here, asking if I'd seen ol' Duke." He picked up his chaw cup and spat into it. "Do you know if they found him?"

Jo glanced at Hank. "Yeah, they found him," was all she said.

"Oh, wow, I'm sorry," Jason remarked. "He was a good dog."

"You're sorry? For what?" She hadn't mentioned anything about Duke's condition.

Jason blinked. "Well, I mean, the way y'all looked at each other, I assumed it wasn't good news, but I'm glad for Mrs. Pearson if he's okay."

"He's not okay," Jo confirmed.

Jason frowned, nodding grimly.

Hank took that moment to change the subject. "You take this dog up with you?" he asked, gesturing at the shaved sheepdog, which had settled in the grass, panting.

"Yeah." Jason shifted on his feet. "Shep rides in the cab when I go up alone, like I did the other night. When I've got people with me, I crate him and put him in the bed."

"You take friends there often?"

"Sometimes," Jason told him with a shrug. "If it works out, we head up a night or two before a game, light a bonfire, get revved up. We've got our own rituals."

"I'll bet you do," Hank said. "You can do a lot of primal screaming on a hundred acres."

"It's an easy drive. I'm thinking the weather's looking decent enough to make another trip. We're supposed to get a full moon tomorrow night."

"That's a good time to howl," Hank quipped.

Jason smiled. "You got that right."

Jo stood there, listening, letting Hank distract Jason with his he-man conversation. As they talked, she pulled a tissue from her pocket and reached down to the asphalt, wiping at the splatter of tobacco juice near her foot. Then she wadded up the tissue and stowed it away in her pocket.

She strolled toward the dirty blanket that Jason had tossed over one of the dog crates just inside the garage. It was stained dark red, all right: small spots here, a few larger spots there.

She hadn't noticed the male conversation stop until she heard Jason yell at her.

"Hey, what're you doing there, Officer? You taking stuff?"

Jo showed her empty hands.

Jason picked up his cup and spat. He wiped a hand across his mouth. "Y'all done with me yet? I've got stuff to do."

They'd been dismissed.

"Thanks for your time," Hank said, tipping an imaginary hat to the kid. "We'll be in touch if we've got any more questions. Take care with that bonfire."

"I will, sir," Jason said, even extending his hand so they could shake. Jo rolled her eyes.

"Thanks," she said briskly.

But Jason kept his back to her, going about his business as if she wasn't there. He went over to the brick wall and turned on the water. The hose bucked on the ground as it pulsed to life, and he picked it up.

Her partner gave a final glance at the pickup bed before he fell into step beside her, walking away as Jason slapped a soaped-up sponge against the window of his truck's cab.

Neither of them said a word until they got to the sedan.

"So he had a dog swiped from his family's country property on the eastern edge of Celina," Hank said as he yanked open the driver's side door. "It's a good bet it's somewhere off FM 455, near where those dogs were found. You think there's a connection?"

"My gut says yes," Jo replied over the roof before she got in. "But is he a victim or part of the problem?"

"He's got those crates and that bloody blanket," Hank said, settling behind the wheel. "Could be as simple as he said, hauling his dog back and forth, going hunting. Maybe he takes the Posse up to toast marsh-mallows and sing 'Kumbaya.'"

Jo sighed. "Thanks for stepping in. I wasn't getting jack out of him. He'd just as soon have spit that tobacco in my face as answer my questions."

"Speaking of wacky tobacky, what were you doing back there, mop-ping up his chaw spatter?" Hank asked as he stabbed the key in the ignition and started the car, which rattled a little at first, like an old man whose bones were shaking.

"I was getting us some evidence." She leaned sideways so she could tug out the wad of tissue from her hip pocket. She opened it up for him, revealing a nasty smear of brown. "His spit."

"Jesus, Larsen." Hank made a face, adding dryly, "If you want a little Skoal, I could buy you a brand-new tin at the nearest 7-Eleven."

"Pass." She laughed, wrapping the slug back up and setting it on the dash. Hank knew as well as she did that this nasty piece of evidence would either clear one of Trey Eldon's posse or point a finger at him.

# CHAPTER
# TWENTY-FOUR

Jo sent Hank back downtown with the tobacco spit in an evidence baggie. He had instructions to hand off to Emma Slater, who already had Kelly Amster's underwear to analyze for blood and semen. Her gut told her there was something incriminating, or Kelly wouldn't have saved them. And now they'd have Jason Raine's DNA for comparison.

She wondered if Trey was running scared. Or was he feeling his oats after his power play last night? Did he think she'd lay off him after that? Didn't he realize he'd only made her want to go after him and his boys that much harder?

Hank had asked if she wanted him back at the station after the drop, and she'd told him to go on home. The commute to downtown Dallas and back would suck up a good couple of hours. It was nearing quitting time for the masses, too, which meant nobody'd be moving anywhere too quickly on any of the city's roadways.

Once her partner had gone, Jo got straight to work. She started with a property records search for Collin County, tracking down the acreage owned by Jason Raine's parents. Sure enough, she found it, right off the Farm to Market Road, FM 455, on the eastern edge of Celina, just as he'd said.

When she Googled the address, she got a beautiful bird's-eye view of a good-sized home sitting a fair piece off the road, near a big pond. There was a large shed or barn with a fenced paddock, though she didn't see any signs of cattle or horses. Trees and brush covered much of the undeveloped land, and Jo figured from Jason's comments to Hank that much of it was used for hunting.

She tried zooming in on an area that looked like a blackened circle within a ring of stones. It was centered inside the paddock, which appeared to cover a good quarter of an acre. Was it the site of the bonfire Jason had talked about, the one he, Trey, and the boys lit up a night or two before a game, beating their chests in order to get their blood pumping?

She sat back in her chair and stared at the screen, trying to reconcile the public persona of Trey Eldon versus what she'd learned of him last night. Was he just a mixed-up young man who'd lost his mother too soon, or was he a spoiled rich kid who thought he could do whatever he wanted without consequences?

"Detective?" a voice said almost tentatively, and Jo looked up.

It was Bridget, holding a laptop that wasn't Kelly Amster's. She'd taken off her knitted hat with the peace sign patch, and her tangled, dark hair resembled a rat's nest. There was a strain around her eyes that Jo hadn't seen before.

"Can I show you something?" she asked, but there was nothing in her face to make Jo figure it was anything but bad news. In fact, she appeared almost ill.

"You okay?"

"I don't know." Bridget shrugged as she moved Jo's keyboard, then opened the laptop to set it on Jo's desk. "I found a couple of the Posse's

Facebook posts archived that hadn't been restricted. There's one photo and a video put up by Dan Trent. I doubt he realized he'd had the privacy settings off, so they could be viewed by friends, not just the four members of the Posse. The video is from last fall. The photo's only a few days old."

She tapped a couple of keys and then stepped back, arms wrapped around her belly.

Jo leaned in, not sure what she was seeing at first. "It's pretty dark," she remarked, hardly able to discern much beside what looked like dashboard lights. "Where are they?"

"Just keep watching."

She heard plenty before she saw anything worth a lick—lots of cursing and laughing, the noise of a beefed-up engine and Hank Williams Jr., wailing about all his rowdy friends comin' over tonight, enough to nearly drown out the voices altogether. "This is how we do it, y'all," someone hollered, and it sounded an awful lot like Jason Raine's West Texas drawl. "Gotta break a few things to get pumped for a game!"

With the near absence of light and grainy quality, it took a few seconds before she knew exactly what she was looking at. Whoever held the phone was recording from the back seat of a vehicle as it bumped down a dark road without headlamps. The camera jostled, and Jo made out a shadowy figure behind the driver, and then the bobbing head of the shotgun passenger.

"Here it comes . . . here it comes," someone whooped, and then the camera panned to the windshield as the headlights abruptly flipped on.

Jo spotted the mouth of a driveway with a mailbox dead ahead on the right. She watched a hand raise a baseball bat, moving it aside as a window rolled down.

"Go for it, bro!" someone cried, and the others joined in a drunken rebel yell.

She glimpsed the shadowy backside of one of the riders, hanging out of the cab before she heard the distinct thwack of wooden bat against metal. The yelling grew louder as the headlights went dark.

"Fucking thing went down flat!" someone yelled, then another, "Rock and roll!"

Then it was over.

Jo checked the timer. The whole thing had lasted a little less than a minute thirty, yet her heart kept on pounding.

*What the hell was that?*

She didn't wait for Bridget to step in and replay it, clicking on that button herself.

Silently, she viewed the video again in its entirety before she fully understood what she was seeing: four people in a moving vehicle, their voices clearly male, one of them swinging a bat and knocking down a mailbox. Where were they? Up in Collin County, in Celina or Weston? Jo didn't recall any kind of similar vandalism around Plainfield last fall. She would have remembered that.

"This was posted to the Posse's closed group?" she asked Bridget, just to be sure.

"Yes." The young woman leaned over her again, tapping keys on the laptop. "It probably appeared on their news feed when it went up, which is why I could find it. But they didn't delete it or change the privacy settings, even though they had to realize friends outside their group viewed it, 'cause it got a couple of dozen likes."

Jo had a feeling they didn't mind at all that others saw it. Maybe that had been their intention, to show their peers that they were infallible. If anyone tried to turn them in, they could deny they were involved. No names were mentioned. There was nothing she'd seen to specifically identify them. Just because Dan Trent posted it didn't make him guilty of anything criminal. Lots of kids shared videos and photos online of acts much worse than this.

"You want to see the photo now?" Bridget asked.

"Does it show more mailbox bashing?"

"No, it's way worse. I can't believe something like this was out there, and no one reported them," Bridget said, pulling up the image and then getting out of the way.

When Jo saw the photograph, bile rose to her throat.

Four figures stood front and center, backlit by the orangey glow of a big honking fire, all with bandanas tied around their heads, hiding half their faces. They either wore hoods or cowboy hats and dark shirts. Baseball bats rested in their arms like babies, and below them, at their feet, lay the carcasses of two dogs, tongues lolling, eyes lifeless.

*Another kick-ass roundup!!!* the caption read.

*Roundup? Was that what they called it?*

Jo felt her stomach lurch.

"Maybe it's staged," Bridget whispered. "Maybe they were just going for shock value, and the animals aren't real."

"How about the photo?" Jo asked. "Is it real, I mean?"

"I don't see any signs of manipulation of the image."

Jo had to look away.

Was this one of the "rituals" Jason had told Hank he and his posse went through on the nights before a game? Where they lit a bonfire and got "revved up"? Did they take dogs to the Raines' hundred acres in Celina and then get their inner cavemen on by banging the crap out of the animals with wooden bats? Had they gone from bashing in mailboxes last fall to beating dogs senseless?

She thought of Jason's story of his missing mutt and kicked herself for feeling sorry for him. She'd thought he was a victim. Had he killed his own dog?

*Damn.*

"Is this all you've got?" she asked, trying to focus on facts, not on her emotions.

"Isn't it enough?"

When Jo glanced up, Bridget had tears in her eyes.

"Did they really do that?" she asked. "Did they really murder them?"

"I don't know," Jo told her. But she aimed to find out.

"Can you make sure to back up everything?" she said, finding it easier to talk shop than address the horror of what she was seeing. "I don't want to risk losing a file because that gang of juvenile delinquents gets wise and deletes everything or infects our system with some virus."

Like they had Kelly's computer, if that was what had happened. Considering Trey's dad had a cybersecurity company, Jo figured anything was possible.

"I backed up everything already," Bridget said grimly. "I just wish I could do more."

"You're doing plenty," Jo assured her. "Just keep at it, okay? If you find anything else online, let me know right away. You turn up anything in Kelly's doc files?"

"I'm sorting through, like, a year's worth of homework and textbooks, and I'm still trying to break the ciphertext in the e-mails from Trey Eldon," she said. "But it's beyond a long shot that I can decrypt them without a key."

"I think he was threatening her," Jo remarked, as her gaze lingered on the dark image of the masked posse with their battered victims. Had Kelly seen this photo or others like it, enough to be convinced that Trey and his pals would harm her if she didn't toe the line?

"I'll forward the AV and JPEG files to you, Detective," Bridget said, reaching for her laptop. "But I need to get this back to my desk."

"Yeah, okay," Jo told her, then looked at the clock and realized what time it was. "No, wait, it's not okay. You should go home. There's a very real thing called burnout in this business."

Bridget shut the laptop and picked it up, hugging it against her. "I want to get these guys. Anyone who can do : . . *that* to poor defenseless creatures shouldn't be walking the streets." Her eyes welled behind her glasses. "Besides, call me crazy, but I'd rather work than go to bars, like everyone else my age. This is what I do for kicks."

"I get it." Jo smiled gently, understanding all too well. "Go dig up more dirt on these bastards. 'Do or do not, there is no try,' right?"

Bridget almost smiled.

"Between you and me and Hank, we'll nail them for something."

"Good," Bridget said, nodding. Then she headed off.

Jo picked up the phone and dialed Hank.

# CHAPTER
# TWENTY-FIVE

"You checking up on me, partner?" Hank said as soon as he'd picked up. "Have no fear, that ugly plug of spit is with Emma. By the way, she says to tell you she'll try to have something preliminary tomorrow. We won't get DNA back, not on the saliva or Kelly's underwear, but we'll find out if there's semen on the pants. That'll be something, at least."

"Something is always better than nothing," she told him. "Where are you?"

"I'm in the car, heading home. You're not still at the station?"

"Yeah."

"You need to git."

"I will, in a bit," Jo said, but first, she wanted to fill him in on what she'd just seen, explain where her mind was going with everything. When she finished, his silence was more telling than words. Hank was rarely ever lacking in smart-ass retorts.

Jo stole the moment to string the facts and assumptions and hearsay together.

"So Kelly decides she wants to be popular, and she knows just the guy to help her out. She contacts Trey Eldon and threatens to expose his family's dirty laundry if he doesn't give her a leg up. He buys her clothes. He invites her to his party, this fifteen-year-old kid who's dying for attention. She gets drunk and passes out, and he takes her upstairs and rapes her, or one of his friends does, or maybe they all do."

Because that was the world they lived in, wasn't it? Just do it. Don't stop and think of the consequences. Satisfy the itch and the urge. Forget about kindness or compassion, or whether the act you're committing is lethal or unlawful or just plain wrong.

"They take her home, dump her on the lawn, and don't realize she's got semen in her underwear and on her blue dress. She starts to fall apart, spilling some of the beans to Cassie. Until Trey starts threatening her, and she realizes she's got evidence. She tells him she has proof of the assault on her blue party dress, except Trey uses the keys she left behind to get into her house, trashing her room to find it. He thinks he's in the clear, but Kelly lets him know that he's not."

Hank remained so quiet that Jo was afraid she'd dropped the connection. She asked, "You still there?"

"Yeah," he muttered. "I'm here."

She went on. "Kelly's got a backup plan. She has her unwashed panties. But Trey's feeling safe, and he's suddenly not so willing to help her out anymore. He thinks his e-mail threats will shut her up. Maybe he even shares a JPEG like the one I just saw, proving to her that his posse means business. Kelly's got someone online calling her a whore, Cassie's burned her friendship bracelet, and her mom's taking care of other people's sick babies. Kelly can't take the pressure and decides to kill herself. Think of her suicide note," Jo reminded him. "'I love you, but it hurts too much to stay.' She feels like she's in this alone, and it breaks her."

"Damn, Larsen." Hank sighed a heavy sigh, which was as good as him saying, *By George, I think you've got it.*

She envisioned him running a hand over his bald spot, rubbing the stubble at his jaw, and feeling as helpless as she did.

"Where do we go from here?" he asked, something she'd done a little thinking about herself.

"We've got to be careful. I don't want to tip them off. I don't want them to think we know as much as we do until we've got enough to arrest their sorry asses."

"They've got a game on Thursday night instead of Friday this week," Hank said. "They're playing McKinney. It's a big rivalry."

"Tomorrow's Wednesday," Jo remarked.

"You figure they already had a roundup?"

Jo thought of Duke and wondered if he'd been part of a warm-up.

"There was blood on that blanket in the back of Jason Raine's pickup truck . . ."

"His folks are gone," Jo jumped in. "He's got no one checking up on him. Why the hell not?"

"He mentioned a full moon tomorrow night," Hank reminded her. "If I were hung up on rituals, I'd want a full moon to do it right."

"Okay," Jo said, trying to calm her racing heart. "I don't want to jump the gun, in case we're wrong. We'll have to wait and see if Jason and the Posse pack up for Celina tomorrow after practice."

"It'll be a light workout," Hank told her. "I'll bet they still do it like they did in my day: helmet only, no pads, game jerseys, shorts, and cleats. They'll walk through the plays and get a down-and-dirty pep talk from the coach, but that's about it."

"So they'll be done early?"

"Yeah. Early enough to head up north and still get home before too late, so they'll get their forty winks."

Jo took a deep breath, expecting to feel the rush she usually felt when pieces of a puzzle started coming together.

But it wasn't there.

Instead, she felt indescribably sad.

"What's wrong with them?" she asked Hank, desperate for some explanation. "What could possibly make them so vicious? They have everything—"

"No, they don't," Hank cut her off. "They don't have everything, Jo, and you know it. Money can buy you a lot of things, but it can't buy you a soul."

"No."

"They're narcissistic clowns who've had too much handed to them," he said, sounding tired and angry. "Affluenza, they call it. You read the papers lately? We breed 'em in this country like gerbils. Commit a crime? Well, boys will be boys, ain't that right? Give 'em a slap on the wrist, and send 'em back home to Mama."

If Jo hadn't already felt sick to her stomach, that was enough to do it. "You're scaring the crap out of me."

"It scares the crap out of me, too," he said. "It's a bad world for raising kids. We used to have a sense of direction, and now we're operating without a compass and no one seems to give a damn."

"You're preaching to the choir, Hank."

"I know," he said. "I know."

"Go home to your wife and kids," Jo told him. "If I need you, I'll call."

"I got a CD full of Barney songs my girls left in here, and I just might put it in. The more I hear about this case, the more I appreciate that sappy purple dinosaur."

"Barney?" Jo grinned. "You are in dire straits."

"Nothing a hug from my girls won't cure."

"Hug them for me, too," she said.

"How 'bout you take your own advice? Hang up, Larsen, and go on home to your boyfriend, but please don't hug him for me. I mean, I like him and all, but that'd be overkill."

Jo laughed. "Will do."

But when she got off the phone, she didn't go anywhere. She put her head down and kept working. A half hour later, her phone pinged.

Adam had sent her a text: Heading to condo. You home?

Not yet, Jo replied. Eat without me.

Everything okay?

Just burning the midnight oil. ILY.

Ditto.

Much as she wanted to see Adam, she had a few things to tackle on her to-do list before she closed up shop for the day.

First, she put in a call to the criminal investigator at the Celina Police Department, leaving a message for her when she wasn't there. She asked about mailbox vandalism dating back to last fall. She also wanted to know if the department had a report filed by Jason Raine regarding his missing dog, Shale, or any other report that involved him or his parents' property.

Next, she e-mailed Hank's buddy Fred at Animal Services, sending him DMV photos of the Posse. She did the same to several other area dog rescue groups. She couldn't help wondering if Trey or any one of his crew had adopted pups, particularly in the days prior to the last two Mustang football games.

Then she e-mailed Jill Burns with the photos of Dan Trent and Scott Gray, asking if she'd ever had contact with either of them, or if they'd ever interacted with her German shepherd, since the high school students lived in her neighborhood next to the dog park.

Finally, she checked her e-mails, finding the examination report on Duke from Dr. Hooks as well as the photo and video that Bridget had forwarded.

She opened up the latter immediately, going over the photo with the department's enhancement software, refining the resolution and magnifying the image, spotting what looked like class rings visible on the fingers of several Posse members. Even with their faces half-covered, Jo knew who they were.

But was it enough to convince a judge to issue a subpoena for the boys' phones and for their laptops so they could look for evidence tying the Posse to Kelly Amster's alleged assault?

Jo wasn't so sure.

She needed more. So she kept looking.

She used the same software to run the video, trying to make the resolution less grainy, the audio less garbled. She fiddled with it until it wasn't worth it to tweak anymore, and then she watched it again at least a dozen times until her eyes blurred.

The voice was Jason Raine's. She felt sure of that much. Otherwise, she could find little to identify the vehicle or anyone in it. There was nothing hanging from the rearview mirror: no rosary, no fuzzy dice, no pine tree–shaped air freshener. She couldn't make out any faces or any features or clothing that pinpointed the passengers. The fact that the video was posted by Dan Trent to the Posse's group page was hardly evidence enough to implicate the boys.

Jo backed up her files and rubbed tired eyes.

Time to go.

I'm on my way, she texted Adam. Be home in ten.

Then she grabbed her gear and took off.

# CHAPTER
# TWENTY-SIX

*Wednesday*

Jo awoke in the dark, lying still for a minute, her heart racing.

She'd heard something, a distinctive ping, enough of a noise to interrupt her less than restful sleep.

Up on her elbow, she saw the light from her phone on the night table, just beyond Adam's chest. The pinging noise certainly hadn't disturbed him. He was snoring like a fiend. Carefully, she untangled herself from his long limbs, an arm and a leg tossed across her sometime in the night. She shimmied from beneath the covers and slowly inched her way to the end of the bed to avoid climbing over him.

When she got to her phone, she had a text. It was from Bridget. Check your e-mail, it read. I found something.

Jo didn't want to stay in the room and risk waking Adam. She tiptoed out and toward the small second bedroom that served as her office. She stumbled over Ernie in the dark, his black hue making him invisible. As she caught herself, she cursed under her breath, moving cautiously through the hallway as Ernie twined around her ankles.

"You're gonna make me break my neck someday," she hissed, but he just purred.

She slid into her chair and booted up her computer, preferring to pull up whatever message Bridget had sent on her laptop screen rather than the small screen on her phone.

"Lie down, baby," she whispered to the cat as she settled herself at her desk, and Ernie wormed his way onto her lap.

Jo let him stay there, dangling across her thighs and rumbling like an engine on idle as she got online and quickly found an e-mail with attachments. It was 2:30 a.m. by her computer's clock. The time stamp showed the e-mail had been sent at 2:20 a.m. Did Bridget ever sleep?

She opened the message and read, thinking all the while that if the captain didn't get the city to hire his niece full-time, he was crazy.

> I might not be able to crack the encryption on the
> notes to your vic from Trey Eldon. But Kelly must
> have gotten wise to the fact that the program re-
> encrypted the e-mails once she closed them out.
> These screenshots were hidden in with her math
> homework. I'm looking for others. I'll let you know
> if I find any more.
>
> —B

Jo downloaded the attached files, which didn't take long. There were only two JPEGs with shots of the brief e-mails from Trey Eldon's Stang12 address. But as she read, her heart raced all over again.

This first was dated a mere day after the party:

> No one made you drink. No one made you pass
> out. He was drunk, too. You should NOT have worn
> a dress that tight. What was he supposed to think?

It's your word against ours. Do NOT mess with us.
Let it drop, or your life will be OVER.

The second, a week after:

You don't have proof, so don't lie. The blue dress
is SMOKE. You have NOTHING. You know about
my posse? Leave JR alone. Shut your trap. Or we'll
take you to Celina.

She read them several times each, enough so that the words and
their intent sunk in. When she'd finished, she realized she was holding
her breath.

With a whoosh, she exhaled, her pulse thumping like Secretariat
on steroids. All the scenarios she and Hank had played out about what
had happened at Trey's party weren't mere conjecture anymore, not
after this.

*It's true,* she told herself, thinking these two short e-mails confirmed
so much.

Cassie hadn't been lying. Kelly had been raped that night, and
Trey was blaming her for it. Maybe he hadn't been the perpetrator of
the assault, but he was pointing a finger at "JR," which very well could
be Jason Raine. Regardless, Trey had threatened Kelly, had told her to
keep quiet or else she'd end up going "to Celina," surely a reference to
the roundup. Kelly must have known that they were killing animals
on Jason's country property. Could it be that she'd seen the very same
picture Jo had seen, or one equally unnerving?

It had doubtless been enough to scare the crap out of her.

If only Kelly had come forward. If only she'd filed a police report
about the assault and the threats. The teenager might still be alive. At
least, she would have had support. She could have helped stop the
roundups, too.

*Why, Kelly?* she wondered. *Why didn't you stay and fight?*

Jo sighed.

She knew why all too well. She'd been there. She understood how small Kelly must have felt in the end, how completely powerless and insignificant. One skinny girl against Trey's physically intimidating crew. What did Kelly have, after all? Not much in comparison. Trey's daddy would have no trouble hiring the best lawyers in Texas. Even if they charged him for being complicit in Kelly's rape, Jo had no doubt he'd walk.

Yeah, Kelly had been screwed from the get-go.

Ernie mewed softly in protest as she dumped him from her lap and drew her knees up to her chest, hugging them tightly. She didn't remember making a sound, but she must have, or else how would Adam have known to come in and put his arms around her?

"You're shaking," he said, his mouth near her temple, his breath ruffling her hair. "What's going on? Talk to me, Jo."

She hadn't shown him the video or the photograph from Facebook. She hadn't told him much about anything she'd learned today. When she'd gotten home, she'd been so tired and hungry. He'd fixed her a sandwich with leftover chicken, some Gouda, and tomatoes, and she'd gobbled it up. Then all she'd wanted to do was get into sweatpants and a big T-shirt and curl up on the sofa with Adam and Ernie. The TV had been tuned to a show about Saturn, and Jo had sat back, staring at the amazing photographs of rings made of dust and ice, but all she had thought about was the underpants Kelly had so carefully bagged and hidden, and the awful photograph of the Posse with bandanas tied around their faces like outlaws from an old B movie, dead dogs at their feet.

She swallowed hard, turning in the chair and opening herself up to him. He sat on the floor at her feet as she talked, his hands on her knees. She showed him the video and the photo Bridget had dug up, and she read him the e-mails that Trey Eldon had sent to Kelly. She wondered aloud if the boys weren't responsible for the nasty remarks on Kelly's social media, too, particularly the one telling her to go back to who she was or jump.

When she was done, she braced herself, waiting for him to say something to undermine her confidence, to subvert the story she'd come to believe was real.

*"You're makin' things up, Jo Anna, and I don't believe a word of it. If you don't watch yourself, I'll wash your foul mouth out with soap,"* Mama had told her once when she was so little, when she had finally screwed up the courage to confess that something bad was going on beneath her own roof. *"Do you hate him so much you want to paint him with tar? And after all he does to take care of you? You should be thankin' him for putting food in your mouth and clothes on your back. That's what you should be doing."*

But Adam didn't go there.

He didn't tell her she was crazy, that she was jumping to conclusions. That she was a foul-mouthed liar.

"I want to help," he said quite staunchly, drawing away so he could look in her eyes. "What can I do?"

She almost said, "Nothing," but realized that she could use his trained eyes.

She asked him if he'd take a look at Duke's X-rays, and he didn't balk. He didn't say he had no time to study the radiographs of a dead dog. He told her that if she could get him the films from Dr. Hooks, he'd look them over. That if Duke hadn't already been cremated, he'd autopsy the pup himself.

"Anything else?" he said, and Jo started to shake her head.

Then she changed her mind again. "Yeah," she told him. "Believe in me."

"I do," he said. "I do."

# CHAPTER
# TWENTY-SEVEN

She was up before dawn and back at the office before her shift began. She even traded in her usual bottle of Coke for a cup of bad coffee, though she hardly needed the caffeine. By 8:00 a.m., she'd gone through her voice mails and e-mails, and she'd gotten hold of Karen Rossfeld, the sole detective in the Celina Police Department, who confirmed Jo's suspicions about the mailbox vandalism taking place up north, not in Plainfield.

"We started getting calls about damaged mailboxes a year ago. We even tried strategically setting up a few cameras on the weekends, but we didn't get squat."

*No,* Jo thought, *because the Posse went on their rampages during the week, before their Thursday- or Friday-night football games, not after.*

"It went on for about ten weeks, then stopped altogether in November. Not sure if the cold made them quit, or if it was all the hard work we've been doing to cut down on underage drinking and

DUIs," Rossfeld told her. "I'm sorry, though, that we never caught 'em."

Ten weeks, huh? Jo estimated that was the entirety of high school football season, which would fit the Posse's MO, too. No wonder the vandalism had stopped in November. They'd played—and won— the state championship game by Thanksgiving. No reason to knock out mailboxes and get pumped up when there wasn't anything to get pumped up for.

"We had them pegged as kids from the area," Rossfeld went on. "I guess, whoever it was, they grew up."

"I think they grew up, all right," Jo agreed. They'd morphed into eighteen-year-olds with a hard-on for bigger and more vicious things. "Have y'all had any reports of missing dogs lately? Probably older dogs, big ones, not the kind you can stick in a purse."

Rossfeld hesitated. "Funny that you're asking, 'cause we've had two that stand out recently. We got a call about a boxer that vanished from its backyard two days ago."

"Have you found it?"

"No, not a trace."

Jo swallowed. "What's the other? You said two stood out."

"Yeah, the other's from about three weeks back. A woman from your neck of the woods came into the station, crying her eyes out and wanting someone to blame for her Labrador that'd gone missing and turned up on the side of FM 455, presumably hit by a moving vehicle."

Jo knew exactly what she was talking about. The dog that had disappeared from Plainfield and ended up dead in Celina, the black Lab that Dr. Hooks had mentioned reading about in a sidebar in the paper. Like Duke, he'd been battered and left for dead.

". . . *a boxer that vanished from its backyard two days ago* . . ."

A few days ago, Jason Raine was in Celina.

Isn't that what he'd told Hank?

The black Lab from three weeks ago fit in with the first week of school, the first big game. There were probably other dogs they didn't know about—the ones in the photograph—that must have come between then and Duke. The timeline seemed a little jumbled, like the Posse hadn't figured out their rhythm yet, or maybe Jason liked to practice his murderous swing between bonfires. Maybe he didn't want to wait between games.

"I think I might know something about the dogs," she said, and the Celina detective was all ears.

Jo told her what she suspected about the gang of four, how she figured they'd gone from bashing property with baseball bats to bludgeoning stolen dogs. "My partner and I believe they're using the Raines' property in east Celina for their roundups, as they call them. Which is why I got in touch. We want to catch them at it, if we can. Maybe you can help us."

"I hope you're wrong," Rossfeld said, "but if those boys got horns holding up their halos, we don't want 'em running wild any more than you do. Let me talk to my LT and the chief, and I'll get back to you ASAP."

Jo thanked her. Before she'd even hung up, she e-mailed the JPEG and AV files so the detective would have ammunition to show her higher-ups. Jo was hoping it would work with Captain Morris, too. She planned to catch him when he got in, so she could finish telling him about the incident with Trey Eldon. Except now she'd add more to it.

But first, she called Dr. Hooks, requesting the X-ray films for Duke.

"Where do you want them?" the vet asked. "I can send the films electronically anywhere you need me to."

Jo gave her Adam's e-mail, and she promised to forward the films right away.

Next, she followed up with Jill Burns, asking if she'd looked over the photos e-mailed the day before.

As Jo had hoped, she recognized one of the faces.

"I didn't get his last name, just his first—Scott. He approached me at the dog park a couple of weeks back," she said. "He asked if he could pet Tucker, and he stayed to play with Tuck for a while, tossing him a ball, that kind of thing. He told me he lived near the park, but that's all I know."

"Did you ever see him again?"

"No," Jill again replied. "But I didn't expect to. My schedule's pretty crazy, and Tuck goes to a doggy day care . . . went to doggy day care." She got a catch in her voice. "You can't think that he took Tucker? Why would he do that?"

"I don't know," Jo admitted, "but I aim to find out."

She touched base with the animal shelters she'd e-mailed the night before, checking to see if they recalled any of the faces or names of Trey Eldon's crew, particularly in relation to recent dog adoptions. Ultimately, she struck out, though she'd pretty much expected it. Legitimate shelters asked for ID, required paperwork, and usually had a waiting period for prospective owners. They also chipped the animals. Jo couldn't imagine any of the Posse wanting that kind of provenance. They were more likely to respond to posts on Craigslist or newspaper classifieds, where dogs were being given away, no strings attached. No worries of presenting a valid driver's license or an animal being micro-chipped and leading the authorities back to them.

But stealing dogs from backyards seemed equally risky, if not more so when thief and owner lived in the same neighborhood. Maybe that was a part of the thrill, Jo decided, tempting fate, seeing how far they could go without getting caught.

And, so far, they'd gotten away with plenty.

If Kelly hadn't jumped from the tower to her death, if Jo and Hank hadn't started asking questions, the Posse's exploits could have gone on and on, possibly until they disbanded or went off to college, leaving a trail of anguished victims in their wake.

When Hank arrived at the station, Jo was on the phone with Emma Slater at the county crime lab. He opened his mouth to start yakking, but she raised a finger to hold him off.

"I haven't gotten far with your evidence, sorry," Emma immediately began to apologize. "I did find a trace amount of semen in the underwear. There's blood as well that matches your vic's type."

"So it's a good bet someone had intercourse with Kelly the night of the party."

"Yes, but I won't even try to pinpoint a timeline," Emma said. "I'll leave that up to you. The specimens did have some degradation from being zipped up in that plastic baggie, but I managed to get viable samples. We're kind of backlogged here, as you know."

She paused, and Jo felt a lump form in her throat.

"So if you need DNA faster than a few weeks . . ."

"I do," Jo told her. "I need it yesterday."

"I could send it to a private lab we're using, as long as your department agrees to pay for it. We outsource to them on occasion, and I'll get the results as soon as they're available. I can try to put a rush on it."

Jo didn't hesitate. "Yes, please. Whatever it takes."

But as she said it, she winced, imagining Cap's less than enthusiastic reaction. He'd give her a lecture and question how she thought he was going to get the city to pony up for an expensive test that may or may not prove Kelly Amster had sex with a high school boy a few weeks before she died. It wasn't like a DNA match would indisputably prove rape when the victim wasn't alive to give her side of the story.

"Do it," Jo reiterated.

"Okay, if you're sure," Emma said. "I'll take care of it right now."

"Thanks."

When Jo hung up, Hank was standing alongside her desk, hip braced on the edge, and arms crossed, patiently waiting.

"What's going on?" he asked. "We about to catch us some bad guys, hoss?"

Jo turned her chair around to face him. "Are you up for it?"

"You got something in mind?"

"Yeah, I do."

She had a plan in place for taking down Trey Eldon's Posse, and once she explained it to Hank, he was all-in. They just had to get the green light from their captain, and they'd be good to go.

# CHAPTER TWENTY-EIGHT

She picked up her laptop and led the way to Waylon Morris's office. The door was wide open, but Jo knocked on the jamb, regardless.

"Hey, Cap, you free to talk?" she asked, noticing that, unlike yesterday, he was tugging the knot of his tie loose. Had he come back from another meeting? She dove right in, telling him, "I just heard from Emma Slater, and she's sending the specimens from Kelly Amster's underwear to a private lab so we get the results ASAP."

"You don't say?" Captain Morris turned around, pulling the tie over his head, like he was removing a noose. If the pinched look on his face was any indication, he wasn't in a giving mood.

"Morning, Cap," Hank offered, even lifting a hand.

"Come on in," Morris told them, pitching his tie toward his desk. "How about you both take a seat. You've got some explaining to do."

Jo looked at Hank, and he shrugged.

"Is something going on, sir?" she said, settling down with the laptop on her thighs while Cap continued to stand. He rolled up his sleeves, then crossed his arms tightly over his chest.

"Yesterday on my way out, you started to tell me about a meeting with Trey Eldon," he began, and Jo swallowed hard.

"Yes, sir. I'd left my card with him, and he called my cell phone at nearly midnight. He had something to tell me about Kelly Amster." Jo shifted in her seat, glancing sideways at Hank. "He seemed okay at first, but then he got a little physical with me."

"Is that right?" Cap asked, eyebrows knitting over the bridge of his nose.

"Yes, sir. He seemed angry that I didn't believe his denials that something happened to Kelly at his party."

"Were you hurt?"

"Just my pride," she admitted, hating that it still rattled her. "It shouldn't have happened."

"No, it shouldn't," Cap said, uncrossing his arms, with such a disapproving expression on his face that Jo felt scolded by it alone.

"It's my fault, sir," Hank spoke up. "I was supposed to be there, too. The kid would've had my boot up his butt if he'd tried anything—"

"So you didn't see what went on?" the captain interrupted.

"No, but I heard," Hank said, adding in a mumble. "Well, most of it, anyway."

"What's up, Cap?" Jo had expected a reprimand, a lecture, maybe. But something was off. The captain seemed unduly angry, and she could think of only one reason for it. "Don't tell me you got a call from Robert Eldon?"

"The chief and I were summoned to the mayor's office first thing this morning. Mr. Eldon claims you've been harassing his boy and his boy's friends. He said his son confessed that you lured him to the park in the wee hours and came on to him."

"Came on to him?" Jo tried to stay calm. "No, sir, that's not true. None of it," she insisted, staring right into his eyes. "Trey set it up—"

"Larsen didn't want to go alone," Hank backed her up. "Why would she have asked me to be there if she wasn't on the up-and-up?" He shook his head. "Robert Eldon must've caught wind of the meeting and got worried that the Third spilled his guts. The kid lied to his dad to save his ass."

"Cap, you know me better than that," Jo said, hanging on to the laptop. "I wouldn't jeopardize the case, much less my career. You believe me, don't you?"

Waylon Morris sighed and sat down on the edge of his desk. "I believe you. But you're on notice, okay? Stay away from the Eldons."

*Stay away?*

"Me, too, sir?" Hank asked.

"They didn't single you out, Phelps," the captain said, jerking his chin at Jo. "Just Larsen here. Eldon threatened to get a restraining order against her if she comes anywhere near Trey . . . their house, the school."

"What?" Hank made a noise of disgust. "Jo was just doing her job."

"They're scared, Cap." Jo bristled. "We've got a growing pile of evidence that someone at Trey Eldon's party assaulted Kelly Amster. We're also starting to piece together a connection between Trey Eldon's crew and the missing dogs."

"The dogs?" Cap repeated. "How's that?"

Jo anxiously opened the laptop, clicking open the photo from the roundup and turning it toward him. "It's starting to look like Trey Eldon, Jason Raine, Dan Trent, and Scott Gray have put together their own billionaire boys club. They call themselves the Posse. They have a closed Facebook group where they can share their exploits. We've got video of them knocking down mailboxes in Celina where the Raines have country property. I think they went from that to something nastier. Stealing dogs and taking them up to the farm to . . . to . . ."

"Beat the crap out of them," Hank finished for her. "Jason Raine admitted to going up to the property for some pregame ritual, and we're guessing it may be tied to some of these dog disappearances. We've had two dogs found near death on FM 455, right near the Raines' property."

"You're guessing? You're *guessing*," the captain said, more emphatically the second time. "So this is all supposition? You got anything concrete?"

He hadn't yet looked at the laptop screen, so Jo stood, holding it out to him.

"Bridget couldn't find a way into the Posse's closed group on Facebook, but she did get this pic of Trey's gang with dead dogs, and there's an AV file of the Posse damaging the mailboxes . . . federal property."

Cap finally squinted at the picture. "This could be a stunt."

"I don't think it is, sir." Jo scrambled to say something more convincing. "Bridget retrieved screenshots of two e-mails that were saved on Kelly Amster's hard drive. They're part of a spate of encrypted e-mails that Trey Eldon sent Kelly after the party. The software is made by Robert Eldon's company, and they've so far refused to help us decrypt."

Jo set the laptop back on her thighs, pulling up the screenshots as she talked. "The e-mails reference a sexual encounter that occurred at the Eldon house the weekend before school started. Trey clearly threatens Kelly to keep her mouth shut. We're not just fishing, Cap. There's something here."

She held out the laptop again, but he didn't reach for it.

"Please, sir, if you'd just take a look."

But, instead, the captain looked right at her. "Bridget's working other cases, you know. She's pretty much dumped everything else for you."

"She's been great, sir," Jo was quick to say. "She feels invested—"

"You can't keep using our resources on a suicide, Larsen," he told her. "And now you've got the county sending evidence to a private lab and sticking us with the bill?"

Jo felt like he'd punched her in the chest.

"I'm sorry, Cap, but it's the only way we'll get results back fast enough. Otherwise, it could be weeks, and we need that DNA evidence if we're going to—"

"She's dead, Detective," he said bluntly, cutting her off. "And it wasn't homicide. She did not die by anyone's hand but her own."

Jo blinked. "Excuse me?"

"I got the preliminary report on Kelly Amster's autopsy not five minutes before y'all walked through my door. There's no physical evidence to suggest anything other than suicide." Cap leveled his eyes on her, a deep divot between his brows, which let her know he was deadly earnest, as if his words weren't enough. "At this point, do you really think it's going to do any good to go after the sons of high-profile members of our community? Maybe it's time to wrap up your investigation and move on."

*Move on?* Her mouth went dry. She'd been about to suggest court orders for all the Posse members' cell phones and laptops.

Jo was used to the captain being direct, and normally, she appreciated it. But this time, it felt more like she was a child being spanked, and she couldn't help wondering just how well Robert Eldon knew the mayor. Hell, with all his money, he could have bought and paid for City Hall.

"You want us to drop this, even if Kelly Amster was raped?" Jo couldn't stop herself from asking. "Even if that's what drove her to kill herself?"

Cap was avoiding her eyes, something he didn't normally do. His rubbed his jaw, which looked unshaven. Also, not like him. Just how much pressure was he under to get them to stop investigating? Robert Eldon must really be turning the screws. Was Mr. Eldon that afraid his son was going to end up in jail?

Hank blew out his cheeks, like he didn't want to get into it.

But Jo wasn't about to give up.

"What if it was Bridget?" she said, knowing she was pushing the envelope by the way the blood rushed into Cap's cheeks. "What if she was at a party where she drank too much and was assaulted? What if those dogs in the photo were kids? Which they are, you know. Just ask Jill Burns and Amanda Pearson. If it was your niece, sir, would you want us to stop investigating then?"

The captain looked ready to bite off her head, but instead, he pursed his lips, seeming to gather his wits before he responded.

"Look, Larsen," he said, gravitas, not anger, in his voice, "the problem with pursuing a rape charge now is that our victim's not here to testify. It's hard enough when we've got a victim willing to take the stand. How do you think it'd go over without one? She can't even tell us her side."

"But we *do* know her side, sir," she insisted, glancing at Hank for support. "The evidence we're collecting will speak for her. We can't let them skate. They're the black hats. We're the good guys." Her chest constricted. "They're out there breaking the law, and we're supposed to turn a blind eye, just to make the mayor and his wealthy donor pal happy?"

The captain had his jaw clamped so tightly, the muscles twitched.

"Cap?" Jo tried again, because it wasn't right, and he knew it.

"Aw, hell." He sighed and slid off the corner of the desk and picked up the laptop. He set it on a crowded blotter and fumbled around for his reading specs, which he plunked onto his nose. Then he leaned forward in his chair. He didn't speak as he read the e-mails from Trey to Kelly and, from the looks of things, read them over again.

Jo didn't move as she waited for him to finish.

Hank shifted in the seat beside hers, clearing his throat. "C'mon, Cap. We just need a little more time to do our jobs."

"All right, a little more time is all you get." Waylon Morris removed his specs and rubbed his eyes. He looked whipped. "Do what you need to do, but do it discreetly, you hear?" He gestured toward the door. "Go on, and don't come back until you've either got enough to arrest those boys, or you're calling it quits."

"Thanks, Cap." Hank gave him a quick salute, ducking out before Jo.

She turned to the captain and swallowed hard. "We're going to get them, sir," she told him. Then she walked out of his office and closed the door.

# CHAPTER
# TWENTY-NINE

The front desk officer caught Jo as she and Hank were leaving the captain's office.

"There's a woman here to see you," he told them. "She said she's the mother of the suicide victim."

"Barbara Amster?" Jo said, as Hank gave her a puzzled look.

"You want an interview room?" the officer asked.

"No, bring her back here," Jo said.

The uniform nodded.

Jo sat down at her desk, and Hank pulled up a chair. They didn't even speculate what had brought Kelly's mom to the station. She appeared not a moment later, with the officer pointing the way.

Barbara was in her work clothes: the polo-collared shirt with the logo monogrammed above the breast and a pair of khaki pants. She shuffled over, sitting down in the chair Jo offered and clutching her bag in her lap.

"Is something wrong, Mrs. Amster?" Hank spoke first. "Other than the obvious, I mean." He had his arms on his knees, kneading his hands together.

"How can we help?" Jo tried, but the woman seemed not to have a voice at first.

She pursed her lips, gaze darting in every direction. "I didn't tell you the truth," she said. "About Kelly and the Eldons."

Jo's mouth went dry. "What about the Eldons?"

"You asked if Kelly had seen John Ross since his mama died," Barb began, only to hesitate. "I lied when I said that she hadn't."

Hank wrinkled his brow. "John Ross?" he repeated. "Who's that?"

*John Ross.*

*JR?*

Jo thought of the decrypted note, and her heart nearly stopped.

"You can't mean John Eldon?" she said, having never heard his middle name before. "Trey's brother?"

"Yes, the younger son," Barbara said, hugging her purse. "He was here this summer, before school started up again. Kelly saw him, all right."

"Where?"

Barbara Amster raised her chin, and her pale eyes met Jo's. "The night before that party you said she went to." She stopped, pushing out a breath. "She was getting ready for bed. She looked up and saw him standing outside her window, just like he had after Mary passed."

Jo remembered what Kelly's mom had told her before about that. *"He must've been twelve, right in the throes of puberty and without his mother to guide him . . . Kelly caught him looking in her bedroom window. He was pleasuring himself."*

"Was he masturbating?"

"I don't know." Barbara Amster flushed, visibly flustered. "I didn't ask."

"What did she do?"

"She screamed, and he ran away."

Hank made a noise of disgust. "You should have called us, ma'am."

"Why?" Barbara said, defensive. "He went back to boarding school the next day. Robert flew him out on that jet of his. He couldn't hurt her."

But when Jo caught Hank's face, she knew he was thinking just as she was: *Did John Ross really go back to Virginia when Mr. Eldon claimed he did?*

What if he'd stuck around for the party?

"There's something else," Barbara said, and her tired voice trembled.

"Go on." Jo waited, wishing the woman had been as forthright from the start.

"Oh, God, it was me," Barbara Amster got out in a strange, strangled cry. "I'm the one who said those nasty things to Kelly online. I'm the one who told her to go back to who she was and stop acting like a whore."

"You?" Jo didn't understand.

Tear-filled eyes met hers. "Angel," she said. "I'm Angel."

Jo looked at the company logo on her shirt. At-Home Angels.

It seemed so obvious. But why would Kelly's own mother troll her?

"Why?" she asked, shaking her head. "Why would you do something like that?"

"I did it for her own good. I just wanted to rein her in," Barbara tried to explain, wiping at her cheeks as the tears began to slide. "I thought she'd listen more to a peer than she did to me. We didn't think we were hurting her, but I guess we were."

"We?" Jo asked, having picked up on the use of the plural. She thought of the anonymous comments on Instagram, wondering if that was Barbara Amster, too, or someone else. "Did you have help trying to rein in Kelly?"

Why did Trey Eldon come to mind?

"No, no, of course not. I meant me, that's all," she said, fumbling in her pocket for a tissue. She found a crumpled one and wiped at her nose.

The more Jo thought about it, the more Barbara Amster as Kelly's harasser made sense. Jo had asked Cassie the previous morning if she knew Angel on Facebook, and Cassie had replied, *"Did Barb tell you about that?"* When Jo had followed up, inquiring if Kelly had told her mom about the mean comments, Cassie had said, *"She didn't have to."*

No, apparently not.

"I didn't know what else to do," Barbara Amster sobbed. "Am I in trouble? Did I break the law?"

Jo stared at her. Was that all she was worried about? *How about "Did I break my child's heart? Did I help to push her off the water tower, even if I didn't touch her?"*

She opened her mouth, ready to berate the woman, to ask how she lived with herself, calling her daughter a whore and a slut. How did a parent do that to a kid and claim to love her? It was messed up. That was what it was. Messed up.

"I let her down," Barbara Amster went on, crying all the while. "I shouldn't have done what I did. But I didn't know another way. I hope she forgives me. I hope Kelly forgives me."

Jo listened to her blubber, and she kept mum. She couldn't do it.

"I don't know what to tell you, ma'am," Hank said, leaning forward. "Being a parent is hard, never knowing what to do from one day to the next. There's not a playbook in the world that's got any tricks worth spit. You live and learn."

"That's what I always told Kelly," Barbara whispered.

Jo turned her head, wondering what he was doing. Was he absolving her of guilt?

"What you did wasn't right," Hank continued softly. "Kelly didn't need more tearing down. After what she'd been through, she needed someone to hold her up."

"I want another try," Barbara said, jaw trembling. "I want to go back and do it over."

"You can't," Jo told her bluntly.

Kelly was dead.

"I'm sorry, baby." Barbara started to sob, bowing her head as her shoulders shook. "I'm so, so sorry."

Hank got up from his chair to pat the woman on the shoulder. But Jo stayed where she was. She sat there in silence, chest aching and mad as hell. Had Kelly known deep down inside who Angel was? Had she suspected? If she had, it was no wonder she'd lost all hope.

Jo spent the better part of the afternoon poring over more of Kelly's social media, finding more instances where Angel had put her down, more anonymous posts chiming in. She'd lost track of time when she got a phone call from the lone detective in Celina.

It was a quarter to five.

"You were right, Jo," Karen Rossfeld said, like they were old chums. "There's been activity this afternoon at the Raines' place."

"Oh?"

"We've been doing a little recon with a drone and spotted someone over at the property, stacking wood for what looks like a bonfire. It's within the paddock fencing, a ways off the barn. We got a name from the side of the pickup truck, and it's a local who does mulch and firewood for area residents. We ran him through the system, and he came up clean, so I don't figure he's involved except for the delivery."

"Anyone else on the property?" Jo asked. "A caretaker, maybe?"

"No one we could see except the mailman."

"Go on," Jo urged.

"I checked with the fire marshal, because the Raines would've had to file a plan ahead of time. They're on way more than the required two acres, so it's perfectly legal for them to burn as long as they notify the marshal. In fact, he's very familiar with the address. He said they do bonfires and seasonal burning pretty regularly."

"Did Jason Raine get a permit for tonight?" Jo asked, feeling her eyelid twitch.

"He surely did," Rossfeld drawled. "I guess he didn't want the fire trucks showin' up and finding him and his friends breaking bad around the bonfire."

Jo felt the flutter of butterflies in her belly.

"You thinking of heading up with your partner to check on them?" Rossfeld asked.

"As long as we're not stepping on anyone's toes."

"Our toes are fine. I heard the chief on the phone a few minutes ago, touching base with your captain. We're here to back you up if you need a hand. But it's your call, and we'll wait on it. Odds are, it'll all add up to nothing."

"We'll see," Jo said, mostly surprised that Captain Morris wasn't putting the kibosh on their little excursion. He could very well have done it, and she wouldn't have blamed him a bit, not with the mayor breathing down his neck. "What's your best advice on surveillance?"

Rossfeld gave her some directions to a patch of adjacent land where she and Hank could park without arousing suspicion. "It's a property for sale, and I've cleared it with the Realtor. I implied we were doing some training."

Jo reckoned it *was* training of sorts, on how to take down a gang of spoiled rich kids.

When she got off the phone with Rossfeld, she asked Hank, "You want to go to Celina?" and he started to scramble.

While he went on a mission to round up a couple of walkies, Tasers, and a body cam, Jo made a call to Amanda Pearson. A young woman answered with a sweet, soft voice. Jo identified herself, and the woman said she was Amanda's daughter.

She put her mom on, and Jo started out by asking how she was faring. Mrs. Pearson sounded tired, her feistiness gone, although she admitted it was good to have her daughter around. She was even thinking of going back to Missouri with her and spending some time with the grandkids, which Jo thought sounded brilliant and told her so.

"You are good to be concerned about me," Mrs. Pearson remarked. "But I'm sensing there's more to this than how I'm doing. Is there something I can do for you?"

There was, in fact, and Jo didn't hesitate to ask for a small favor.

"Can you keep an eye out for Jason Raine's truck?" she said. "I know you can hear it when he goes by. You remarked that it rattled your walls."

"Has he done something wrong?" Mrs. Pearson asked.

"He might have, yes, ma'am," Jo replied diplomatically.

"You think he took Duke, don't you?" Before Jo could answer, Mrs. Pearson added, "I remember something that didn't strike me until now. You'd wondered if I'd seen any cars on the road that night Duke disappeared, ones I didn't recognize. I told you no, which was the truth. Because I didn't *see* any strange cars at all. But I heard a truck, that awful roaring engine, while I was putting on my nightgown. I'd grown so used to it that it didn't register. He could have tossed Duke right into his pickup, with me being none the wiser."

"We're not letting this go," Jo assured her. "When you hear that truck tonight, would you please call me on my cell?" She recited her number again, even though she'd left a card at the house days ago. "Hank and I need to know when Jason leaves his house. It's important."

"I will sit by the front window and watch for him," Mrs. Pearson assured her. "If he's the one who hurt Duke, I want him punished."

"I do, too."

Jo glanced at the time. It was already close to six.

*Hurry up,* she told herself, gently bidding goodbye to Amanda Pearson, who wished her good luck, whatever she was up to. Jo said she'd take it.

*Ticktock, ticktock.*

She got up from her desk, glancing down at her clothes. She had on dark jeans, a broken-in pair of Lucchese boots, and a navy-blue T-shirt. Not a bad uniform for an evening stakeout. The more she could blend into the night, the better.

She took a few minutes to study the Google photos of the Raines' property, getting a sense of the lay of the land and where everything sat—the house, the barn, the fenced-in paddock where the bonfire would burn—and how best to approach it. She wanted to be close to the fire, able to quickly intercede before things got out of hand. Hank would be near enough to keep a visual on her and the paddock, but at a safer distance.

Jo wanted to be in position before the boys arrived. She didn't want them to see her until she needed to be seen.

"You got everything?" she asked as Hank returned to her desk. He had a canvas knapsack slung over his shoulder.

"Everything and then some." He patted the bag. "You sure you don't want a vest?" he asked, not for the first time.

"He's not going to shoot a cop."

"Not on purpose," Hank replied. "But he's a hunter. He's probably got guns up the wazoo. And we don't have a warrant, so we're not exactly marching up to the front door . . ."

"They're not using guns on the dogs. They're using baseball bats," she said. "And we won't be empty-handed."

Hank looked resigned. "All right. I need to go grab us some wheels. Give me a few minutes more," he told her, picking up the canvas knapsack before he disappeared.

Going with Hank to Celina, Jo texted Adam, knowing he'd be worried. Be back by midnight.

He texted back in record time: If you're not, I'll call the cops.

Funny guy.

Saw Duke's X-rays, he went on. I concur with Hooks. It looks like severe abuse.

It was, Jo texted back. It definitely was. She was as sure of that as she was of anything.

She checked her phone's battery, which still had a strong charge. She had her sidearm locked and loaded in her shoulder holster, and she'd tossed a few extra plastic cuffs into her jacket pocket. All she'd forgotten was a trip to the bathroom. Once accomplished, she was out the back door, stopping at the curb just as her partner rolled up in a truck from the impound lot: a very dirty late-model Ford Ranger with tinted windows.

"Nice ride," she remarked upon opening the door. "It's from the drug bust two weeks back, yes? Heroin dealer from the Audubon Apartments?"

"I'm giving the battery a chance to charge."

"Right."

"I figured that old sedan would stick out like a sore thumb in horse country, but nobody'll give this rig a second glance."

When Jo got in, she noticed he'd made a pit stop at the vending machine, too. A cold Coke and a Mountain Dew sat in the cupholders. Wedged in the well beside Jo's feet was a plastic bag filled with assorted junk food.

She buckled her belt, then inspected the items on the menu for dinner. "Nutter Butters, honey buns, and cheese crackers. The three essential food groups."

"Hey, don't bite the hand that feeds you."

"Ha," she said, watching him grin. She looked around her, spotting some fingerprint dust on the dash.

"You ready to rodeo, partner?"

"I guess I am."

"Then let's do it."

With that, he put the truck in gear and pulled out of the lot.

# CHAPTER
# THIRTY

The sun slowly slipped lower toward the horizon as they headed north on Preston Road. With rush-hour traffic, it took forty-five minutes instead of the usual twenty-five to make it to Celina. By then, the dull blue sky was tinted pinkish-purple. The same hue colored the blanket of clouds settling in to smother the stars.

Despite the predicted full moon, it would be a moonless night, for sure. In another hour, twilight would descend.

Was that when Jason and the Posse would arrive? Under the cover of impending darkness, when the rest of Celina was eating dinner and watching *Wheel of Fortune*?

"Okay, Siri, where are we headed?" Hank asked, and Jo directed him.

They found the lot for sale easily enough, though the GPS tried to lead them straight into a good-sized pond instead of a barely visible dirt path off the farm road.

"You sure this is it?" Hank said, pulling onto the shoulder.

"That way." Jo gestured toward a trail of tire tracks cutting through the bare earth, a lot of weeds in between and everywhere around them. The undeveloped land looked a lot like cow pasture surrounded by brush and trees. It was what Plainfield had been half a dozen years back, Jo thought, before the developers had set in.

"So we park here and walk over?" Hank asked.

"That's the plan."

"Hear that, my friends? We're walking," her partner said, reaching beneath the steering wheel to pat his knees and sigh.

Jo ignored him, having no sympathy for any of his bum joints at this point. For the next couple of hours, they both needed to suck it up.

A billboard to the left screamed, LAND FOR SALE! and touted the 104-plus acres as RAW LAND, CURRENTLY UNZONED WITH WATER FRONTAGE.

The truck bumped along the uneven path as Hank went in just far enough so they weren't sitting out in full view of the cars that sporadically passed, zipping along FM 455 like it was a racetrack. Jo didn't want Jason or his buddies spotting a strange truck on the side of the road near the Raines' land. They couldn't afford to tip them off, or the Posse might turn tail and run back to Plainfield.

The Raines' place was due west. They'd gone by the entrance a quarter mile back: a metal gate with PRIVATE PROPERTY—NO TRESPASSING signs on either side.

Jo had been surprised not to see it surrounded by barbed wire, although she couldn't imagine fencing in a hundred acres of country property for nothing. It wasn't like they'd lose cattle without it, as it wasn't even a working ranch.

"We going over now, or waiting until dark?"

"I'm waiting on a phone call. We can go once I get it."

Jo took off her seat belt, rolling down the window to let in some air. Even hot, it felt better than nothing. She rolled up short sleeves to her shoulders so her skin could breathe. Then she dug into the plastic bag for a Nutter Butter, passing one over to Hank as well.

They went over her Plan A for the hundredth time, until Hank finally said, "And what's Plan B, if we need it? You got one of those, don't you?"

"Yeah, I've got one," she told him. "It's called improvise."

Hank mumbled as he ate a cookie, "That's a little too detailed for me to remember."

She hadn't even taken a bite when her phone began to trill. Unlike Hank, she was too nervous to put anything in her stomach, so she shoved the uneaten cookie back into its wrapper, put it in her pocket, and answered her cell.

"It's Amanda Pearson," said a familiar voice. "He just left in that abominable truck of his, and if he had anything to do with Duke, I hope to hell that he doesn't come back."

"Got it. Thanks," Jo replied and hung up, looking at the clock and then at Hank. "They're on their way."

It was 7:30 p.m. on the nose. Traffic had probably eased quite a bit on Preston Road. Jason and his pals could conceivably reach Celina within a half hour.

"Okay, partner," she said. "I think this rodeo's about to start."

They got out of the truck, decently concealed from the busy route by brush and stunted trees. If anyone spotted it, Jo hoped no one would think too much about a truck parked on a lot for sale.

Hank retrieved the knapsack and set it on the hood, removing the pair of walkies and handing them over so Jo could set the frequency. She clipped one to her belt, and Hank did the same with the other.

Jo added a Taser to her holster and clipped on the body cam. The camera had night-vision capability, she knew, which was exactly what she needed. She wanted every bit of what happened tonight to be recorded. If what went on was nearly as ugly as that photograph, Jo figured they'd have evidence enough that even the mayor couldn't protect his buddy's kid, evidence enough to get warrants for the closed Facebook page and the boys' cell phones, too.

Hank offered up a pair of night goggles, but Jo didn't want them. She wouldn't need them if she was near the fire. She intended to be close enough to see the boys' faces. Hell, she wanted to see the whites of their eyes.

Hauling out a can of bug spray with DEET, Hank doused his arms and the legs of his jeans. "Don't want to get mauled by bloodsuckers," he remarked, offering the can to Jo.

But she didn't need the stuff. Mosquitoes didn't like her blood much. Adam had once jokingly told her that it was because she was a type A through and through. It seemed that bugs preferred O.

Jo checked her weapon, a .38 that fit her hand like a glove and that she was reluctant to part with despite the prevalence of 9mm on the force. If she'd been a rookie anytime sooner than she had, she would have had no choice. But she wasn't giving up her trusted revolver, not for a semi that could jam. Besides, she hadn't used it once since joining the Plainfield force. She hoped she wouldn't need it tonight.

"We're good to go," Hank said and slung the knapsack over a shoulder, following after Jo as she trudged through shin-high weeds toward the trees that continued onto the Raines' property.

She used her phone's compass app to move through the wooded landscape. The house was due north. The barn was slightly west of that, beyond a large pond. That was where the drone had seen the bonfire being built. That was the spot Jo was aiming for.

She heard Hank breathing hard behind her, twigs snapping underfoot. Cicadas hummed in the air around them, growing louder as the sky turned dark. Frogs began their melodic croaking, and somewhere off in the distance, a coyote howled.

"Hey, Dorothy, I don't think we're in Kansas anymore," Hank muttered from behind her, between his huffing and puffing. "I'm used to hearing sirens and car alarms going off, not all this nature racket, which is pretty loud, by the way."

"It's not the only thing that's loud," she said, and he got the message, piping down.

A vague light loomed ahead through the trees, and Jo kept moving toward it. In another few minutes, she came to a clearing, keeping tight against the trunk of a tree as she peered out, spying the back of the house. A floodlight had come on above the steps to the rear porch. A few seconds later, it went off.

Her heart pounded, thinking someone was there, manipulating the switch. Then a breeze picked up, blowing a tree branch so that it swayed near the porch, and the light went on again.

*Ah,* she realized. *Motion sensor.*

She skirted the yard, spying the pond in the darkness, so flat and black without the moon's reflection. The dirt drive snaked around it, leading up to the house. Another hundred feet, and they were in the woods beside the barn. She waited for Hank to catch up with her, then motioned him forward, toward a spot in the trees where he could view the fenced-in paddock and see the barn, yet still remain concealed.

Jo paused to check the time on her phone. It was almost 8:00 p.m. The Posse should arrive at any moment.

She found a tree stump, brushing it clear of debris so her partner could take a seat. If he used the night-vision goggles, he'd have a decent visual, kind of like sitting in an orchestra-level box to the side of the symphony. Except no pretty music to hear.

Hank settled down eagerly, dumping the knapsack beside him and rubbing his knees. "You sure you want to be in the barn?" he asked in a near whisper. "What if they decide to go in there?"

"I'll be fine," she told him. "I'm the po-po, remember?"

Hank didn't seem to think that was funny. "They rape underage girls. They beat dogs with bats . . ."

"I'll be fine," she said again. "And if things get nasty, then you call the Celina PD. Ask for Detective Rossfeld."

Jo thought she spied a flash of light beyond the paddock fence. Headlights?

She figured it was time to get in place.

"Keep radio silence unless it's absolutely necessary," she told Hank, and he nodded, the whites of his eyes looking blue in the dark.

"Be safe," he told her.

"I'll do my best."

Jo took off, sticking with the trees and skirting the fence line until she came up behind the side of the barn. By then, the faint glow bumping along the horizon had turned into a bright glare.

The Posse had arrived.

She hurried across the open terrain between the woods and the structure, hugging the walls of rough-hewn boards until she'd reached the barn doors. They weren't closed, much less padlocked, and she slipped through the opening into the darkened interior just as she heard the rumble of Jason's truck approach. The bass beat of music thumped loudly for a minute, pulsing through the night air and drowning out the cicadas before it stopped.

Jo tried to calm her fast-beating heart, breathing in the smell of dust and hay as she let her eyes adjust and looked around her. There were empty stalls, partitioning the space, and a storage area beyond, housing a large riding mower, three or four ATVs, and some dirt bikes, attesting to the fact that the country property was used mostly for recreation.

She raised her gaze, checking above her and seeing the hayloft and the ladder leading up to it. She started toward it when she heard a noise, a whimper coming from somewhere close.

*Was it human?* she wondered, as she instinctively reached for her holster, but she slid her hand away when she recognized what the sound was and where it was coming from.

Two cages sat in the nearest stall, covered by stained blankets like the one Hank had found in the bed of Jason Raine's pickup. Nearby, she saw a slew of wooden bats lined up like soldiers, looking bruised and bloodied from previous battles.

She inhaled the stink of excrement, of fear, and she swallowed hard.

She pulled back a corner of a blanket on the nearest cage to see a large dog cowering. A German shepherd, she realized. "Tucker?" she said instinctively, and the pup inched toward her slowly, clearly afraid.

She reached in her pocket for a peanut butter cookie, and she offered it to him through the bars. He opened his mouth, and she thought, at first, that he would take off her fingers, but he merely grabbed the food and gulped it down, like he hadn't eaten in a while.

Had anyone come to care for them recently, or had they been left alone?

From the looks of their empty water bowls, Jo guessed it was the latter.

The other dog began to whine, and Jo peered past the bars to see a boxer, likely the one Karen Rossfeld had mentioned disappearing from its backyard. She offered up the second cookie in the package, dropping it into the cage when she heard a shout from outside.

"Sorry, guys," she said, feeling a horrible pang in the pit of her stomach. "I've got to go."

She stared at the frightened dogs and second-guessed herself, thinking that she should just put an end to it all now, not let any part of this roundup go on. They could call in the Celina cops and charge the boys with stealing dogs, but she knew it wouldn't work like that. Their lawyers would spin it. "They found the poor dogs," she could hear them protesting. "They were going to take them to the vet to check for chips. Hell, they weren't harming them. They were saving them!"

So she pushed down her self-doubts and whispered to the skittish animals, "I won't let them hurt you. I won't."

Not any more than they were hurt already, being ripped from their homes, thrown into crates, and taken somewhere foreign, left without food to sit in their own feces.

They whimpered softly as she took off, then one began to bark. Jo ran to the ladder leading up to the hayloft and climbed quickly, as though escaping a fire below, which in a way, she was.

With a groan, the barn door slid open, pushed wide enough to drive a car through, and Jo scrambled up the last rungs, flinging herself onto the dirty wooden floor of the loft. Her heart slammed against her rib cage as she picked up voices from below.

She half crawled toward the large window, open to the air beneath the hay hood. A big iron hook hung above, tied to a rope that wound around a pulley, then ran back along the hay track. There were no hay bales, nothing to suggest any of it was still being used.

Jo came up to the edge of the window, daring to peer out as the immense teepee of logs ignited with a whoosh, fire rushing up from the brush around its base and in its center, engulfing the pyre in flames that leaped into the night.

She saw two of the boys then, dressed to match the darkness, bandanas on their faces, ball caps on their heads. They whooped and hollered, arms raised to the sky, as if praising some unknown god of destruction.

Then the other boys appeared, bringing with them the cages, which Jo realized were on wheels. They rolled them forward, toward the fire, and the dogs' whimpers changed to howls and snarls.

Did they sense what was to come? Did they know that they'd be fighting for their lives?

Jo reached for the walkie on her belt, tempted to signal Hank now, to tell him she was going to end this, that he should call for backup pronto. Instead, she raised her fingers to her chest, where the body cam rested in the vee of her collar, between her breasts.

Quickly, she turned it on.

She angled her body against the side of the window, tipping the camera so it could capture the scene unfolding below, lit up so brilliantly. The fire was like a dragon's breath, blowing flames of illumination toward the starless sky.

Jo could see everything.

She didn't worry that they'd look up. They were too engrossed in their own theater, handing out the baseball bats, tossing pieces of meat around their arena, banging the cages and screaming obscenities until they were fired up enough to let the dogs out.

The animals began to run, darting haphazardly, unsure of their surroundings and what was going on. Finally, they scented the food and ran toward it, unaware or uncaring that the young men awaited them, circling, chasing, toying with them, and then taking a swing.

"Holy shit," Hank's voice hissed from the speaker of her walkie.

She let go of the body cam and snatched it up. "Call for backup now," she told him, feeling her own disgust rise above all else, snapping her like a rubber band stretched to its limits.

She reached up for the hay bale hook, felt it give, and pulled it down.

Then she screamed at the top of her lungs, jumping from the hayloft window, the rope in her hands, burning her skin as she rode it down.

She hit the ground hard, throwing herself off her feet as she landed. She'd bit her tongue and tasted blood but didn't pause. As she got up, she reached for her holster, tempted to grab her sidearm. Instead, she removed the Taser and turned it on as the dogs ran toward her, trying to get away from the bats.

It was then that Jo saw the boys swivel on their boot heels, wondering where the high-pitched scream had come from.

Jo picked out Jason Raine, the ringleader, all six-odd feet and two hundred–plus pounds of him, and she let out an anguished cry, running straight at him with all her might. She threw her shoulder into his chest and felt like she'd hit a brick wall, bouncing off, falling down to the dirt as he pulled down his bandana and laughed at her.

"Remember, Detective, you hit me first. It's only self-defense," he said and raised the bat.

Jo rolled on her back, Taser still in hand. She fired it, hitting him square in the belly.

He cried out and went down, kicking and flailing.

She backed away, breathing hard, keeping hold of the Taser, which only would stun the second time around, but she wouldn't even need that.

She heard Hank's voice, yelling that he was the police and directing the boys to get facedown on the dirt. A siren wailed in the distance, the sound small and then louder and bigger, fast approaching, and Jo picked herself up, her hands on her knees, trying to catch her breath and find her balance. The dogs came around her, sniffing at her pockets and whining, but they looked okay.

She put her Taser away to sling her arms around the pups, hanging on as they whimpered, hoping to hell the body cam clipped to her shirt had captured every shot.

# CHAPTER
# THIRTY-ONE

They split the boys up, putting the first two in separate interview rooms. The other two were kept apart and babysat by uniforms so they wouldn't get up and wander, finding each other to intimidate or coordinate stories about what had gone on.

Jo left Trey Eldon by himself for a while. *Let him stew,* she mused, as he probably had the most to lose of them all.

She went inside the room that held Jason Raine.

He gave her a sneer as she entered, and he leaned back in the plastic chair, looking extremely pleased with himself. "Go ahead and charge us, Detective. What have you got?" he said, a hollow smile on his lips. "Animal cruelty? Punishable by a fine, I'll bet, or better still, any charges will be dropped once we get our lawyers involved. You'll see."

"You forgot about the rape charge," she told him, pulling up a chair on the other side of the table. "We've got your DNA."

He raised eyebrows at her. "How?"

"From that chaw you spat at me yesterday."

For an instant, his face clouded. Then, as quickly, he was giving her another grin, even sloppier than before. "You've got nothing," he told her, leaning forearms on the table, his shoulders hunched forward so they were closer than Jo would have liked. She could smell the stink of his perspiration and his fetid breath. She could see the brown stain of tobacco on his teeth. "I didn't rape anyone. I didn't go near that chick after Trey took her upstairs."

"Then who did?"

"You know what? You can talk to my lawyer," he told her. "He should be here any minute."

Then he pressed his mouth shut, making a big gesture of zipping it.

Jo stared at him stonily. She thought about a hundred ways she could wipe that smirk off his face if she didn't care about losing her job. But she was interrupted by the door coming open.

"Larsen?" Hank leaned in. "Can you come out a minute?"

She turned her head. "Now?"

"Yeah, now."

Jo swiveled back around, figuring he was right. She looked long and hard at Jason and realized she wasn't making any progress, not with this particular son of a bitch. Maybe her partner wanted to give it a crack. He was better than she was at dealing with chauvinists.

She got up and walked out, not acknowledging Jason's cries of, "Hey! You're not leaving me in here, are you?"

Once she'd cleared the room and shut the door, she rubbed damp palms on her jeans. "You're right. I'm not getting anywhere. You should probably take over."

"You've got a phone call from Emma Slater," Hank said, such a grimness to his tone that she was sure it was bad news.

"Is she working late, too?"

"I guess so. Why don't you ask her yourself?"

"You take it," she insisted. She would deal with bad news later. She still had work to do. She had to get something out of these despicable boys before they all lawyered up.

"I talked to her already," Hank said and grabbed her wrist. "I really think you'll want to hear what she has to say."

❖  ❖  ❖

Jo took the call at her desk, bracing herself as she picked up. "Hey, Emma," she said. "I'm almost afraid to ask what's up. It's way past quitting time."

"I've got your results back from the private lab."

"Oh." Jo got quiet fast.

"We got a match on the DNA. It was in the database."

"How?" Jo had run background checks on the members of the Posse. Except for minor traffic offenses, they were clean. What had she missed?

"Your unsub was arrested three years back for solicitation. He's in the system."

"Jason Raine?" Jo said, confused.

"No," Emma corrected. "The name's Eldon."

"Robert Eldon the Third?" Jo said. Had Trey gotten caught hiring a hooker at fifteen? She wasn't really surprised, not considering how messed up he said he'd been when his mom died, and how his dad started having affairs.

"No, not that Eldon . . ."

"John Ross," Jo said. The younger brother who'd masturbated outside Kelly's window before he'd been shipped off to Virginia?

"No, not that one, either. It's Robert Eldon Junior," Emma told her. "Age forty-three."

*The father?*

Jo sat there, phone in hand, stupefied.

The *JR* that Trey had mentioned in the encrypted e-mail to Kelly wasn't his brother, John Ross, or Jason Raine.

It was Robert Eldon Junior.

But he hadn't been at the party that night, or had he? Mr. Eldon had told them that he'd gassed up the private jet and taken his younger son back to school that very day. So either the lab was wrong, or Papa Eldon was lying through his teeth.

Jo put her bet on the latter.

"Are you a hundred percent?" she asked Emma bluntly.

"It's a clean match," Emma said. "All thirteen markers. They don't get any better than this."

"Thank you." Jo breathed, a feat in itself, considering she'd just had the wind knocked out of her.

She nodded, feeling stronger somehow, her anger and frustration at not getting anywhere with Jason slowly ebbing. She finally had some honest-to-God leverage. No, more than that. She had concrete evidence. Kelly hadn't been lying when she'd told Cassie she had proof.

"We're gonna get him, sweetheart," Jo whispered to no one but the walls, and then she did something she should have done earlier instead of taking Robert Eldon's word as gospel. She went online to track down his flight plans, filed with the FAA, and even called the private airstrip to confirm what she found.

His plane had not lifted off before Trey's party. He had not flown out of the metroplex until the next morning at dawn. For all she knew, he could have been the one to dump Kelly in her yard on his way to the airstrip.

No one made you drink. No one made you pass out. He was drunk, too. You should NOT have worn a dress that tight. What was he supposed to think? It's your word against ours. Do NOT mess with us. Let it drop, or your life will be OVER.

They would fight the charges, Jo knew. Robert Eldon would hire the best defense attorney in Dallas to get his ass off the hook. He would point the finger at Kelly, say it was all her fault, that she'd been consenting—albeit underage—and that she'd asked for it. To him, Kelly was nothing but leftover party trash, a crushed Solo cup with beer in the bottom.

Daddy Eldon would grease some palms, and if the case went to court, he'd do his damnedest to make sure a judge was assigned who was known for his leniency toward upstanding white guys who had friends in high places. And he might very well get off, too, considering it was his word and his boys' word against that of a dead girl, one of "those girls" from the wrong side of the tracks.

Jo swallowed hard, the taste in her mouth more than bitter.

"You okay there, hoss?" Hank said, putting a hand on her shoulder. "You look like you're coming down with something."

"I am," she said.

"You pick up mad cow when Jason Raine knocked you on your ass in the paddock?"

"More like I'm suffering from an acute case of disillusionment."

Hank grunted. "Hey, it's not over yet."

"No," she said. "But I think I know how it ends."

"Stop it, okay?" He turned her chair around so she faced him. He even squatted on those banged-up knees, so she knew how much he wanted to get through to her. "If we don't try, if we throw up our hands, what's left? You want the bad guys to win?"

She lowered her head to her hands.

"C'mon, Jo. Where's that hard-ass cop I know, the one who's like a dog with a bone, who never gives up, no matter what's against her?" he said, sounding pissed. "She's not a quitter. She's the kind of woman I want my girls to be when they grow up. Resilient, compassionate. Tough on the outside and soft in the middle."

Surprised, Jo looked up and met his gaze. Her own eyes teared with appreciation. "Me as a role model?" she said. "I don't know if that's wise . . ."

"I disagree, partner. If not you, who? The hot mess of self-absorbed idiots on reality television and half-dressed pop princesses?"

"Well, if that's my competition . . ." She laughed dryly, brushing at the damp on her cheeks.

"We're the good guys," he told her. "We help each other. We don't give in."

"I know." She bit her lip, nodding. "You're right."

"I'm always right." He put his hands on his knees, still crouched low on his thighs. "Now, if you'd help an oldster stand up straight, we can get back to work. Let's go talk to the captain and see how he wants to do this. We've got to go by the book if we're going to arrest a man like Eldon, not to mention his asswipe kid and his kid's asswipe friends. Gotta dot all those *i*'s and cross those *t*'s, you know."

Jo smiled at his use of the captain's own words. She was tempted to reach out and touch his sweet face with all its middle-aged creases.

Instead, she stood and held out her hands, taking his and giving a heartfelt pull. And when he was upright again, after a lot of grunting and groaning, he gave her hands a squeeze before he let them go.

# CHAPTER THIRTY-TWO

Trey glanced up as she entered.

He straightened his back, putting his hands on the table, palms up. Where Jason Raine had looked anything but vulnerable, Trey appeared visibly shaken.

Jo settled into the opposite chair, putting a file down before her and setting her hands atop it, clasping them. She gave herself a minute before she spoke. "Last time we met, it was on your terms, wasn't it? You lied to me, and you lied *about* me. Big Brother's watching now, Trey, so I wouldn't pull that crap again if I were you."

He stared at her, saying nothing.

She settled back. "It's my turn to tell the stories. I have a really good one, too, and I want you to listen."

"Detective, I told you, I didn't—"

"Shut up, son," she said. "Kelly Amster goes to your party. She hangs outside with your boys, who keep giving her drinks. Hard liquor, beer, whatever's handy. Except Kelly can't hold her booze, not like your posse. She gets sick, and they leave her out there by the pool. You hear about it, and you don't want her puking on your dad's expensive patio furniture. So you bring her in. How'm I doing so far?"

Trey pulled his arms off the table, dropping his hands into his lap.

"You take her up to a guest room and lay her down on a bed. Maybe you clean her off a little so she doesn't soil the pretty linens."

He cocked his chin, his eyes narrowed, not sure where she was going with this, which was just what she wanted.

"But then you left, and someone else went in. Someone who didn't care that Kelly was unconscious." She shook her head. "What I think is that Kelly awakened sometime while he was raping her. Worse for you, she remembered." Jo paused, sighing. "She trusted you, Trey. She trusted your family."

He opened his eyes wide, opened his mouth to refute her. "I told you, I didn't do anything—"

"Oh, it wasn't you." Jo leaned forward. "It wasn't you. But you weren't any less terrified, because she had the dress with the semen. She had DNA. She had leverage, and you were afraid she'd use it. So you stole the dress, but you forgot something equally damning." She whispered, "She had a pair of underwear with her blood from the rape and your father's semen."

Trey sucked in his cheeks. His hands came back on the table, palming it. "I went to wake her up," he murmured. "I wanted to take her home, but Dad was in there."

"They hadn't flown out that day, had they?"

"No. The weather was bad in Alexandria. They were canceling flights and rerouting, so Dad and John came home from the airport during the party." Trey wet his lips. "My father . . . he hasn't been the same since my mom died. None of us have."

Jo opened the folder, shuffled a page and then began to read aloud:

"'No one made you drink. No one made you pass out. He was drunk, too. You should not have worn a dress that tight. What was he supposed to think? It's your word against ours. Do not mess with us. Let it drop, or your life will be over.'"

She paused so she could look at him, see into his eyes. If they were the windows to his soul, they were full of splintered cracks, about to shatter.

Then she read a little more: "'You don't have proof, so don't lie. The blue dress is smoke. You have nothing. You know about my posse? Leave JR alone. Shut your trap. Or we'll take you to Celina.'"

Trey ran his fingers through his hair, making little choking noises. "I didn't do anything wrong. I had to protect him."

"You stole her dress. Did you take it to the bonfire and burn it?"

He pursed his lips.

"You protected a rapist," Jo said, the thought piercing her heart. "What about Kelly, huh? She was a victim."

*Who protected her? Who looked out for Kelly?* Jo asked herself, though she knew the answer.

No one.

She closed the folder, clasping her hands atop it to mask their trembling. "You put her panties on backward, and you pulled her dress back down before you loaded her into your car and took her home. When she got in touch later, did she turn the screws? Maybe ask for more than you'd bargained for? So you threatened her. For all I know, you lied to her, told her there was a video or photo, something out there that she'd be humiliated for all the world to see, pushing her closer to the edge." Jo's jaw clenched. "We'll get your phone, Trey, and we'll get your father's, too. Pretty soon, we'll know everything that happened. We'll have the truth, and you won't be able to squirm out of it."

He turned red-faced, his body shaking. He wrapped his arms around himself, but it did little to still him.

"Your dad raped a fifteen-year-old girl, then you victimized her all over again. Did that make you feel good? Did you feel like a bigger man?"

"No! God, no," he blurted out through snot and tears and abject fear for himself and his future and everything he had to lose.

He hung his head, hands holding on to it, as if to keep it down. And as he fell apart, he started talking, angrily telling Jo that nothing was the same after his mother got sick. His father turned to other women and booze, spending money like water and traveling, leaving him and John to deal with it, trying to fill a void that his sons couldn't fill.

Jo didn't interject. She just listened, wanting to feel even a sliver of pity for a family torn apart by loss. But what the Eldons had done was inexcusable. They had broken the already fragile soul of an innocent girl, and no amount of explanations or apologies would ever make up for that.

# CHAPTER THIRTY-THREE

It was midnight before Jo could leave the station.

She was beyond tired, beyond hungry. Her insides felt like they'd been ripped out and wrung out. All she could think of was getting home, crawling into bed, and holding Adam. She wanted to pull the covers over her head and forget all the things she'd seen today, all the horrible things she'd learned.

But as she passed the server room, heading toward the rear exit, she saw a light and stuck her head in, just to be sure that Bridget had gone. But she hadn't.

"Hey," Jo called out. "You should be home asleep."

The dark head turned around. "I couldn't sleep if I wanted to," she said. "I was hoping to see you, but I had to wait for the circus to die down."

Jo gave her a weary smile. "You can ease up now," she said, "and get back to working on other cases. This one's as good as closed."

The wide brown eyes behind the thick lenses just stared at her, like she hadn't heard a word. She didn't have her headphones on, didn't seem to notice the noise or anything else around her. The young woman looked pained.

"Bridget?" Jo's smile went away.

"It isn't over, Detective Larsen," she said. "It's not closed, not yet. I found more saved screenshots of messages that Kelly had stashed away . . ."

Jo waved her off. "We're getting subpoenas for all the Posse's phones and their computers. Trey and his father will have to produce the key for the encryption. We'll have all we need to press charges."

"No," Bridget said staunchly. "It's not even e-mails. This has nothing to do with the Posse or the party. But it might help explain why."

"Why what?"

"Why she killed herself. Isn't that what this was really all about?"

She moved her chair aside so Jo could see what was on her three monitors, a triptych of text messages blown up so large, even the captain wouldn't need his spectacles to read. And every word, every phrase made Jo's heart ache:

You're a slut
You're worthless
You're a liar
You deserve what you got
No one wants you
No one loves you
You've got no dad, and your mom's barely got time for you
Go fucking kill yourself
Go jump from the tower and be done with it
No one will miss you
No one will care that you're gone

It was worse than the stuff posted by Barbara Amster as Angel. And it wasn't even from Trey or his boys.

"Brutal, huh?" Bridget said in a sad little whisper.

"Yeah, brutal," Jo agreed. The worst part of all was that the texts were from Kelly's BFF, someone she'd grown up with and loved like a sister.

Cassie Marks.

Jo was up bright and early the next morning, despite hardly having slept.

She called the high school as soon as it opened and asked Helen Billings for her help again.

By the time the first bell had rung, she was waiting for Cassie in the conference room, where just days ago, Cassie had spilled the beans about Trey Eldon's party and the night that had changed Kelly forever.

Except that wasn't the whole story, just the part that she'd cared to share.

No wonder the girl had been so interested in whether or not they'd found Kelly's phone and so insistent that they let Kelly rest in peace.

*"Maybe it's better, you know, not to dig too deep. Maybe you should just drop it."*

Jo heard the tap-tap-tap of approaching footsteps before the door opened, and Cassie Marks stood there, hesitating.

"Come in, please," Jo told her.

Cassie took her time. She nibbled on her glossy lips and turned to close the door. She walked toward the table slowly, to the place where Jo had spread out the copies of the text conversations where Cassie had methodically beaten down Kelly.

She didn't sit but stood there, staring at the pages. She stopped gnawing on her lips. Instead, her mouth began to tremble.

"I loved her," she said and began to cry, fat little teardrops sliding from her eyes. "I loved her, and she was leaving me behind. She wanted to move up, but she didn't want to take me with her. I was hurt, so I lashed out. But I didn't mean it."

Jo didn't believe that for a moment. Cassie had meant to destroy Kelly, and she had done a damned good job.

"She wanted you to go to the party, too," Jo told her, having heard it from Trey himself. "She asked Trey to invite you. He said no. It wasn't Kelly's fault that you were excluded."

"You're lying!" Cassie's eyes flashed, angry and accusing. She didn't even bother to wipe at the bubbles of snot that snorted from her nose. "Kelly told me I couldn't go with her. She never mentioned Trey—"

"She was trying to be kind, to spare your feelings," Jo said, wondering if it would sink in, if Cassie would realize what she'd done.

"No," the girl insisted. "No, she wasn't trying to spare me. She thought I wasn't good enough."

*Good God.*

"You're the one who cut the bracelet off," Jo reminded her. "You cut *her* off when she needed you. She was raped, and you flat-out didn't care. You left her to deal with the aftermath on her own."

"That's not true!"

"You broke her heart—"

"She broke mine!"

Cassie grabbed the pages off the table and tore them up, threw them onto the floor and headed for the door, but Jo sprang up from the chair, catching her arm.

"Do you know what you did to her?" she asked, getting right in Cassie's blotchy face. "Do you even understand?"

"I didn't push her! She jumped."

Jo made a noise of disgust. "You might not have been there that night, but you walked her to the edge with your words. You might as well have thrown her over."

"I didn't mean for her to die!" Cassie bawled. "I just wanted her to feel as bad as I did, to feel as alone."

"Well, you did a bang-up job."

Jo watched her fall apart. The tears coming faster. Did she get it now? Had the truth sunk in? Was she grasping the fact that she had not been betrayed, that she was the one who'd done the betraying?

Jo wanted to feel sorry for her, but she couldn't. Kelly was the one who'd suffered. Kelly was the one who'd needed compassion. But she hadn't found it anywhere, not in her best friend, not in her mother. Certainly not with the Eldons.

*"The girl is dead. Kelly's dead. She offed herself, and that's all there is to it. Nobody pushed her. Nobody made her jump. So get off my back, keep away from my bros, and leave my family the hell alone."*

Jo couldn't decide which offense was worse—that Kelly had been raped by a grown man she'd known and trusted, or that she'd been goaded to her death by a girl she'd considered family.

It wasn't possible to pick one, to weigh one evil against another. Each was horrific in its own right. Both had caused a girl to die.

She couldn't bring Kelly back. She couldn't tell her that everything would be all right, that she just had to hang in there long enough to see that her life wasn't over. Jo could only do her job. She could only pick up the pieces victims left behind and make sure that all the guilty parties paid a price.

Even if that price was never high enough.

# CHAPTER
# THIRTY-FOUR

*Monday morning, a week later*

The woman looked a lot like Mama: thin white hair cut at her chin, the baby-fine strands revealing plenty of her pink scalp; pale skin that hung loosely at her jawline and neck; blond-lashed blue eyes ringed with puffy, brown shadows. Eyes so bright but so vacant, like the lights were on but nobody was home.

"I knew Verna back before you were born," she said as she came to settle in the chair beside Jo's mother at the dining room table. "Your mama was such a pretty girl. Rather like a southern Grace Kelly." She sounded deceptively lucid, something Jo was sure she wasn't, or she wouldn't have been at Winghaven, not on the dementia floor, where nobody but the staff had all their marbles. "We were stewardesses with TWA for years and years, and your mama loved to travel. It hit her hard when her folks died, and she went home for a while to take care of things."

*Mama was a stewardess?* Jo mused, because it wasn't a story she'd ever heard. She didn't know much about Mama's life before she'd met Daddy, and almost as little about the time before Daddy left.

"I don't think I saw her again until we ran into each other at Neiman Marcus years and years later. She was working the cosmetics counter, and I was there to buy lipstick. I always did like Le Rouge. Was that Chanel? No, no, it was Yves Saint Laurent." The woman paused and smiled. "Such a pretty red, don't you think? I never leave home without it."

But she had no lipstick on. Just pale pink skin, slightly chapped.

"Your mama, she was in the circus once," the woman went on. "She trained elephants."

"Ah," Jo murmured, realizing then that the woman might not even have known Mama at all. She turned away from the stranger, looking at Verna, whose rheumy eyes seemed to be staring far away, at something Jo couldn't see because it probably wasn't there.

"Mama?" She touched the blue-veined hand. "Do you want something to drink? It's about time for lunch, but I could find you some lemonade, I'll bet."

They always had lemonade. And ice cream, too.

Verna reached a hand in the air. "Do you see it?" she said. "There's a bird on the branch there. It's so little."

But Jo saw only an empty hallway, a potted plant, and the shiny doors of a closed elevator. Instead of correcting her, she nodded. "Sure, I see it. Very pretty."

Mama smiled. "I love birds," she said. "They come visit me."

Jo sighed, glancing up at the clock on the wall. She'd been there for only fifteen minutes, and it felt like an eternity.

"I knew your father," the woman in the opposite chair went on, and Jo settled back, turning to look at her again.

"Is that so?"

"Oh, yes. Handsome man," the woman remarked, blue eyes glinting. "Very quiet, though."

"Ah."

"They didn't approve of him, you know," she said, and Jo wrinkled her brow.

"Who?"

"Your mother's parents. They didn't like him one little bit."

Jo swallowed, reminding herself the woman didn't know what she was saying. It was like Mama seeing a bird where there was none. The past didn't exist for these folks anymore, not in a true sense. Memories got jumbled up with fiction.

Except there was a sliver of truth in those words. Mama had confessed once, when she'd been too drunk to censor herself, that her folks had not approved of Jo's father, that they'd cut her off when they'd found out she'd gotten herself knocked up. Jo had never heard exactly *why*. She had always assumed it was because Mama and Daddy hadn't been married when she'd been conceived, and Verna's parents had been ultraconservative and uptight.

Jo had not even started kindergarten when her dad left them, divorcing Verna. She had barely known him, not enough to remember much. She had never known her grandparents on either side. Mama had claimed they were all dead whenever she'd asked.

A part of her wondered now if any of that had been true, or if Mama had just made it up to suit herself. Jo looked at Verna now, staring at things that weren't real, and she wasn't sure if she'd ever know anything for sure.

"I remember seeing Verna with him once, though she tried to pretend he wasn't her beau," the woman went on, clicking her tongue against yellow teeth. "He had very dark eyes and dark hair, much like yours. He kept it short, of course. He had to, so no one would know." The loose skin at her jaw wobbled as she nodded in Jo's direction.

*Know what?* Jo nearly asked but didn't. She was getting tired of this game. She was ready to go.

She glanced at Mama, who wasn't paying any mind to the woman. She had been particularly withdrawn since she'd returned from the psych ward at Presbyterian. She hadn't said much, except to comment on the invisible bird. Jo almost missed the usual babble that made no sense. If they'd put her on some kind of medication to keep her calm, afraid that she'd push a resident again, Jo hadn't been told, and she didn't ask.

Her white hair was carefully brushed away from her brow and pulled into a ponytail. One of the caretakers, a young woman named Egypt, said Mama had been grabbing the strands that fell into her eyes and yanking them out.

"I believe your father was a boxer," the garrulous woman went on. "He was very famous. He had a funny foreign name that's on the tip of my tongue . . ."

*Good God.*

"Excuse me," Jo said, having heard about enough. "But I don't even know you."

The woman laughed, a soft cackle that made Jo think of a fairy-tale witch, something she vaguely resembled. "Everyone knows me," she answered. "I'm Irma."

"Of course you are," Jo said, angling her chair so her back was mostly to the woman, trying not to be rude, but she was tired of hearing her nonsensical stories that only reminded Jo of how much she did not know about her own past.

The woman reached over to stroke Verna's brown-speckled arm. "Oh, Lord, I am so happy to have found such an old friend here," she remarked. "She's going to take care of me, you know. She said she'd drive me wherever I needed to go. Isn't that sweet?"

"Very," Jo said dryly. Sweet and impossible, since Mama hadn't had a car to drive for longer than she'd had Alzheimer's.

Jo checked the clock again. Noon on the button.

"Ladies, it's lunchtime," a staffer trilled, walking over and interrupting the very one-sided conversation.

She had on the bright blue shirt with a dove on the left pocket that all the employees at Winghaven wore. Jo had been told the color was supposed to be calming, but she didn't feel calm. She felt like a trapped bird, ready to flee.

"Irma, are you dining with Verna again today? How great," the caretaker said, doing her best to smile and play perky. She turned to Jo. "Will you be staying for lunch?"

"No," Jo said, when she really meant, *hell, no*.

She pushed away from the table.

"Goodbye, Mama," she said, addressing Verna but not making a move to hug her or kiss her. Why should she do that now when she'd never done it before? Mama's illness didn't change a thing.

"He's gone," Verna whispered, hand outstretched.

"Who's gone?" Jo asked.

"The bird," her mother said sharply, looking angry. Then she set her chin on her chest and closed her eyes, seeming readier to nap than to eat.

"Verna and I, we're going to have such a lovely time together, aren't we?" Irma insisted, patting Verna's shoulder this time. "Perhaps after lunch, we can go see a movie. You'll drive, won't you, darlin'? I don't seem to have my keys."

Jo sighed, giving up.

She went to the elevator, trying to remember the passcode so she could get out. It was always something easy, like 1234*—simple for the visitors, but impossible for the patients to recall when they tried to escape now and then.

Adam was waiting for her by the car.

She hadn't asked him to come with her, but he'd wanted to. He'd even offered to go upstairs to see Mama. While Jo had so appreciated the offer, it would have made things more awkward, not less.

"How is she?" he said, holding the door open for her as she approached. "You weren't in there for long."

"Oh, I was," Jo remarked. "Long enough."

She had her belt on when he eased himself behind the wheel of his Jeep, and he reached over to squeeze her hand before he started the car.

"Where do you want to go?" he asked. "Anything you want to do?"

They had each taken some PTO so they could spend the day together.

"A museum, maybe?" he suggested when she didn't answer. "A nice cool movie theater? We can sit and neck in the back row."

"A movie?" Jo smiled. "But we might run into Mama and her new pal," she said, having to explain when he didn't get it.

"If it's okay with you," she told him, "I just want to go home."

He didn't respond, merely pulled the car out of the garage and headed north on the freeway, back to Plainfield.

Adam had an old CD in the player and cranked it up loud. Jo recognized the notes in the intro even before Geddy Lee started to sing. She knew it was Rush's "Fly by Night," having listened to the song often enough before. Adam belted the lyrics at the top of his lungs. They spoke of knowing when it was time to stop trying, time to leave, and start a new life, to move on.

Jo felt a tug in her heart, like the words were instructions. She and Hank had closed a rough case. She should be feeling lighter now, shouldn't she? Knowing she'd done her part in getting justice for Kelly Amster. The Dallas County District Attorney had filed sexual assault charges against Robert Eldon Junior, and she'd heard they were considering charging Trey with complicity in Kelly's rape. Trey's entire posse was facing prison time for animal cruelty, which was the least that they deserved.

Though it didn't look like the DA was seeking to punish Barbara Amster, they were still debating going after Cassie Marks for cyberbullying.

Jo made herself take a deep breath and exhale. *Let it go,* she told herself. She didn't want to dwell on the darkness anymore.

Despite the blowing AC, she rolled down her window a crack, craving the warm wind on her skin and in her hair. She needed to feel something moving, not stillness, as she closed her eyes and leaned her head back.

She listened to Adam's voice, so happily out of tune, and she focused on that, on remembering Jill Burns's tear-stained and smiling face when she was reunited with Tucker; on the memorial service that Kelly's school had held for her in a packed auditorium, with the principal asserting to the heavens, "We will not forget you."

Jo hung on to those thoughts, the weight on her chest easing. She didn't open her eyes again until they were home.

As soon as she exited the Jeep, she spotted mail sticking out of the box on her porch railing, something in a big white envelope. While she unlocked the door to let them in, Adam picked it up for her. He tossed it onto the skinny console as they entered, though the big white envelope slipped to the ground. Ernie spotted it instantly, racing over to bat at it, pushing it around the wood floor as though it were a toy.

"Hey, that's mine," Jo said and picked it up, squinting at the unfamiliar return address until she realized it wasn't really unfamiliar after all.

It was from the lawyer that Ronnie had sent her to, the one helping her go through the legal end of Mama's life, sorting out the insurance policies, her savings, and the pension still trickling in from the man who'd ruined Jo's life. They were working to get Jo power of attorney, too, so she could make more decisions and ensure there was money enough coming in to cover all of Mama's expenses.

Ernie followed her to the sofa as she slid a finger beneath the gummed flap. As large as the envelope was, she expected documents requiring her attention, something with those tiny Post-its indicating the pages to be signed or initialed.

Instead, there was a handwritten note:

*Found these in your mother's papers and thought you'd want them.*

*Them* being old birthday cards, clearly meant for a little kid.

The first was for a five-year-old, a big green frog on the outside and a bad poem about leaping forward a year on the inside, along with an unfamiliar scribble.

*Dear Jo Jo,* it read. *Happy fifth birthday. I wish I was there. Love you, Daddy.*

She opened up another, this for *A Princess Turning Six!* There was a similar scrawled note within: *I miss you. I love you. I wish I was there.*

Jo couldn't breathe.

She couldn't move.

Something tugged inside her chest, and she let out a whimper. Then Adam was beside her, asking if she was all right, but she wasn't.

"What is it?" he was asking.

"Birthday cards," she told him, her voice sounding so strange, "from my father."

"You hadn't seen them before?"

She shook her head, biting her lip, remembering all the times Mama had angrily responded, *"Daddy left us, Jo Anna! He doesn't love us anymore. Don't you get it?"* whenever she'd asked, *"Where's my daddy? Why isn't he here?"*

Her father had taken off before she'd turned five. Mama had remarried just after she'd turned six. Those two birthdays and the year that connected them had changed her life forever. They were to her what Trey's party had been for Kelly: a monumental turning point. Nothing was the same thereafter. *She* was not the same thereafter.

She'd been cast into her own living hell, just like Kelly. The only difference between them was that Kelly had jumped to end it.

Jo had held on.

"Can I take a look?" Adam asked.

She handed the cards to him, watched his eyes as he read, saw the questions in them as he looked at her again. "Why would your mother keep these if she was never going to show them to you?"

"I don't know," Jo started to say, but that wasn't entirely true. A soft breath escaped her. "She didn't want me to know that he was out there somewhere, missing me. She wanted to cut him off, to punish him, because he'd let her down . . ."

"How?" Adam asked.

This time, Jo answered, "I don't know," and it was the truth.

*"They didn't approve of him . . . Your mother's parents. They didn't like him one little bit."*

She took the cards from Adam and read them over again, and all she could think was that her mother had lied. And if Mama had deceived her with something as small as birthday cards, what else had she kept hidden?

"What do you want to do?" Adam asked.

Jo shook her head. She reached back into the envelope the cards had come in, hoping to find something else. There was no way to ascertain a return address. Though, the cards had been mailed so long ago, her father could have moved by now—several times, in fact.

"Have you ever thought of finding him?"

"Oh, God, so many times, when I was younger," she said. "When I still hoped he'd come rescue me, take me away. But then"—she paused, sucked a deep breath in before she finished—"I gave up on him. I just quit."

Adam squeezed her arm gently. "Whatever you decide, I'm with you," he said, and Jo leaned her head against his arm.

"Thank you."

She was not alone, she told herself. She didn't have to be afraid of looking back, of learning all the things she didn't know. Maybe it was time she acknowledged more about herself than just what her stepfather had done and what her mother had ignored. Maybe it was time to find out the truth about who her father was, what she'd meant to him, and him to her.

*Do or do not . . . there is no try.*

She thought of Kelly Amster again, and she wondered if the girl had felt such a distance from her own father. She doubted Barbara Amster had done a single thing to remedy it. Instead, she had given Kelly one less person to love who could love her back, just as Mama had done with Jo and her daddy.

That, in itself, was unforgiveable, as messed up as claiming to love a child and then calling her hateful names "for her own good."

Jo held on to Adam's hand, squeezing her eyes closed, trying so hard to remember a face that her memory blurred. She hardly knew what he looked like, not with Mama having cut him from their photographs. Jo had so very little of him to cling to. Or did she?

*"He had very dark eyes and dark hair, much like yours."*

Irma's words worked their way into her head again, unsettling her as much as they gave her a part of herself, a piece that had been long missing.

*"He kept it short, of course. He had to, so no one would know."*

So no one would know *what?*

Maybe it meant nothing. Maybe it was more nonsensical talk from a woman too far gone to know the difference. Still, it was time, Jo realized, to get some answers.

What if she was that invisible bird Mama had seen, sitting on a branch, before it flew away? Her wings weren't clipped anymore.

Mama couldn't hold her back now.

No one could.

# AUTHOR'S NOTE

We live in rough times, where kindness can often seem distant, but there is always someone willing to listen and help. Please do not suffer in silence. If you or anyone you know is being victimized or needs emotional support, there are resources out there to assist you. All you have to do is reach out:

National Suicide Prevention Lifeline: 1-800-273-8255
National Sexual Assault Hotline: 1-800-656-4673
The Trevor Project: 1-866-488-7386
Loveisrespect: 1-866-331-9474

> "Although the world is full of suffering, it is full also of the overcoming of it."

—*Helen Keller*

# ACKNOWLEDGMENTS

Thank you, as always, to Christina Hogrebe for your unflagging belief in me and my work. I am so fortunate to have you guiding my career.

Thanks also to Megha Parekh and to Jacque Ben-Zekry for being Jo Larsen's cheerleaders (and Kjersti Egerdahl!). It has been a wonderful journey thus far, and I look forward to more adventures with Jo to come!

*Merci beaucoup*, once again, to Caitlin Alexander, for being such a vigilant reader and developmental editor. You push the bar ever higher with your invaluable insight.

A big hug to everyone at Thomas & Mercer and Amazon Publishing who have been so supportive: Sarah Shaw, Gracie Doyle, Laura Barrett, Oisin O'Malley, Laura Costantino, Gabrielle Guarnero, and the rest of the magnificent crew. You seriously rock.

To my friends who listen to me gripe about deadlines: What would I do without you? Ditto my amazing family, who puts up with my odd hours and exhaustion and brain drain throughout the year as I work. I am beyond blessed.

And to the readers who have fallen in love with Jo and cheered her on, thank you so much. I hope I never let you—or her—down.

# ABOUT THE AUTHOR

*Photo © 2015 Sarah Crowder*

Susan McBride is the *USA Today* bestselling author of the Debutante Dropout Mysteries and the River Road Mysteries. The debut of her Jo Larsen series, *Walk Into Silence*, was a #1 Kindle bestseller in the US and the UK, and #3 in Australia. She has penned three women's fiction titles: *The Truth About Love & Lightning, Little Black Dress,* and *The Cougar Club.* She has also chronicled her bout with breast cancer in the short memoir *In the Pink: How I Met the Perfect (Younger) Man, Survived Breast Cancer, and Found True Happiness After Forty.* Susan lives in Saint Louis, Missouri, with her husband and daughter.